Island Shadows

Phillip Strang

BOOKS BY PHILLIP STRANG

DCI Isaac Cook Series
MURDER IS A TRICKY BUSINESS
MURDER HOUSE
MURDER IS ONLY A NUMBER
MURDER IN LITTLE VENICE
MURDER IS THE ONLY OPTION
MURDER IN NOTTING HILL
MURDER IN ROOM 346
MURDER OF A SILENT MAN
MURDER HAS NO GUILT
MURDER IN HYDE PARK
SIX YEARS TOO LATE
GRAVE PASSION
THE SLAYING OF JOE FOSTER
THE HERO'S FALL
THE VICAR'S CONFESSION
GUILTY UNTIL PROVEN INNOCENT
MURDER WITHOUT REASON

DI Keith Tremayne Series
DEATH UNHOLY
DEATH AND THE ASSASSIN'S BLADE
DEATH AND THE LUCKY MAN
DEATH AT COOMBE FARM
DEATH BY A DEAD MAN'S HAND
DEATH IN THE VILLAGE
BURIAL MOUND
THE BODY IN THE DITCH
THE HORSE'S MOUTH
MONTFIELD'S MADNESS

Sergeant Natalie Campbell Series
DARK STREETS
PINCHGUT
ISLAND SHADOWS

Steve Case Series
HOSTAGE OF ISLAM
THE HABERMAN VIRUS
PRELUDE TO WAR

Standalone Books
MALIKA'S REVENGE
VERRALL'S NIGHTMARE

Dedication

For Elli and Tais, who both had the perseverance to make me sit down and write

Chapter 1

Cockatoo Island conjured up an impression of a tropical paradise set in the Barrier Reef in Northern Queensland, but it was not. Situated west of Sydney Harbour Bridge, it had been used as a harsh and unrelenting prison in the fledging colony of New South Wales due to its isolated location in Sydney Harbour. It was feared by the convicts incarcerated there, even more so by the wrongdoers who were not.

It had been called Wareamah by the Indigenous Australians who traditionally inhabited the land before European settlement, although no physical evidence of Aboriginal heritage had been found on the island. Initially, the island was thirteen hectares, but it had been extended to eighteen in the subsequent two centuries. From 1839 to 1869, it was a prison for those who reoffended in the colony. And then concurrent with the prison for its first twelve years, the site of one of Australia's biggest shipyards from 1857 to 1991. The first of its two dry docks was built by convicts. The island has been managed by the Sydney Harbour Federation Trust since 2010, and its prison buildings have been World Heritage listed since 2010.

None of which concerned Sergeant Natalie Campbell and Inspector Gary Haddock as they looked down at the body.

'I didn't hear anything, nor did I see anything, pitch black up here of a night,' Claude Liddie, the island's caretaker, said as he stood alongside the two officers. The man was unsteady, and his breath stank – Liddie was drunk. Drunkenness was not a crime, but murder was.

Thirteen grain silos had been hewn out of the sandstone by convicts, although only eight remained, and of those, most were no longer intact. Three prisoners had died during the construction of the grain silos. There was a small entrance at the top, through which the convicts were lowered to where they chipped away at the sandstone, creating a spherical hollow to store grain during drought.

It was near the entrance of one of the silos that the body lay. The area was floodlit, a crime scene tent was erected to one side, and three investigators were conducting their investigation.

In a pocket of the man's trousers, a driving licence identified the victim as Alan Greenworthy, the lead singer of the starring act at the heavy metal concert on the island that night. Haddock had heard the tail end of the concert when he and his sergeant had arrived on the island and knew he could not blame the caretaker, forced to endure the noise, for drinking more than was good for him. Haddock had arrived from Parramatta by water taxi, the wharf a short distance from his one-bed apartment. Natalie had the relative luxury of a Water Police patrol boat that had picked her up on the western side of Finger Wharf in Woolloomooloo, the suburb's name an obvious derivation of an Aboriginal word, but nobody knew which.

The prison was high on the island, up a gently inclining road, or up one of the three sets of stairs on three sides of the rocky escarpment.

Since the shipyard's closure, the island had become a place for open-air concerts, and the former prison officers' accommodation had been renovated and was rented out nightly. Below the prison was a grassy area where tents on platforms were rented for a day, a weekend, or a week.

Most gave scant thought to the island's early history, those who had suffered, and those who had died. Natalie Campbell knew more than most, an interest in early Australian history she had acquired since the murder of Sasha Cornell, whose body was discovered on Pinchgut, another island, smaller than Cockatoo but no less violent.

Haddock had noticed the pungent smell of marijuana as they passed the tents and realised that more potent drugs would be on the island. Another day, the drug squad might be interested, but he was not. A rock concert was enough for him; he could only imagine what occurred when the concert ended, and the island was empty apart from those who had paid to stay. But not that night. A murder had been committed, and there would be a police presence.

The concert would have been hell for Haddock, who had not been there when it was in full swing; to Natalie Campbell, it might have been fun, better than staying at home with a bottle of wine and a soppy movie on the TV.

Neither officer had heard of Alan Greenworthy's group, the Maligned Manglers, but that was not unexpected. They had never been on television, played for the joy of it, not for the money, appealing to a disparate group of would-be anarchists and an independent online radio station that broadcast their music.

Saturday night's line-up was the Maligned Manglers, the Desperados, the Youthful Yobos. Another group that had come up from Melbourne, driving all night to be there, not enough money for airfares with all their equipment.

According to the island's caretaker, the audience was in the hundreds, and to him, after thirty-one years as the caretaker, they were a motley bunch. But then, Natalie Campbell could see a man who had gone to seed, too many years living in the cottage that had been the prison commandant's when discipline and cruelty had been dished out in equal measures. Without the ghosts, which Liddie had said his wife believed in, the nights would have been lonely, a furtive mind conjuring up all manner of doom and gloom.

'Knife to the heart,' one of the crime scene investigators said. One of the better CSIs, in Haddock's estimation, even though the man had stated the obvious.

The sight of the body had not disturbed the caretaker. Natalie would want to know why later that day, but for now, there were other things to attend to. A team of uniformed officers was on the way, due to arrive within the hour, and it would be for them to take the witness statements, record the names of all present on the island, and confirm their contact details. It was more than likely that a few would not want to help the police, either due to their political views or they had something to hide.

Those from Greenworthy's band and the other bands would be interviewed by Natalie and Haddock.

Natalie's promotion to inspector was not yet confirmed, and Haddock's promotion to chief inspector was on hold, not that he knew that officially. Natalie had been told by Superintendent Payne, their commanding officer at State Crime Command in Parramatta, that the man had neither the qualifications nor the aptitude for the additional responsibility. Natalie had argued that he did, but Payne told her that she was sentimental about him and was not being objective. She knew Payne was right, but her inspector was a good man who deserved it. Payne's response had been to say that he would try to sway the Promotions Board, but Natalie knew he would not.

The small café near the ferry wharf was doing roaring business, with the additional persons on the island, and extra staff would be laid on for the breakfast shift.

The murderer might be on the island unless he or she had taken the last ferry at 1 a.m. If that person had, then solving the murder would be doubly difficult, but they were prepared. A well-honed team, the inspector and his sergeant, with the junior on the promotion ladder and the inspector, stalled in his career, balancing policing and family responsibilities, succeeding at one, failing at the other. His hoped-for return to the family nest was now thwarted by another murder, which should be easy to solve but probably would not be due to inevitable complications as the evidence accumulated and persons were interviewed.

What had been ascertained so far was that the dead man was a loner, naturally shy, introverted off-stage, and dynamic when on. That was what another of the band, Jeb Barton, who had avoided the police cordon, said on the phone.

'Alan, strange guy, likeable if you got to know him.'

'Why the change?' Natalie asked.

'Jekyll and Hyde. It concerned him, but he didn't talk about it much. Up on the stage, transformed, one of the boys, charming, able to find a woman, but once the adrenaline dampened, he went back into his shell. Highly intelligent, unlike us. We're a bunch of reprobates trying to pretend we're contributing to the art form.'

Natalie thought Barton sounded intelligent and that his self-deprecation was a defence mechanism designed to throw off suspicion and be seen as the police officer's friend.

'Where can I find you?' Natalie asked.

'Ryde County Council, first floor. Civil servant, boringly normal.'

'Boring sounds fine. We assumed those on the stage would be ne'er-do-wells or amateur anarchists.'

'Well said, Sergeant. Everyone is anarchistic to some extent, but most are worn down by the system, which sucks. I'm sure you would agree.'

Natalie, aware of political incompetency worldwide, might have agreed that change was necessary. Still, the reality was what people had to deal with. Singing banal lyrics to banal musical compositions might have been one way to deal with the injustice, but murder was neither anachronistic nor banal. It was factual, and death was permanent. Someone was answerable for their crime regardless of their political persuasion.

'A friend?'

'Alan, I suppose so. I saw both sides of him, but I can't say I know much about him. He lived alone, and I rarely went to his place. I reckon he had money.'

'Why?'

'Which question?'

'Both.'

'He had more money than you could make in a dead-end nine-to-five job working for the government. He didn't have a job, but a wallet full of money, not that he opened it that often. He told me the house where he lived, which was run down but worth plenty, was his. I rarely went because he did not want me to go. But sometimes there were things to discuss about the band. He was on a high with the band and often picked up a woman, not that he ever saw them afterwards. As I said, a strange person, a barrelful of intrigue.'

'Later today, State Crime Command, Parramatta. I will need you to make a statement. Can you identify the body?'

'I can come out to the island now if that helps.'

'Parramatta's better.'

***

Haddock stood alongside one of the crime scene investigators. The caretaker had returned to his cottage. 'Sexual intercourse?' Haddock asked.

'Pathology to confirm, but I would say probably. That is visual, judging by the clothing and the impressions on the grass. Two people; I assume it is a woman.'

'According to Sergeant Campbell, the man was adept at picking up women, so assume it was. The murderer could be a disgruntled boyfriend or the woman's husband.'

'Or someone who fancied his chances with the woman, and the victim beat him to it. Not the caretaker; too old.'

It was an interesting thought, Haddock knew. A man who had not been concerned about a murder, living on an island with a violent history, enough to turn the most stable slightly mad. Noises in the night, a bird in a tree, the wind rustling through the trees, the abandoned engineering workshops, the former prison cells, the place where punishment had been meted out, where people had died. The setting for a horror movie.

Later, enough time for Claude Liddie to have washed his face, brushed his teeth and gulped down two cups of black coffee, Haddock and Natalie sat in his cottage, which had the look and the feel of a man who lived alone.

'My wife died twelve years ago,' Liddie said.

'Here, on this island?' Natalie asked.

'In this room, but she had been ill for a while. I offered to go to the mainland, but she was adamant. It was on this island that she wanted to die. An amateur historian, she knew the history of this place, the names of those who had been here, their fates, good and bad. She would have been the person for you now, tell you where the skeletons are, metaphorical and literal.'

'Are there some, literal that is?' Haddock asked. In his hand, a piping hot enamel mug of tea. The mug looked as though it could belong to the convict past, darkened by tea stains and chipped around the rim.

'Time glosses over most of them. Nobody wants to remember the crimes committed by those sworn to uphold the law, and the convicts out here, the most incorrigible.'

'You seem unmoved by the murder,' Natalie said.

Even though the cottage lacked charm, its history interested her. Another time, she would ask for a guided tour, the caretaker's tour. He would know much more than the tourist brochures.

'Young lovers up here before?' Haddock asked.

'Not the first time, if that's what he was doing. I've seen it all, and they shouldn't be up here, but down there, those concerts, alcohol and drugs. I'm surprised some haven't fallen in the harbour. I don't mind the opera, but the motley would-be overthrowers of the police and the government, not a clue as to what is going on,' Liddie said.

'My question,' Natalie reminded the man.

'I was in Vietnam, doing my bit for Queen and country. I saw death there and then, up here, enough stories to turn the stomach. Another dead body isn't going to faze me.'

'You didn't see him. How often do you do a round of the island?'

'When it's empty, late at night, early morning. If there is a concert, I stay here and check after they've gone or when they're winding up. That's when I found the body, and if there had been violence, how could I have heard with the racket down below?'

'Up here?' Natalie asked.

'Noise rises and echoes through the empty buildings and up the rocky escarpment. However, here in the cottage, it's quiet. I don't walk close to the silos; they are not as stable as you would imagine. Most have been weakened by the rock face being chipped away over the years to put up new buildings. The island was busy in the past, with a few destroyers built here for the Australian Navy and then refitting submarines. It's as quiet as a grave when no one is here, deathly at night. You would not want to believe in ghosts, not of a nighttime.'

'Are there?' Haddock asked.

'My wife thought there might be. Not that it concerned her, and I never believed it.'

Haddock, a sceptic, would agree with Liddie, although Natalie was more susceptible. In her early teens, a family trip to Tasmania, a midnight ghost tour around the convict prison of Port Arthur, the cold winds, doors blowing open, the rattling windows, an owl hooting. That was enough for her, and then, in 1996, a crazed madman with automatic rifles slaughtered thirty-five people during daylight hours. To her, Port Arthur and Cockatoo Island represented a link with the past that was both interesting and macabre.

It was two in the afternoon before Natalie and Haddock left the island, this time by ferry, which had been authorised to take on persons but not to allow others to disembark, two constables standing on the wharf to sign off those leaving, in case some had slipped through the net and not been interviewed. A few were grumpy and argumentative. The police had heard all the excuses before and were not listening. It was a murder, not a minor disturbance. The discomfort of a few held little weight in a murder investigation.

"If Greenworthy was killed by a jealous lover, where is the woman? Does she know? Is she concerned, or was she high on drugs, committing an indiscretion, or was it more?' Natalie said on the ferry heading towards Parramatta.

'Find the woman,' Haddock replied. He had a murder to deal with but was distracted by a troublesome daughter and her frantic mother. In his forties and going to seed, the weight was starting to pile on due to his lifestyle. A daughter of sixteen, going on twenty-five, in love and lust, exploring the forbidden, a mother who looked to an absent and estranged husband and father to discipline the child. Haddock could see no resolution other than to battle on, hopeful that his occasional chats with the daughter would ease her through the worst excesses of adolescence.

Chapter 2

Jeb Barton, the Manglers' drummer, arrived at State Crime Command at four in the afternoon. Regardless of the group he played in, he was clean-cut and wearing a suit.

'Not the look I expected,' Natalie said.

Haddock was in the other room on the phone, attempting conciliation between mother and daughter, wanting to pull out his hair, wanting to tell his wife that shouting at the daughter was not going to help, and in the eyes of the law, she was no longer a child, but an adult, even if she was a pain in the rear end. In tears on the party line, the daughter explained that she knew what she was doing, and it was love. And why couldn't her mother accept the fact instead of complaining? Haddock wanted to bang their heads together, but he had a murder to solve, a crucial witness in the other room giving his sergeant the eye. Which was the most important? Solving the murder or bringing harmony to the family? The latter was impossible; the former had the makings of a convoluted investigation, false hope, distorted evidence, and a missing woman. Pathology had confirmed semen on the man's underwear, almost certain proof of sexual intercourse. Two persons needed to be found and fast – the woman and the person with the knife. Were they one, or was the woman oblivious to the murder? The media had reported the murder and were now allowed restricted access to the island, but not up to the murder scene. Superintendent Payne was on the island to read a statement but not to get involved in additional comment due to a scurrilous press sensationalising the murder, the concert, and the violent death.

Claude Liddie was in his cottage, a constable stationed outside, in case any of the media slipped through, although Liddie had been adamant that he didn't know anything. Natalie wasn't sure of the man's affirmation, knowing that the reason he hadn't found the body earlier or heard the murder was due to a bottle of Johnnie Walker Red Label.

Liddie was a drinker, whether due to his wife's demise or habitually alcoholic. Not that it mattered, but Natalie knew that if she had to spend a night on the island alone, she would need something more substantial than a police officer's warrant card and a mobile phone.

Barton spoke, comfortable in the police station, clearly a weekend anarchist – or was he? Natalie wasn't sure. 'It's the music, the vibe, certainly not the lyrics,' he said.

'The majority there, would-be anarchists, down with the police, the government, the corrupt society?'

'If they don't have money to burn, some would be, but Alan had it in plenty. He felt guilty about it.'

'Did he tell you that?'

'Sometimes, once, to be more precise. It was a few years back, a gig in Brisbane. Alan would smoke a joint, wax lyrical, not about his money or where it had come from. We're all philosophers when we're drunk or drugged.'

'Are you about to incriminate yourself? Remember, this is a police station; what you say is on record.'

'Not incriminate, no harm in recreational drugs, or don't you agree?'

'I'm a police officer sworn to uphold the law. My personal views don't come into it.'

'Well said. I asked him once where the money came from, and he told me it was old money, a grandfather who had made it as a pastoralist, a property that would take a day to ride across on horseback. That was it; I don't know if it was true. It's one thing to be dirt poor and believe in the utopian state, but what do you get? 1984, Orwell's classic. But up on that stage, belting out our songs, a few drinks in us, a few drugs, and if I'm honest, you start to believe it. I asked him why he didn't hand it around if the money was a curse.'

'His answer?'

'Easier said than done, and he was right. If I had money, I wouldn't be working for the council, not sure if I would be better off for it, idle time to get up to mischief.'

'Criminal record?'

'You must have checked, and no, apart from speeding a few years back. I lost my licence for six months. Since then, nothing, other than noise pollution from the row we make.'

'You were the headline act,' Natalie said, appreciative of Jeb Barton's self-deprecating humour.

'Headline of what? You didn't hear the others. We could hold a tune, but one of the other groups had no idea why they were there, instruments out of tune, unable to hold a note, flat on some. Even so, the audience was raucous.'

'Drugs?'

'Rudimentary check on entry, a declaration that those disembarking from the ferry weren't carrying drugs.'

'Which means they were.'

'No need to. On the other side of the island, there's a marina, easy enough to sneak in drugs and alcohol. Plenty of dark areas on the island, a roaring trade for those who had the concession.'

'Concession makes it sound official.'

'Not official, no papers signed, no agreements given. You either pay for the privilege to sell drugs or get your head bashed. Those selling weren't lovers of the music; they were in it for the money.'

'You're remarkably honest. You could get yourself into trouble.'

'I won't,' Barton replied. 'There's no point in feeding you lies and platitudes, not when Alan's dead. Someone killed him, but why?'

'We believe he had a woman with him.'

'Would she have killed him?'

'It's possible, psychotic or high on more than recreational drugs. Crack cocaine, fentanyl, easy to purchase on the island?'

'Maybe. A joint is my limit, and Alan wasn't keen, torn between having plenty of money and the guilt of it, not that I have that problem. Money doesn't bring happiness, only conflict, and he had it in bucketloads.'

'You said that before. This introversion, why did it go away on the island? With a woman? What do you reckon?'

'There is one, but she seemed to be able to get through to him.'

'Girlfriend?'

'Sort of. She has more than one man in her life, and she's classy; butter wouldn't melt in her mouth if you met her. She didn't appeal to me, nor me to her. She saw me as working class, which I am. She is a gold digger, a rich man's fancy, even though Alan didn't throw his money around.'

'Where can we find her? Would she be the mystery woman?'

'Unlikely, can't stand to associate with the plebs. Easy with her morals.'

'Your belief?'

'Of her morals?'

'Yes.'

'I met her once, in Sydney, down by the Opera House. I'm there, walking along, minding my business, and taking in the sights. It was over a year ago, and Alan appeared. He's got a woman hanging on his arm.'

'"We've just been to the opera," he said. "By the way, this is Alice."'

'I shook her hand, the obligatory response from her, but she had a sneer. I'm not negative about her, but she's got a dark side.'

'Occupation?'

'High-class whore. Believe me, she could carry it off, a stunner.'

'How do you know this?'

'Alan suggests we go to a bar, plenty by the Opera House. There are the three of us, and Alan's paying. Alice starts to talk, unsure why, as she doesn't reckon much with me. Or maybe she wanted to show off or try to shock me. She's drinking a cocktail. Alan and I were drinking beer. The normal chit-chat, what I did for a living, what she did. I'm not afraid to say that I'm one of the humble minions working for the council, although I'm hopeful of improving myself.'

'And her?' Natalie asked, leaning back in her chair, enjoying her conversation with the man, realising that he was a good person, even if he played in an awful band and sang stupid songs.

'She tells me that she's fond of Alan, gives her a sense of reality, but she's an escort, older men, some good, some bad, all generous with their money.'

'Were you shocked?'

'It's not something you expect to hear, but no, each to their own. Alan didn't seem to care; she was the closest he ever came to a girlfriend. Talk to her, find out what she has to say, but she's not the woman on the island.'

'Would she know?'

'No idea, probably not. I imagine the woman was a stray he picked up. Even us, not that we're famous get groupies.'

'You've taken advantage?'

A wry smile. 'What do you reckon?'

***

As a result of the witness statements taken on the island, several persons required follow-up. One of those, reluctant to give his name, was a minor politician in the New South Wales government, and either way, he had a right to listen to whatever music he wanted, although the anarchist overtones of the lyrics were of concern to the police. If the man harboured opinions contrary to the electorate that voted for him, did that indicate someone with a hidden side of the public persona?

Also, a woman who had spent time in prison for grievous bodily harm to a boyfriend who cheated on her. He had subsequently spent three months in hospital, another two convalescing, before he could return to work and resume his life. She interested Haddock more than the others, a possible midnight romp with Greenworthy, capable of having sex with the man and then killing him.

Natalie wasn't fixated on the woman; she was in her forties and no longer considered violent. Haddock didn't see either characteristic as exclusory in the crime of murder.

Apart from that, the remainder of those interviewed on the island were a disparate group; some enjoyed the music, were fans of one band or the other, and others enjoyed the ambience of an island with music, alcohol, drugs, and the opportunity to indulge in wanton uncomplicated sex.

Even so, the woman who had been with the dead man was important, and the politician could wait, as could the convicted woman – a clean slate for six years since her release from prison, and now married, and her husband had been at the concert with her, alibis that seemed to stack up.

Neither of the two, politician and convicted felon, seemed relevant, and according to Jeb Barton, groupies were more likely; no need to spend time in meaningful conversation, just take hold, whisk them off to somewhere secluded, no need for sweet words or dialogue, do the deed, and back in time for the second time up on the stage. Although where Greenworthy had died was at the high point of the island, reached either along a gently-sloping road or up the side of the rock escapement, with metal stairs and handrails. There were more convenient places closer to the concert: the disused and decaying engineering workshops or in the dog-leg tunnel that connected one side of the island to the other, a number of alcoves in there. Or, as Barton had said, groupies were often exhibitionists; they didn't crave privacy for sex, nor did they restrict themselves to one band member.

Beth Sukkin proved to be one of the latter. She was thirty-one, twice married, with two children from different fathers. Her address given at the concert proved correct: a small apartment in Blacktown, named after the indigenous persons that had once lived there. Little remained of the original settlement, and it was not regarded as affluent; low-rent, low socio-economic status, battlers to use an Australian colloquialism, persons doing it tough, doing the best they could, some succeeding, others failing miserably.

Beth Sukkin appeared to be one of those failing. The apartment was a mess, with clothes strewn around the place, a television in the corner turned up loud, and a bottle of vodka on a table in the middle of the room. In the kitchen, a sink was full of dirty dishes, and in a frying pan, bacon congealed in its fat. She was living below the poverty line, and the welfare of her children, six and eight, was under investigation by Community Services; a strong probability they would be taken from her and placed in care.

Haddock sat in the main room, pushing a mangy cat off the chair. Natalie wasn't so keen and would have preferred to stand, but they needed the woman calm, not ranting and raving. A cigarette dangled in Beth Sukkin's mouth, ash about to drop onto the floor.

'It's a dump,' she said.

'The children? When you were at the concert?'

'With my mother, not that she likes it, but what option does she have? They're her grandkids, and their fathers don't come near, nor do they give me money.'

'Are they forced to by law?' Natalie asked.

'Both deny paternity, but I know who the fathers are.'

'How?' Haddock asked.

'I know,' the woman replied. It was evident that she thought she did, but nothing was certain. DNA testing would have proved it one way or the other, but the men weren't about to comply.

The woman's parlous state was not Homicide's primary concern, although murder was.

'Did you know the dead man?' Haddock asked, once again brushing the cat to one side.

'I saw him there but didn't go near him, not that night.'

'Someone else?'

'Someone else, any ship in a storm. Poetical, an island in Sydney Harbour.'

'Do you often sleep with band members?' Natalie asked, ignoring the woman's attempt at levity.

'Not often, but I've got to get away from this dump and have some fun. Or is that a crime?'

'Neglect of your children would be, but having fun isn't.'

Natalie had little time for the woman, obviously a wastrel, committed to self, easy with her virtues, not considerate of the resulting dilemma, which in the woman's case was two children of indeterminate parentage, the fathers long gone, possibly ignorant of the fact, and almost certainly not caring. No more than dogs on heat to Natalie. Even so, it was unlikely that this was the woman who had been with the murdered man. For one thing, she had gone to the concert with a friend and had returned with her, and that woman's alibi was strong.

Haddock knew that his daughter was at a crossroads in her life, and even though she had been brought up in leafy North Shore Sydney and was better educated than Beth Sukkin, she was at a susceptible age. He did not know how to resolve it, which affected his policing so much that he did not speak for a while.

Eventually, 'Miss Sukkin,' Haddock said after he had cleared his throat and stroked the cat – better to have it as a friend than scratching his trousers. 'We need to find the woman who was with Alan Greenworthy. Earlier, you said it was not you that night. Does that mean that on other occasions, you have had sex with him?'

'I might have. I've been there at other gigs, seen him and his band up on stage, and been backstage with them afterwards, plenty of alcohol, marijuana, and cocaine. All of us high, and then pairing off. None of us too fussy who with, but not with him on a grassy knoll with my arse in the air.'

'You're smarter than you make out,' Haddock said.

'I could have made something of myself, but I'm low-rental, from the wrong side of the street, a father in prison for abusing my mother, a mother permanently drunk, and I've not mentioned my uncle.'

'Sexual, underage?' Natalie said.

'Never charged, unsure if my mother knew, but she wouldn't have cared. Not much of an upbringing.'

'You could turn your life around,' Haddock said.

'Could I? As you said, smarter than I make out. I've read books on the subject, the formative years. Give me the child, and I'll give you the man. We're shaped by our childhood; not so easy to break free, mentally scarred, and then as soon as I was old enough, screw anything in trousers. I'm a lost cause.'

Natalie could see a woman with issues and two children who needed to be in care. It was her responsibility to inform the authorities of the parlous state of their upbringing, the conditions in which they lived, and the irresponsibility of the mother, who blamed her childhood for what she had become as an adult. Although, if it was as horrendous as she said, it would be wrong to blame the woman. But how much was true? Did the woman deserve sympathy, or was she playing a game with them?

The crime scene investigators, based on what they had found at the murder scene, had concluded that the woman with Greenworthy was of medium height and had dark shoulder-length hair. Forensics had found traces of perfume on his clothing. Also, Pathology confirmed bright red lipstick on his neck.

'Fast and furious,' the CSI had said at the scene.

Beth Sukkin would have qualified on the fast and furious but not on the red lipstick or perfume. Natalie had excused herself and checked in the bathroom – a cheap scent from the supermarket and no lipstick. An unattractive woman starting to put on weight due to her unhealthy eating habits and slovenliness, she was a woman whose life was mapped out for her. A few more children, bad men, drunken nights, and possible prison for a crime yet to be committed.

Chapter 3

The Maligned Manglers – the name grated with Haddock – had four in the group. The lead singer Alan Greenworthy, although Haddock thought 'singer' was subjective after listening to a recording of one of their songs. To him, it was wauling, lyrics that made no sense, a drum solo midway, banging and clanging, and then a guitarist going mad with the instrument, attempting a Jimi Hendrix and failing badly, and another who either played the guitar or blew a trumpet. It was torturous to Haddock's untrained ear, especially to Natalie, who had come to appreciate finer music.

Greenworthy had been the lead singer, Jeb Barton on drums, Gus Gomulka, the would-be Jimi Hendrix, and Igor Minsky, the bass guitarist.

'I came from Russia eighteen years ago,' Minsky said. His accent was harsh and strong, his English precise even if his voice was hard on the ear. 'I was classically trained, but in Australia, there were no opportunities; besides, classical music was what my parents wanted. But here, I play what appeals to me, and, yes, the Maligned Manglers are not very good; no idea why people pay to listen to them.'

'Why not find a better band?' Haddock asked.

They had met the man in Balmain, close to the Birchgrove Shopping Centre, close to the harbour, west of the Sydney Harbour Bridge, not far from where the murder had occurred.

'I am free to make my own decisions, and I teach music, contract myself out to functions, even to the Opera House when they need me. I will play their bourgeois music; otherwise, I can play what I want, experiment, and enjoy myself.'

'The Maligned Manglers, your idea of music?' Haddock asked.

'To some, they are popular, but not to me. I have little to do with them besides the opportunity to see if their crude musical compositions can be improved.'

'Can they?'

'They can, not that they would know. Alan Greenworthy was a reasonable singer but untrained. Jeb Barton hits the drums like old tin cans, and Gus Gomulka has a natural talent and would benefit from tutoring.'

'Which you could do,' Natalie said.

'I could, but it requires discipline, and Gomulka does not have it. Besides, I do not talk to them about my past, nor do I play their games, drinking, and taking drugs, nor their prevalence for women of loose morals.'

'According to one of the women who went backstage, you did,' Haddock said.

'I am one of the band; do as they do. The Manglers served my purpose, but I intended to leave in the next few months. It was Greenworthy they came to see.'

'An unusual character,' Natalie said, taking a long, hard look at the man. He was above average height, with jet-black hair parted in the middle. His hygiene was questionable, with a faint odour of garlic, and he wore a tee-shirt, even though the weather was cool, a pair of jeans, and open-toed sandals, the look of a hippie. However, Natalie thought that might be the affectation of a serious musician, slightly eccentric, and he was probably prejudiced, especially against Gomolka, who was of Polish heritage, and historical animosity existed between the two nationalities.

'I could respect the man, not his singing. He was educated, not like Gomulka, who is a bear of a man, uncouth and poorly educated. And unlike Jeb Barton, who attempts to portray himself as better than he is but is a slug of a man, weak and whimpering, getting high on bad drumming and drugs, screwing whoever he could, which in his case wasn't very many.'

Natalie had liked Barton, surprised to hear Minsky bad-mouthing the man. 'I found him not as you've described.'

'Russian honesty, plain speaking. Your opinion might differ, and I saw him only when we practised or played. Alan wasn't a great singer, but he had charisma on the stage.'

'But not Gomolka?' Haddock chipped in.

'He's a crude man, on or off stage, although a natural talent, could be somebody. As I said, that requires discipline. Meet with the man. You will discover what I am telling you is the truth.'

Honesty was what a murder investigation required, but whether it was what Minsky had given was unknown. He was clearly educated and spoke flawless English, albeit with a strong guttural accent. Haddock thought he could be a man capable of violence, and Natalie intuitively did not like him and thought there was something intangible about him.

'Beth Sukkin, do you know the name?' Natalie asked as Minsky got up to leave.

'I know a Beth who turns up at various gigs. Barton was partial to her; I don't think the others were.'

'You?'

'A pretence, if you like.'

Natalie wasn't fooled; the man had enjoyed Beth Sukkin, even though he would not admit it.

'Crystal Andersson?' Natalie asked, looking down at her phone and seeing a message from Barton. Why he had sent it to her, she didn't know, but she thought it might be that he was trying to ingratiate himself. And if he was, then Minsky's evaluation of the man might be correct.

'Blonde, Scandinavian background, attractive. Yes, I remember her.'

'Not your style?' Haddock asked.

'She came to the gigs for Greenworthy. Not a groupie. He might have met her outside of where we played, but I wouldn't know. Nobody knew much about Alan, never spoke about his family or where he came from, or why he wanted to be involved with a bunch of losers.'

'You were involved.'

'I was, but I had a reason, a chance to see if the music played could be made into something worthwhile. Experimentation, the creative mind, see what is possible, a diamond in the rough.'

'Did you find any?'

'I'm working on a symphony, incorporating some of Gomulka's improvisation and Barton's rhythmic smashing on the drums, even though he broke more than a few sticks, tried to portray himself as the angry rebel.'

Haddock thought Minsky was spouting hot air; Natalie was unsure. She had listened to heavy metal in her teens, a passing phase, and even though the music could be crude and grating, there was an underlying rhythmic pulse to it, and the lyrics, with expletives included, could have a poetic symmetry. If Minsky was as bright as he portrayed himself, investigating other forms of music made sense.

***

Crystal Andersson sat at her desk. She had been informed earlier in the day to expect a visit from Inspector Haddock and Sergeant Natalie Campbell.

'Yes, I knew Alan. He was quiet and sensitive, not like the others. You've met Jeb?'

'We have,' Natalie replied, realising that Minsky's description had not been wrong. Across from her and Haddock sat a young woman, confident in herself, occupying an office, the sign on the door stating Crystal Andersson, Human Resources Manager.

'A good job,' Haddock said, although he struggled with the concept that such an accomplished and attractive woman would want to associate with a heavy metal band of indifferent quality.

'It is. I'm sorry about Alan, more than you would believe.'

'Try us,' Natalie said. She was not as easily swayed by a pretty face. So far, Jeb Barton, who she had thought charming, had been told by Minsky that he was anything but, that Alan Greenworthy was a mediocre singer but wealthy, and that with Gus Gomolka, what you saw was what you got. The verdict was still out on Minsky. Beth Sukkin had been open, one mark in her credit, although she was a lousy mother and possibly a worse person. Why should Crystal Andersson, even if the packaging was attractive, be what they saw before them?'

'Worked hard,' Crystal said. 'A degree from Sydney University, but it's my father's company. Not that he was dishing out favours, had to convince him that I was up to the job, even put me on probation for six months.'

Outside the office was a walkway, and down below, the engineering workshop.

'Mining equipment,' the young woman added.

'Business good?' Haddock asked.

'Tighter than before, but we've got a cushion of orders, two years' worth. We should be fine, but I've had to lay off ten per cent of the workforce, another five in the next month.'

'You've been painted as one of the band's women,' Natalie said, looking for a reaction. She was not about to be seduced by a pretty face and a pleasant office.

'I was Alan's woman if he wanted me, which he didn't.'

'Then why be there?'

'Alan was a strange person, independently wealthy, introverted, unsure of himself. I only saw the inner man at a Manglers' concert. Awful band, I'm sure you'd agree.'

'We do,' Haddock said.

'Alan knew they were, told me so. But with them, he's a changed person, the person he wanted to be. He hated his alter ego, which had plagued him all his life, but we are creatures of circumstance. His was solitary, an emotionally uptight mother who never hugged him or tucked him into bed as a child; a father who was stern and not often there.'

'The money?' Natalie asked.

'Old money, new money, it makes no difference. I met Alan at a concert, not as a groupie.'

'It sounds like love to me.'

'For me, and I loved Alan at the concerts, could not at any other time. He was a contradiction, resulting from bizarre parents.'

'Where are they now?'

'Both are dead, his mother before the father. He rarely went out, apart from the concerts and to meet Alice.'

'You've met her?'

'I know of her but never met. You can find her on the internet; a fortune for her time, but Alan didn't pay. I have no idea why, or maybe I do, creatures of our environment and our upbringing. Regardless, I adored the man, but outside of a concert, he was a disaster when we met. For some reason, he responded better with Alice.'

'Marriage?'

'If he had asked, but he wouldn't. The most I could hope for was time with him at a concert.'

'Did that include having sex with him?'

'It did, but it wasn't me the night he died.'

'You're remarkably calm, the love of your life, murdered,' Haddock said.

'I'm not, but I was conditioned, not for his murder, but to not see him again. I could not afford the wasted emotion. I had decided to move on, go overseas for a few years, and see if I could forget. I intended to tell him that night, but he wasn't there when I wanted to, off with another woman, and then he's dead. Now, I won't be able to forget him, doomed to a few lonely years until time and distance separate me from him.'

'Any idea who this other woman was? Do you know Beth Sukkin?'

'No idea who, and I do know Beth. A life destroyed, barely able to cope, sleeps with band members, gets drunk and whatever else. We all have our demons to deal with. Mine was loving a person who couldn't reciprocate.'

Natalie could see the power of a beautiful woman and that Haddock, an experienced police officer who should have known better, had swallowed the woman's story, hook, line, and sinker. It was a convincing story that might even be true, but it would need to be checked by evidence and talking to other persons. Until then, Natalie remained sceptical; the reference to Beth Sukkin appeared disingenuous.

***

Alice Minchin's website confirmed what Jeb Barton had mentioned, which Crystal Andersson had sneeringly confirmed. Long legs and provocative clothing, members only for the more revealing photos, phone number not given, but a contact form if someone wanted to meet her, either for sex, a massage or to accompany them on a business trip, to act as the man's woman.

Natalie understood that business and act were euphemisms for sex. And that having a website implied that Alice was not a tart off the street, a blowjob down an alley, or a quick screw in a seedy hotel.

Natalie and Haddock were surprised on meeting the woman in a penthouse apartment close to the city. 'One of my gentlemen friends,' Alice Minchin said when Haddock asked if it was hers. Dressed in an evening gown, even though it was ten in the morning, the woman exuded sexuality.

'Early in the day,' Natalie said, aware that her inspector had been taken aback by the woman when she opened the penthouse door.

'My friend is coming within the hour. I would appreciate it if you would keep your visit short.'

'As short as we can,' Natalie said, unsure if Haddock would add much to the meeting. She had started to worry about him; the stress of his wife and daughter weighed on him, and he was once again spending time with Theresa de Klerk, eating fast food too often, and his appearance was inappropriate for a police inspector.

The previously sharp investigative mind had dulled, and he had become an encumbrance to her as she was at the top of her game. Her skills were improving in leaps and bounds, and the reality was that someday, she would have to tell Superintendent

Payne that she was ready to accept a promotion and advance without the man who had mentored her. To her, it would be gross disloyalty, and it troubled her, but there seemed no other option.

'You want to talk about Alan?'

'We do. We've been told that the two of you were friendly.'

'By that, are you asking if we were lovers?'

'We are,' Haddock mumbled, looking away from a message on his phone.

'It was more than that,' Alice said, pulling up the top of her evening gown.

Natalie was unsure if she was using her obvious attributes to fluster Inspector Haddock or if she was a painted hussy. Regardless, the woman was in her early thirties and had probably been under the surgeon's knife to accentuate certain features, to remove others. But, overall, the somewhat prudish Natalie could not dislike the woman.

'He's dead, murdered at Cockatoo Island. We believe that he had been with a woman before his death. Whether she murdered him, we can't be certain.'

'I knew about him and the group he played with. It was his outlet. Some people need alcohol or drugs to reveal their true selves or the self they would prefer, but with Alan, it was that group and the concerts.'

'From what we know, you were his only true friend,' Haddock said. He had put the phone to one side and refocused on the woman.

'I cared about him as he cared about me. We met when we were both young. I was a brat, took advantage, and was unpleasant to him. With maturity, I realised he would always be there for me.'

'Your gentlemen friends?'

'Generous with their money, but they offer no emotional support, nor should they. It's a commercial transaction. I give them what they want. They give me what I want.'

'A bordello in the sky,' Natalie said. She wasn't sure why she said it, although she didn't want to hear about how the woman's life had been burdensome, nor did she want a lecture on humankind's oldest profession. Whether on a street corner, skirt hitched up around her arse, or swanning around in an evening gown at ten in the morning, it was still prostitution.

'Not that. The person I'm expecting rarely wants sex, prefers to sit and talk, put his feet up, and enjoy the ambience I provide.'

'Expensive way to relax,' Haddock said.

'Money is not a consideration for some. Normality, if only for a short time, is a luxury they crave, to be free of others looking to them for money or asking favours, waiting for them to fall flat on their faces, their assets there for the taking.'

'You're an escort, a fancy website, plenty of men. Does he agree? Did he agree about Alan?'

'I rarely see others, and there are other women I can send. As for Alan, that was between him and me, no one else; there couldn't be.'

'Then explain,' Natalie said.

'I came from a dysfunctional family, parents I loved but didn't love each other. I'm not about to give you a lecture, six children, a house in the bush, and barely enough to eat. We were financially sound. My mother was a university lecturer, and my father worked for Alan's father. No cruelty, no hunger, and good schools. Alan looked out for me and ensured I was safe. It isn't prostitution, and I wasn't contemplating it as a career choice.

'We had become each other's therapeutic drug of choice. Pure love for another individual, without complaint or criticism. Although what ailed him continued when I wasn't with him, and I was materialistic and sexual.'

'Alan knew you were sleeping with other men?'

'He did. He worried about me. A woman at Cockatoo Island does not come as a surprise to me. Have you found her?'

'What do you know of the other band members?'

'Not a lot. I met Jeb Barton and thought him polite but nothing more. Alan never saw them apart from when they were rehearsing or playing at a concert or a pub. There was always a woman. Over time, our relationship became more platonic, and we weren't ripping off each other's clothes every time we met. Sex has become mercenary to me, and Alan, he was almost a big brother.'

'Would you have married him?' Haddock asked.

'In an instant,' Alice Minchin said.

Five minutes later, the two police officers were hustled out of the penthouse. They could have said it was a murder investigation and used authority to remain, but for now, they would leave the woman alone with her benefactor.

Natalie said as they left the building, 'Were we told the truth?'

Haddock knew the answer. 'She's selling herself for a reason. Find out what it is.'

Chapter 4

There was one more person in the band to interview, Gus Gomolka, the guitar strumming Pole, but he would have to wait. Another development, possibly minor, but it needed immediate attention.

At State Crime Command, a visit by another politician. Not as well-known as the politician who had previously visited, the then prime minister of Australia, Ralph Davidson, who had attempted to use the police to deflect suspicion away from him in a murder investigation and then made a hash of it in a television interview that night.

Sam Galea, thirty-six years of age, the son of Maltese immigrants, had entered the New South Wales parliament at the last election. He arrived at the station in a late-model BMW, parked it in a place reserved for police vehicles only, unapologetic when a sergeant of twenty-five years standing with the police had bawled him out and told him to move his car.

Arrogant when he had no right to be, short and stocky when he thought he was attractive and charismatic, he had a powerful voice, a firm handshake, and a lopsided smile.

He was, Natalie thought, the person most unlikely to be elected to parliament by his electorate, but he had commanded a substantial majority. Labour party, an ardent advocate for the working man, those newly arrived in the country, and dismissive of the liberals, who represented right-wing ideology. He had been ejected from the chamber twice for abusive comments across the political divide.

The man, for his faults, was a seasoned debater, an astute political animal, and he exuded confidence.

In the station, he sat at the head of the table in the conference room, his arms open, ready to take on all-comers.

'Why are you here?' Haddock asked.

'I was at the concert. You will want to interview me at some stage, even though I was there as a private citizen,' Galea said.

'We don't believe you to be involved in the murder,' Natalie said. 'You gave your name at Cockatoo Island, reluctantly, we're told.'

'Not that I had any issue with being there, but a duly elected politician and heavy metal rock bands are not a suitable mix for a politician. Professionally, I must be serious and upstanding, but I enjoy the music and ambience in my off time. However, as you know, there was a fair amount of drug-taking and mud sticks. Political points, smearing the opposition, all too easy, parliamentary privilege.'

'Which you've used,' Haddock said. Galea represented the electorate where he had grown up, and the man was a divisive character. Some loathed him; some did not. Haddock had no thoughts either way, although the man had been arrogant when he arrived at the police station. When Ralph Davidson, the former prime minister, had visited, he had been friendly and appeared genuine to those in the station, but Galea did not. Some might have seen it as strength of character, but not Haddock, and he thought the man abhorrent.

'Do you intend to make a statement after you leave here?' Natalie asked.

'I will make a statement in parliament if it becomes necessary. I am not guilty of any crime other than my taste in music. I can also say that I was in the audience and gave a statement to the police at Cockatoo Island and, subsequently, at State Crime Command. No doubt the opposition will take the opportunity to rip me to shreds, but I'm more than capable of dealing with them.'

'You play it tough,' Haddock said.

'Politics is not for wimps, but you must know that.'

'We do,' Natalie said. 'Did you know the deceased?'

'On stage, but not personally. I watched them play, as well as the other groups. They were the best, but that's not much credit to them; some of them were lousy. It was a chance to unwind after wrestling with the opposition and ensuring the interests of the electorate I proudly represent.'

An impassioned speech by Galea held little weight at the police station. The man wasn't there as a concerned citizen, doing his civic duty, but protecting his political career. There had to be another reason.

'The truth, Mr Galea,' Natalie said. 'Time out from politics. You're a young man who grew up in Bankstown, exposed to alcohol and drugs, slept around, and made a fool of yourself. You're not unique in this, but now you're an up-and-coming politician, aiming to make your mark, future leader, and a possible seat in the Federal Parliament in time. And here you are at the first hurdle; a murderer throws you into the centre ring. What's the truth? We will find out in time, interview those there with you, and surely some must have recognised you.'

'Very well. I had more than a few drinks, smoked a couple of joints, high on the music, high of life, met up with a female, the usual.'

'Did you know her?'

'Casual hookup. It often happens at concerts. Incognito, the chance to let off steam. The pretence of being an upright citizen is hard, no doubt the same with a police officer. We're all guilty of sin, but I'm expected to be squeaky clean, and sometimes I'm not.'

'This woman?' Haddock asked.

'What I've told you, will it be in confidence?' Galea asked, the previous arrogance gone. The man was no longer a formidable political animal but caged and subdued.

'What have you told us,' Natalie replied, 'other than you are human?'

'There is an election next year. I must fight for the right to represent the electorate. An admission of drugs and casual sex could damage my chance.'

'In this day and age?' Haddock said.

'It's politics. Those against me will use it as a weapon, even if they are guilty of the same sin.'

Haddock had little sympathy for Galea; Natalie had none. To her, the man was guilty of more than he would admit to, although she did not regard murder as one of his crimes. The man portrayed a clean image, as most politicians would, but his dark side would be revealed if it became relevant. A heavy metal concert, drinking and smoking a joint, would not necessarily preclude him from political office, but he could become the butt of jokes, facing the mirth of others.

***

At ten that evening, a meat processing plant in Strathfield was the best place to meet Gus Gomolka. As had been described, he was a bear of a man with beefy hands, which Haddock thought would have been unsuitable for playing the guitar, but Minsky had said that he was accomplished and, with training and the requisite disposition to hard work and practice, he could be great. But Gomolka had a disregard for strenuous mental agility and discipline.

The three sat outside the plant on a bench. The night was cool, but Gomolka was adamant that he needed a cigarette, even if forbidden at the premises, and that cutting up cattle into their composite pieces was hard physical work.

'Minsky reckons you are accomplished on the guitar,' Haddock said to the man wearing white overalls, a hairnet, and covers on his shoes.

'I play what I like. He told me, but what does a Russian know?'

Natalie thought to say 'more than you,' but desisted. Prejudices which should have been left in the homeland migrated with the individual.

Physically imposing, taller than Haddock, Natalie could see that the man was muscled, resulting from repetitive heavy, sweaty, and dirty work.

'Alan Greenworthy, what can you tell us?' Haddock asked, looking at Gomolka's cigarette, wanting one but holding firm not to succumb.

'A decent guy who didn't say much, and I knew nothing about him. Barton said he had money, but he didn't flash it around. He always managed to find himself a woman. The classy one, the blonde, she was keen, but he could be dismissive of her, preferred them more earthy. Not sure he was killed because of a woman.'

'Explain earthy,' Natalie said.

'Rough, easy with her favours, a quick leg over, and then back to the gig. The blonde, she was serious, could have fancied her myself, but she wouldn't go for me.'

'Why not?'

'Look at me. Big, burly, no class, although I make good money out here. Also, I'm a drinker, vodka mainly, make a fool of myself sometimes, more than once fined for drunk and disorderly.'

'Pub brawls?'

'Too often, rarely lose.'

Gomolka, as with the others in the group, was a contradiction. He was a competent musician, although he had neither the look nor the manner of someone who should have been. Jeb Barton, the government employee, who Natalie thought had an innate charm, but others had regarded as below contempt. Minsky, the classically trained musician in Russia, taught music to reluctant children and spun a yarn about how heavy metal gave him inspiration. And then, Alan Greenworthy, dead and in the morgue. That man was more of a contradiction than the others combined. Well-educated, private schools, a privileged upbringing, even if a sterile household. Those in the band considered him wealthy, but it was more than that. It was serious money, enough to allow Greenworthy to travel the world ad infinitum, the best hotels, women, first-class airline tickets, and an exotic car in the garage. But, Natalie and Haddock had been to the man's house, an edifice perched on choice land close to Bondi Beach, on a headland, up high. However, once inside, it was in poor condition. This was where Greenworthy had lived, deprived of creature comforts, a place few had visited.

And whereas the motive of a disgruntled boyfriend or husband discovering his woman with Greenworthy at Cockatoo Island, in flagrante delicto, seemed the most likely, there might have been other motives.

Gomolka had mentioned the possibility, but he had come from a country where conspiracy abounded, death was a weapon used too often, and he was a seasoned fighter and an accomplished musician. And what of Jeb Barton, seemingly innocent? Was he what he made himself out to be? Was there a dark side to his persona, jealous of Greenworthy's easy ways with women, of Alice's and Crystal's love of the man?

These were questions formulated in Natalie Campbell's mind, although Haddock saw it as black and white, a fraught lover finding his woman in Greenworthy's clutches, drawing a knife and stabbing the man in the heart. But what of the woman? Where was she? What had happened to her? Was she dead?

It was food for thought; it was time to revisit Cockatoo Island.

***

Claude Liddie was in his cottage when Natalie and Haddock returned the following morning. They had taken the ferry; there was no need for the Water Police launch. The ferry from Circular Quay maintained a half-hourly schedule, and there had been plenty of opportunities for the murderer to further cover his tracks, conceal evidence, and be sure that the crime would not be solved.

Natalie realised that referring to the murderer as male was based on statistics. Murder was invariably a male's domain, but women had murdered, and it had been a woman with Greenworthy that night. Not Alice Minchin, not unless she had a reason to want her man dead, willing to wipe the expensive makeup from her face, lather her body with carbolic soap, and change out of the evening gown into clothing more suitable for a heavy metal concert. Natalie could not believe the woman would degrade herself, even if violence was in her mind. And as for lying down on the island, a quick fumble and sex with Greenworthy seemed incongruous unless she used it as a tactic to try to understand the man and his predilection for groupies and easy women. And even if she had loved and wanted Greenworthy, why would she choose him? Surely, she must have been conscious of how he lived: frugality an understatement. Did she have a means of getting his money? Was it more important than the man? Had she secured it?

'Not the first,' Liddie said.

Natalie caught the comment but not the context. 'First? Clandestine lovers? Murders?'

'The island's history, more than a few deaths here over the centuries. Cruel place back then, and have you seen inside the grain silos? Three convicts died in them, and nobody cared; others were strung up on the island, justice meted out by a corrupt military. Violent times, no alcohol back then, no drugs, and no tourists.'

Natalie realised that Claude Liddie was old school, had spent too long on the island, and his views on society had not adjusted to modern reality. And that Haddock was playing along with him, realising that Liddie would say more if he thought he was talking to someone attuned to his outlook on life.

She excused herself and left the men in the cottage. She would not be surprised if the Johnnie Walker Red Label was opened, the two men drinking and regaling each other with stories of their lives, and then Liddie, comfortable in Haddock's presence, saying more.

She knew her presence was counterproductive; better to walk around the island, get a feel for the place, and understand why Greenworthy thought up high near the silos was the best place for sexual congress. There were other places on the island, more than a few cottages, and the disused workshops had secluded rooms with basic creature comforts. Why a barren piece of land instead of somewhere cosier? Why not behind the stage?

The other band members would not have cared. They would have given them privacy. Or was it that the woman wanted secrecy or that Greenworthy didn't want them to know who it was?

Alice Minchin had admitted she would have married Greenworthy; Crystal Andersson had more than a passing interest in the man and had wanted a more permanent arrangement with him. Had they met? Were they aware of the contradictions with the man? Was it his money or him? Why would two attractive women, one selling herself and the other working for her father, want a man with psychological issues?

On the other side of the island, there was a small café. Natalie ordered a latte and a bun that had seen better days.

'Good to see you,' a voice from another table.

Natalie looked over and saw the smiling face of Jeb Barton. Alarm bells rang, consternation that the man was on the island.

'What are you doing here?' Natalie replied, putting her bun to one side. It was stale, but she did not intend to complain.

'The same as you,' Barton said. 'I've been out a couple of times since, trying to make sense of it, to see if I could remember who the woman was.'

'Have you?' Natalie replied, hoping that the man wasn't following her around. There was something about an attractive female police officer that made certain men interested. The only problem for her was that, so far, it had been the wrong kind of man. She didn't want a subservient man looking to her for authority and direction but a partner in life and love. Jeb Barton was not going to fill that position.

Barton moved over, sat opposite Natalie, and looked at the woman behind the counter at the café. 'Two lattes,' he said.

'Why did he not stay down below at the concert?' Barton said as he sipped his latte.

'Had you finished for the night?'

'We had. No one would have cared, and there were plenty of dark spaces nearby. I came here two days ago and took the last ferry off the island. It was dark then, and up where he had died, there wasn't much light, the worst place to choose.'

'It's hard to fathom. Do you have any idea how he lived?'

'Where, I know. I've already told you that. As to how, I can't answer, but it was a miserable existence.'

'What did you think? Did you ask?'

'Ask, I did. Think, I didn't. We're a motley bunch. You've met Minsky and Gus?'

'We have. Igor Minsky told us how he intended to take the heavy metal lyrics and rhythm and mould them into a symphony. Gus Gomolka told us he was a brawler who got into fights, but Minsky tells us he's a competent musician.'

'Gus is. I'm mediocre, and Minsky's up himself. Classically trained he might be, but on stage, he's a wet fish, rarely gets into the spirit of it.'

'What spirit? Literal or metaphorical?'

'Literal. We're meant to be anti-authoritarian, anti-whatever, bite the head off a chicken. But Minsky stays serious. Alan was wild on stage, and I smashed the drums, broke more than a few sticks, and there's Gus, doing his Jimi Hendrix. Igor tries, but he's incapable of the gay abandon. Not sure why, could be a result of growing up in Russia, trouble if you rebel too much over there.'

'We've been in Alan's house. Utilitarian. He lived in a few rooms, no luxury, purely functional. Alan Greenworthy had serious issues.'

'He did. Alice was a beautiful woman and keen on him. But at a concert, any slapper he could find. There was also the blonde woman, Crystal. No slouch in the beauty department, spoke well, and obviously came from a good home.'

'Did she come to the concerts?'

'Once or twice, but she didn't fit in. We thought she was a groupie initially, but it was Alan she always wanted, not that he always took her. I have no idea why she persisted, but Alan told me once that she was keen, but he wasn't about to commit, and then there was Alice, but that wasn't possible. Look at me; I would have taken either, but they don't look at me. I'm reliable, dependable, and a decent catch, but they're drawn to him for some reason. Sure, he had money, but as you said, he lived abysmally, never spent what he had, drove a bomb of a car, and dressed downmarket. What made him tick? What made them?'

'That's what we need to know. Any insights on your visits here to the island?'

'The man who looks after the island and lives in the cottage at the top of the island. He's a pervert.'

'I know him,' Natalie said.

'It was that time I stayed late on the island. I've got twenty minutes before the ferry comes. It's dusk. People stay overnight in tents and rent them for the night. There's a couple, obviously young and in love, or maybe it was lust. I could see they hadn't secured the opening, and it was flapping in the breeze. The caretaker, or whatever he's called, is sitting on a bench not far away. He's got a pair of binoculars trained on them, seeing more than he should. Decidedly creepy.'

'And you?'

'I thought it was gross. I could see what he was looking at: the two in the tent naked and going for it. I didn't stay, but he did. I could have disturbed him, but it wasn't for me to complain. Besides, who knows, the two could have been exhibitionists, doing it on purpose.'

'He wasn't far from where Alan and the unknown woman were. If what you are saying is true, would he have been watching?' Natalie said.

'Unlikely to have missed the opportunity, but as I said, dark up there,' Barton replied.

Chapter 5

Natalie considered informing Haddock what Jeb Barton had said about Claude Liddie. However, she did not, realising that camaraderie between the two men was more important than a hostile interrogation. Liddie would go on the defensive if accused, and was Barton's denunciation valid?

Liddie was the caretaker. He needed to know what was happening on the island, and carrying binoculars and a strong flashlight would have been expected. An amorous couple might not have been unexpected, and Liddie would have seen that more than once on the island. But Barton had lingered and taken a good look? It was evident he was lonely.

Any of those interviewed could be a murderer. Gus Gomolka's late-model Audi showed that the man had some money. Jeb Barton didn't and lived within his means, but was that because he was honest or timid? Was there a malicious undertone to the man, jealous of Greenworthy's success with women? Minsky was neither charismatic nor friendly, and he was a solitary character, composing obscure symphonies based on heavy metal music, which, to Natalie, grated on the ear and offended the sensibilities.

Natalie left Barton at the ferry. And, yes, they could meet in a few days to continue their conversation, and if he wanted to pretend to be Sherlock Holmes, that was fine by her if he didn't interfere with evidence, or conduct an interrogation of persons, or intimate that he had de facto authority from Sergeant Natalie Campbell of State Crime Command, Parramatta.

Free of the man, who had shaken her hand on parting but would have lurched forward for a kiss on the cheek if he could have got away with it, she continued her investigation of the island, first checking the tents where Barton had seen Claude Liddie. Even though it was mid-week, a few tents were occupied, and one scantily-clad female was hurrying over to the shower block. Natalie was conscious that the modern generation did not have the conservatism of previous generations and that naked flesh wasn't to be covered at all costs.

She had been camping in her youth, knew that people relaxed when sleeping under canvas and that an open flap on a tent could have resulted from that relaxed approach, not due to exhibitionism at what should have remained a private act.

Continuing, she reached the road to the island's highest spot. It was a road suitable for a truck, but since the navy had moved out, there was no motorised transport other than Liddie's electric golf cart and a front-end loader based over the other side of the island where the boats, sailing or motorised, were stored, for those who could afford them or had the interest to deal with the upkeep, and, Natalie assumed, with the resultant pleasure.

The light was burning in Liddie's cottage, the two men visible through the window. They were laughing, which boded well for more information. A caretaker sees all, and the man had been on the island for a long time. He knew all the nooks and crannies and had seen more than he should, whether in a tent or where the grain silos were. Indiscreet behaviour, cheating couples, and snatched romance were universal through the ages, not only on the island. But Liddie was in the box seat. The question was, would he reveal it to a police inspector? If he didn't, Natalie knew she had ammunition to shake him, an accusation that he abused his responsibility and was a peeping tom.

***

Margie Williamson was irate. Four years in prison for violently attacking a former lover in the kitchen of the house they had shared.

'I moved heaven and earth for that man, and there he is, after I come home early, in our bed with her next door. A shameless hussy, lucky she didn't get caught in the ensuing action. And now there's a murder, another cheating bastard, and the entire police force descend on my door.'

'Apologies,' Natalie said. She hadn't intended to interview the woman with her husband at the concert, as her alibi was strong. However, she had a criminal record, and it would be remiss not to meet with her. 'I believe that apart from giving your name and address at Cockatoo Island, you've not been harassed by the police.'

'Even so, I'm still on your database, and it was years ago. I'm in my forties now, holding down a good job, a husband I'm devoted to, and three children. How long before I'm left alone?'

Haddock could sympathise. He firmly believed that if a person had served their sentence, they should not be implicated or harassed as a potential suspect. Although Margie Williamson's crime bore similarities to the murder of Alan Greenworthy.

'Unfortunate that we've had to approach you, but you must understand that due to the murder, we must interview all persons, regardless,' Haddock said.

Natalie could see that, for some reason, the woman had been charmed by him but was dismissive of her. Was it the Haddock charm, attractive to women of a certain age? Natalie had seen it with Theresa de Klerk and now Margie Williamson.

'It wasn't me. The Maligned Manglers, an atrocious noise. Have you heard them?'

'Only a recording, and yes, we would agree, so would they. A disparate bunch, who, for various reasons, some sound, others extremely odd, would get together and try to belt out a tune. If you thought they were bad, what about the others?'

'My brother plays with the Desperados. His band had third billing. He thinks he's the reincarnation of one of the greats; don't ask me for a name.'

'Is he?' Natalie asked.

'Third billing to the Manglers, what do you think?'

'He's serious with his music?'

'The Manglers might have realised it was rubbish, but he doesn't. He's my brother, holds a steady job, and fancies himself as a star. The only star he'll see is when he stage-dives into the crowd. He was lucky that night; he didn't hit the ground hard, just bruised his ego. No one rushed to grab him, clearly indicating what they thought of him and his band. I've told him enough times, but it has fallen on deaf ears. No much more I can do, and his wife couldn't go, expecting their third child.'

'Did you see the Manglers?' Natalie asked.

'I did. I read that the dead man was with a woman. Is that correct?'

Haddock and Natalie had read that in the newspaper and realised that someone had been talking out of turn, a couple of hundred dollars for information given. Natalie thought of Claude Liddie, Haddock's drinking buddy. Haddock thought of Jeb Barton, his sergeant's would-be paramour. Whoever it was, it wasn't important, just unwise if too much was revealed or a hitherto unknown fact was revealed that the police were not cognisant of.

Regardless of someone making money on the side, the focus remained on Margie Williamson. Natalie could see she was a reformed person, a neat and tidy house in a neat and tidy suburb, although signs of her past life remained, the crudely inked tattoos on her arms. The woman had had a history before she attacked her lover, before he had spent months recuperating from the wounds inflicted with a carving knife. The man still bore the scars but now lived on the other side of Sydney, working from home and creating websites for those who could afford the quality work he produced.

Haddock had phoned him to gain an understanding of the woman. Bitter and resentful, he said that he had never forgiven her, and although he was guilty of cheating on her, he had never expected violence. He had not seen her in years, but his answer had been unequivocal when asked if she could harm another person. 'Riled, she would. Has she? What I did with the other woman was unforgivable, but Margie wasn't a shrinking violet. I'm certain she was playing up where she worked. Do you reckon she's involved?'

'No, just getting a background on her. Bad singing and fumbling attempts at sex on a cold and windy night hardly justify killing a band member.'

It had been a short conversation after Margie Williamson had been run through the database, as had all the other names and addresses of people at the concert, and her conviction had sounded alarm bells.

'Margie,' Haddock said, 'we believe you have a temper, quick to rile, quick to calm down. Is that correct?'

'It is, or should I say it was. Anger management keeps it under control. Are you trying to bait me? I was the wronged person, not him. Maybe I shouldn't have used that knife, but what was I to do?'

'Your reaction was understandable,' Natalie said. 'Only we have a dead body and no clues. What do you reckon?'

'A criminal mastermind, I ain't. A woman with him?'

'We believe so, proof that sex occurred.'

'Then she did it, which seems unlikely, or her disgruntled lover. Find her, solve the murder.'

Natalie wasn't sure why she asked for the woman's opinion other than Haddock was starting to irritate her. The woman had paid for her crime, and there was proof that her brother had been playing with one of the other bands. Unless there was evidence to the contrary, the woman was innocent of the murder of Greenworthy.

'What perfume do you use?' Natalie said as the two officers left the house.

'4711.'

It was the same perfume that had been found on Greenworthy. It wasn't proof, as it was relatively cheap and used by many women. It would be written up in her report, but apart from that, it was coincidental. Natalie hoped it would remain so.

***

The investigation had stalled. The realisation that without the woman, the investigation could not proceed. And that, if the person had been a groupie, she hadn't been seen around the stage or at the rear of it. Which meant that Greenworthy had met the woman elsewhere on the island, either prearranged or a casual pickup. Prearranged would require prior contact. His emails and his phone had been checked, but nothing apart from a message from Crystal, attempting to meet with him, and a message from him to Alice to say they should meet in the next week. Neither message indicated anything untoward. The reason that Natalie and Haddock were at Greenworthy's house early on a Thursday.

Hundreds of names and addresses were taken on the island, but it was impossible to interview each person in-depth, and if they did, what questions would they ask? Did you know the deceased? Did you kill him if the interviewee was male, or did you have sex with him if the person was female? It was a pointless exercise. The persons involved could have left the island or found a hiding place on the island, kept their heads low, waited for the furore to die down and then taken a ferry, but that would indicate premeditated murder rather than impulsive action. If that were the case, that would lead to the conclusion that the woman was there to weaken the man, to distract him, and then for her or another person to kill him. And there had been inconclusive evidence of another person. Even that was open to conjecture, as the CSIs had been vague about the possibility of another person. Where Greenworthy was found, the grass was short and dry, and to create an impression, it needed a maintained pressure for ten to fifteen minutes, and another person could have slipped in, stabbed the man once with a knife and retreated, a small boat waiting somewhere on the island.

There were plenty of places to tie up, to slip in under darkness, to draw Greenworthy off to one side, and then, after his death, for both persons or for one to slip away and over to the mainland. The vessel would not have needed to be motorised; a rowing boat or a kayak would have sufficed.

Natalie would take the ground floor at the house, Haddock, the second. What they were looking for, they weren't sure.

Before they started, the two reviewed what they had discussed the previous day. What they knew about the man; what they did not.

Natalie outlined the known facts. 'Reclusive, independently wealthy, keeps to himself, apart from Alice Minchin, who appears to have some sway over him. Enjoys heavy metal music and being up on a stage.'

'And we must regard the man as having mental issues. It's one thing to be introverted and shy; it's another to not have them on a stage. And then there is his predilection for loose women at the concert. There are issues, especially after meeting with Crystal Andersson, who appears normal, and Alice Minchin, apart from her lifestyle, appears an ideal mate for the man. Yet he chooses neither and avoids the possibility. This house, reflective of the man?'

'That's an opinion, not a fact,' Natalie said. She looked around the kitchen and realised someone had tidied it since the man had died. It was no longer taped off, although the padlock remained on the front gate. Someone else had a key.

The emphasis changed. The person with the key was important. The two looked through the house for information that would lead them to that person, but none could be found. On the second floor were four bedrooms, three of which had a bed with a mattress but no sheets or pillows. In the fourth, the master bedroom, the bed was made, the sheets were clean, and the air smelled fresh.

'Someone's living here,' Natalie said. 'A woman.'

The house had been checked after the man's death, and no sign of another person had been found. Whoever it was had moved in after his death. It was suspicious.

On the bed, a Stephen King novel. Natalie, who had read some of his books, wondered what sort of person would read a horror novel in the depressingly neglected home of a murdered man. Someone with a morbid outlook, someone who could be a murderer.

Haddock disagreed as he had read the novel, one of the author's more benign. Even so, finding a woman in the home was important. But who was she? Where was she? A lover or a relative, or someone who had no relationship with the man, other than she knew that the house was empty and how to get in? After all, there was a padlock at the front gate, no electric fences surrounding the property, no savage dogs, and it would have been possible to clamber up a tree, stretch out to the top of a wall, and jump into the front garden. It was also a neighbourhood where people minded their business and did not get involved.

In a wardrobe, a woman's clothes, a small suitcase at the bottom. Whoever it was, they intended to make themselves comfortable.

Natalie looked in the bathroom. The shower was still wet, and a towel hung on a towel rail, a collection of bottles next to the sink, a toothbrush in a jar, and an opened tube of toothpaste.

It was an unexpected development. All that was needed was the woman. Downstairs, the sound of a door opening. Natalie moved first and was down the stairs in an instant, securing the door from the kitchen to the backyard. 'Sergeant Natalie Campbell, Homicide,' she said as she flashed her warrant card.

'Surprised you took so long finding me,' the woman said. 'Fancy a cup of tea?'

'Who are you?' Natalie blurted out, taken aback by the woman's gall. Breaking and entering, and they were police officers, but there was no fear in the woman, only cordiality.

Natalie shouted up the stairs. 'Come on down; the situation is under control.'

Haddock appeared, looked at the woman, and sat down. 'How long?'

'In the house?' the woman, in her mid-thirties, dark-haired, and Chinese, said.

'Three days. Alan wouldn't have appreciated my presence here.'

'What are you to him? A friend, another lover?'

'I'm his wife. Sorry, you would not have known that. But that was Alan, excessively private, preferred solitude, and should have been a monk, but there was this other side to him, wanting to break out. That was the man I married, not the man he was.'

'We agree that he was a complicated man to understand, but a wife. Can you prove it?'

'Yes, I can. My name is Melinda Greenworthy. I grew up in Hong Kong, moved to Cambodia, and met Alan there.'

'This house in your name?' Haddock asked.

'It is or soon will be. We were married overseas and lived as a couple for a while, but then Alan reverts to type, and I return to Hong Kong.'

'When was the last time you saw him?'

'Two years, maybe three, a brief reconciliation, three weeks in Cairns, love under the palm trees. We realised we couldn't make a go of it. I was stuck in my ways and enjoyed the bright lights, whereas he was solitary, and we parted. We've kept in contact; no reason not to.'

'Yet your husband is here, living in this house, singing in a band, having sex with groupies, and a prostitute. Weren't you concerned?'

'For Alan, no. We stayed married and supported each other. We rarely met but spoke often. Alice, that's who you're referring to?'

'It is. Do you know her?'

'She was special to him; they had known each other for years. She didn't know about me, or I don't think she did. Alan kept his cards close to his chest and didn't discuss his private life. There was another woman keen on him, Crystal. Have you met her?'

'We have,' Haddock said. 'Your plans?'

'I'll fix up the house. I might sell, but I'm not sure yet. I need to see to Alan first.'

'A formal identification?'

'If you want. Sugar, milk?'

Three people sat around a small kitchen table, one of them unexpected. If proven to be his wife, she would inherit the man's estate and provide additional input into who or what Alan Greenworthy was.

Natalie took a photo of the marriage certificate the woman had shown her and sent it to Victoria Adderley in the legal department at State Crime Command. If the certificate was validated and recognised in Australia, then without a will from Alan Greenworthy to the contrary, the woman would inherit. Natalie did not believe that there would be an issue. And that Melinda – it seemed hard to afford her the title of Mrs or the surname of Greenworthy – came across as capable and astute, expecting the police to find her at some stage.

'You don't seem upset,' Haddock said.

'Stoic. My grandparents suffered during the cultural revolution in China, and my parents experienced the aftermath. Outward displays of sorrow were not permitted in my family. You would understand if you have read the history of China's recent past. Alan was a good person but did not show emotion, nor will I.'

Natalie thought it was an adequate explanation, although it did not explain why nobody knew that Alan Greenworthy had been married. Melinda's explanation, when pressed, was to say it was complicated, and Alan had hidden parts of his life that he did not want to reveal. However, Victoria Adderley phoned after fifteen minutes and confirmed that the marriage would be recognised in Australia. The only issue was, why Cambodia? Who was Melinda Greenworthy?

For now, there was a motive: a woman who, by her own admission, gained a lot by her husband's death, someone who knew of his love of heavy metal and loose women, a person who could have been at Cockatoo Island, meeting with her husband, making love to him, and then stabbing him in the heart.

Why she had remained hidden and then become visible concerned both officers, although, as Natalie saw it, she would have had to reveal herself at some stage if she intended to claim the inheritance. If she was a murderer, she had played a strategic game and had a hidden side to her.

The murder investigation had taken another turn, but now it showed the possibility of a solution if only someone would tell the unvarnished truth, but who was that person to be? Certainly not Melinda Greenworthy.

After two hours with the woman, Natalie and Haddock left the house, more confused than when they had entered, realising they had not completed their search of the place, concerned there might be more hidden. And now, the added complication of a search warrant if they wanted to enter again.

Chapter 6

Superintendent Payne wanted an update, not from a report but from the two police officers and Victoria Adderley, who Natalie suspected was having an affair with Payne. Not that it worried her, but she regarded Victoria as a friend, and didn't want to see her burnt on the fire of public opinion, the butt of jokes and sneers in the corridors of the police headquarters.

Behind closed doors, Payne, affable at night, although he could be officious during the day, handed Haddock a can of beer, another to Natalie, and a soft drink to Victoria. 'The usual?' he said.

Haddock had not warmed to Payne initially when he replaced the previous incumbent, but after several murder investigations, he had found respect for the blunt-talking man, realising that when the heat was on, he would be protecting his officers, ensuring they had support and the freedom to do their job.

'The usual,' Haddock replied as he sipped his beer. 'A further complication, unforeseen, a wife.'

'Legit?'

'She is. Victoria's checked it out. The woman's claim to the estate appears valid, and she will inherit.'

'And Greenworthy had plenty.'

'Old money, stocks and bonds, real estate. Greenworthy did not get involved, left it to a trusted colleague of his father.'

'Who cheats if he can.'

'Fraud has been out there,' Victoria said. 'Generous payments for work done and skilful investments have expanded the Greenworthy family's wealth. Alan Greenworthy had the opportunity to sit back, enjoy himself, travel, and live like a king.'

'Yet he lived like a pauper,' Haddock said.

'Reason?' Payne asked. One word sufficed.

'Psychological,' Natalie said. 'It is, or was, the only explanation.'

'Ambiguous statement. What does it mean, Sergeant?'

'This wife, legitimate from what we can see. But why is she at the house? Why didn't she contact us on arrival into the country? If we are to believe the woman, she was fond of him. She's got his wealth, is living in his house, and we have no reason not to allow her.'

'But suspicious,' Payne said.

'Exceedingly. We know Greenworthy was with a woman the night he died and that his wife wasn't concerned, nor about the other two that were trying to get him to commit.'

'Which he could not have if he was married. Do these other women know, and why was he overseas? Backpacking around the world or living it up? He's a hermit in Australia who often came out and made a fool of himself. Could it be a fabrication, hiding away for fear of something he had done? Crime overseas, underage children, drug running, or even guns. Or could he be involved with ASIO?'

'Australian Security Intelligence Organisation? Far-fetched, don't you think, Superintendent?' Natalie said.

'I agree, but what was it with the man? Bizarre behaviour. There must be an explanation.'

Both Natalie and Haddock knew there was and that it was critical to find out. In the meantime, the woman who claimed to be Alan Greenworthy's wife would stay in the house, drawing on a joint bank account in their names. She had woven a convincing tale, but was it fact or fiction? It was important to know as she was the person who had gained the most financially. But murder was not only about money but also about love, lust, anger, and hatred.

***

Sam Galea did not enjoy the day. He had arrived at the New South Wales parliament house in Macquarie Street in Sydney full of confidence, the speech rehearsed, willing to make an impassioned speech that he was, as were others, allowed a private life if their electorate had faith in them, and that no laws had been broken, moral or legal.

If willing to admit it, he was aghast at the headline that had appeared in a scurrilous newspaper and the subsequent social media condemnation.

Politician involved in sordid murder. A love triangle, was he involved?

The headline drew attention, but then the paragraph below explained that Sam Galea, an up-and-coming member of the New South Wales Parliament, was at the heavy metal concert and had given his name and address to the police. If it was that, the love triangle had occurred elsewhere on the island, and he was not implicated. But the damage was done: the headline was sensationalist and deceiving, guilty as charged, political career dashed or soon would be.

After all, he had criticised and lambasted opposition members for the slightest infraction and had been ejected from the chamber twice for not withdrawing his comments. But now, the shoe was on the other foot. It had been easy to lambast and use rhetoric to demean another. It was a different matter to be on the receiving end.

'I wish to make a statement,' Galea stood up, awaiting a nod from the speaker's chair to continue.

Howls from the opposition, mild cheers from Galea's side of the chamber.

'Please continue,' the speaker said.

'My name has been maligned by a scurrilous press and biased social media,' Galea said in a firm voice. 'It is true that I was on the island on the night in question and that a murder was committed. However, I do not consort with criminals or commit illegal acts.'

Howls from the opposition. Galea knew his political life was on the line, and his defence was weak. If it had been an opera that he had attended, that would have lent credibility, but it wasn't; it was heavy metal, the starring act, the Maligned Manglers, and their singer dead.

As a representative of the people, a serious-minded individual should always conduct themself with decorum. There was no day off, a chance to let the metaphorical hair down, get drunk, use recreational drugs, or fornicate with random women. All crimes that Galea had been guilty of at one time or another.

He had considered not going to the concert, but at the last minute, unable to sit quietly in the apartment he owned in the electorate, he had accepted the invitation of two of his closest friends, friends since his teens.

Not only had he not enjoyed the night, but now he was defending himself, hoping to salvage his political career. If he could defuse the situation, it would be old news in two weeks, another disaster for the government, or another politician committing an indiscretion.

Hadn't that been the situation for Robert Gardener, the opposition's spokesman on the environment, caught in his parliamentary office with his trousers around his ankles, literally, with his personal assistant, while his wife was at home looking after the children.

The next day, on the parliament steps, Gardener and his wife holding hands, the loving couple, and the man saying that it was a misunderstanding and that he loved his wife.

Galea had known the truth and used parliamentary privilege to denounce the man and to offer proof that Gardener was a serial lecher and that the personal assistant was using him as a stepping stone to advance herself.

He had been ejected from the chamber for bringing it into disrepute, compliments from his side of the chamber, derision from the other. And then, three weeks later, Gardener was on his feet in the chamber, outlining his party's policy on the environment and global warning, his wife in the gallery looking down at him with a beaming smile. Galea, not having known that she had been his personal assistant before the latest one.

Seduction and illicit affairs were to be tolerated; murder was not, not even by association, as it leaves a stench in the parliament, a cloud hanging over it.

Galea did not finish his speech; the derision from the other side of the chamber was so much that the speaker had to declare that Sam Galea would need to enter it into Hansard's, where it would be recorded.

Three hours after his ignominious attempt at making a speech, he met with Inspector Haddock and Sergeant Campbell.

'You called us here,' Haddock said.

'You're aware of the slurs against my name?' Galea said.

'And your speech in parliament,' Natalie said.

'Not my finest hour,' a humbled Galea said.

Natalie didn't take to the man, slippery and sleazy, an opportunist who would do and say whatever if it was to his advantage. Haddock gave the man credibility as he was the state member of parliament for the electorate where he grew up. He was controversial but still held the majority in the electorate, and he had been a positive influence, promoting the area as a fine place to bring up a family, business-friendly, multicultural, and inclusive.

Natalie had come across his sort before; and the man would lie, even to the police, if he could.

The three sat at a café close to Hyde Park. Galea had ordered for them.

'Why here? What can we do for you?' Natalie asked.

'I am not involved in the murder, that you know,' Galea said.

'We are willing to concede that possibility. What is unclear is why you went to the concert. You must have realised that it was an inappropriate venue for a person in your position.'

'I didn't expect there to be a murder. It was nighttime; most would not have known me, and if they had, they would not have criticised or used it to slur my name.'

'Which you do if given a chance.'

Galea smiled. 'Touché, Sergeant. In the bear pit of parliamentary debate, it's dog eat dog. I play the game, better at it than most. Maybe it will backfire, but it's good fun, and I'm friends with some I lambast.'

'We would,' Haddock said. 'It still doesn't explain why we are here,' Haddock said.

'I know Alice Minchin.'

'How?' Natalie asked. Haddock, not as naïve, knew the answer.

'The occasional luxury. Sometimes, I need the best. The same as a Cuban cigar and a fine bottle of brandy.'

'An expensive whore,' Natalie said, understanding what the man meant.

'I wouldn't call her that, but she's available at a price. With her, discretion is assured. Mine is a crafted persona that serves me well, and I see no reason to change, but that's why Alice is so expensive. She's non-critical, listens, and does not condemn. In parliament, in public, and especially in my electorate, I must be an attentive ear, a dynamic force, fighting for the underdog, taking on the dishonest property developers, attempting by rational debate to moderate their activities, and if not, to use legal means. Occasionally, the chance to relax, whether at a heavy metal concert with friends or in a penthouse with Alice, they are both vital to me.'

'If we concede that your relationship with Alice Minchin is therapeutic,' Natalie said, 'it doesn't explain how you know she is part of our investigation.'

'Pure chance. I saw her dressed downmarket at the concert and talking to a man. It was only afterwards that I realised it was Alan Greenworthy.'

To Haddock, it seemed the breakthrough they were looking for. To Natalie, it was another avenue to explore. Was Alice the mystery woman? Was it her on that island who had made love to the man, then killed him?

There were too many ifs and buts and not enough facts.

'Did you speak to her?'

'No. Only that she was at the concert, although why she was talking to Greenworthy, I don't know.'

'Friendly, animated, loving?' Haddock asked.

'I saw her briefly. I didn't want to let her know that I had seen her. All I know is that she was there.'

'And if it comes out in parliament, more derision,' Natalie said.

'As you said. I can deal with it. Alice does not deserve to be involved. We all have our secrets. You know mine, and now, you know Alice's. I will never mention it to her, and if you decide to talk to her about it, which I'm sure you will, please don't use my name.'

***

The first concrete lead had come from an unexpected quarter, from Sam Galea, whose troubles continued, more abuse in the chamber at parliament house, a stern talking to from his political leader, and questions were being asked in his electorate from those who had championed his selection. The man was worried, but the persona he showed was confident, and he was sure he would survive and become a political heavyweight within a few years.

Natalie and Haddock had seen the other side to the man, as had Alice Minchin if what he had revealed was true. Alice Minchin's name had not been taken on the island, but it was obvious that a few would have slipped through the cracks and left the island before the body was discovered, the alarm was given, and the police arrived on the island.

Melinda Greenworthy, the previously unknown wife, had given a press conference in front of her house, stating that Alan had been a good man and that their relationship had been complicated yet loving.

Not that Claude Liddie thought much to it as he sat with Haddock on the porch of his cottage. It was a weekday, tourists walking by, looking in this window and that, even his if the light was on.

'Damn nuisance, sometimes,' he said. 'This angle you're talking about, a disgruntled lover. Do you reckon it's possible?' The Johnnie Walker Red Label was open, and both men had a glass. Haddock would have preferred not to drink so early in the day, but if he wanted Liddie to talk, he needed to join him in what seemed his only pursuit. The man was a drinker, probably due to his wife dying and lonely nights on a foreboding island.

'It's a possibility, only you've been sparing with the truth,' Haddock said.

'I've been honest.'

'Honest with what you've told, but what haven't you told us yet? Not the first lovers up here, and what about the accommodation, the tents down below? More than a few drugs, plenty of alcohol, easy to get an eyeful. Can't be helped, a man on his own, walking around the place, knowing where to hide. What say you? Greenworthy up here, an odd place; why there, why not below? Could it have been the two of them walking up here, discussing, making plans, cementing their love with an embrace, and then sex? You must have seen it more than a few times, easy pickings with the tents, and then there are the rented cottages. A man like you, on your own, I can't blame you. Level with me, man. It's murder, not musical chairs or postman's knock. Someone has died violently. You're the caretaker. Surely you've got something to say.'

'I'm not sure what you want from me,' Liddie said as he topped up Haddock's glass.

'Look, it's only natural. An innocent person, the police asking questions. That person gets nervous. They start to consider what to say and keep facts to themselves, which could be vital. We've just met with a man in the last twenty-four hours who told us that a woman associated with the dead man was at the concert.'

'And she said she wasn't?'

'Precisely. It might mean nothing, but she could be the woman with him, even the murderer. We can't discount any possibility.'

'You think that I saw them. That I am a peeping tom.'

'Are you?'

'No. My job is to ensure that this place is secure and that nobody vandalises, steals, or commits murder. And no, I didn't see the two where the man died.'

'But you did see them up here. The truth is preferable.'

'A few come up, even at the concert. I might have seen them, but I couldn't be sure. I did not go over to where the man died; I only discovered him later. Not sure how much later, but the music was still going on down below.'

'Fifteen, twenty minutes, according to the CSIs and Pathology,' Haddock said, although they could only be precise to within an hour. 'Is it a place where young lovers go?'

'Not the most comfortable, better places up here. I've seen more than a few over the years, and you get used to them, and if they're not causing trouble, I leave them alone. Why would I intrude?'

Haddock had to concede the man the last point. He was responsible for ensuring the island was looked after, not to deter loving couples. He couldn't be sure whether the man saw more than he should.

And besides, he couldn't stay long with Liddie, who looked like he was settling in for a night with the whisky. He had promised to go to the family home to try and calm his daughter and console a distraught mother. Life was tough, and he wasn't sure when it would end, only that he had to continue, to hope there was a light at the end of the tunnel, but so far, he hadn't seen even a glimmer.

Chapter 7

Due to the sensitivity of the subject matter, it had been decided that Natalie should meet with Alice Minchin. The woman might be guilty, but first, she needed to be allowed to explain why she was on the island, whether she had lain with Greenworthy, whether she knew of Melinda Greenworthy, and if she did, why she was pursuing the man.

The penthouse was the agreed-upon location, and it had been confirmed that no gentlemen friends, whether the person who owned it or those who rented its occupant's time, would be coming for three hours.

A bottle of wine was open on a coffee table, a couple of glasses alongside.

'I'm aware of certain facts,' Alice said. She was dressed casually, with a loose-fitting blouse and a pair of jeans. She was barefooted. 'You want explanations; I'm unsure I know all the answers. I know it focuses guilt on me, but I am innocent.'

Natalie wasn't willing to concede the woman's innocence. As with others, there was a depth to her, hidden facets that she might not want to reveal but would. This was a murder investigation. The truth, unblemished and forthright, no shillyshallying, was critical.

'What facts?' Natalie said as Alice poured herself a glass of wine, attempting to pour one for Natalie, who put her hand over the glass. She was with the woman for answers. The time for a friendly chat was long gone. Alice had been on the island; she was a potential murderer.

'Melinda.'

'You knew, yet you failed to mention it.'

'I thought it was over between them. Alan said it was a sham marriage, not legal in Australia.'

'It's a legal document. We've checked, and according to the woman, they had remained married out of choice, even though they had infrequent contact.'

'It appears I've been duped. I had hoped that he would one day want me permanently. Who is he? I don't know, and I believed I knew him better than anyone else.'

'Did Melinda contact you, or did you visit the house, which would mean you had a key?'

'I chose him long ago as a husband and would have married him, but then he disappeared. He came back after a few years, a wife overseas, but he was distraught. What had happened, and I don't know, had worsened his condition. With my love, he would have slowly reengaged with society. Believe me, he was not as bad as you've been told. But I wasn't the sanity. It was that goddamn band and their music that worked for him.'

'Could Melinda have caused the change in him and that you were tarred with the same brush, Alan unable to trust another woman?'

'Alan wouldn't talk about her; only said she wasn't to blame. And now she will inherit if there is no will.'

'Is there? The man had a lawyer and people looking after his money. Did Alan trust them?'

'He trusted them, because they were either indebted to his grandfather and father or tied up in so much legalese, they wouldn't have dared to defraud.'

'Regardless of Melinda and Alan's deception, there is another more pertinent fact that we need to discuss. I suggest you pour yourself another glass of wine, and if you don't answer truthfully, you will be taken to State Crime Command. The interrogation there will not be cordial but precise and exhaustive.'

A nervous woman poured another glass of wine as instructed and then sat back in her chair, attempting to look relaxed, but was anything but.

'You were seen,' Natalie said.

'Where?'

'Cockatoo Island, dressed downmarket, talking to Alan. We have a witness who will sign a statement that you were there. If you deny, we could find others who will identify you.'

'I couldn't tell you before, could I? What would you have said?'

'Back then, the truth would have weighed in your favour, but now, I have to believe you are an unreliable witness.'

'And possible murderer,' Alice added.

'Precisely. Either here or State Crime Command, your choice.'

'Not much of a choice,' Alice said as she gulped down the contents of the glass. 'I wanted him and knew of his history, of Melinda, but not in detail. He told me they had met in Cambodia, fallen in love, married, and then he realised that it was his money, not him, that she wanted.'

'Which is what she has got. Planned?'

'I wouldn't know. He lied to me; we would have had a serious talk about it if I had known. He was a child in some ways, letting others look after his interests. He didn't even pay the house bills, leaving it to others. They might have fleeced him, but he would not know.'

'I thought a complex set of agreements and charitable and financial intent towards the grandfather and father held those persons in check.'

'Do you believe that? I'm sure they were dipping their hands into the cookie jar.'

It was an interesting question, Natalie thought. If there was money to be had, did she have a price? She knew of police officers who took bribes, but she was realistic: everybody has a price.

'Why did you go to the island?'

'Alan had been avoiding me. I was concerned his condition was becoming worse. We spoke on the island. He was surprised to see me and told me he wasn't himself, and I could see a woman looking over at him. I knew what he had lined up.'

'A groupie? Were you concerned?'

'You ask me, a woman who sells her body to whoever has got the money. Was it that slimy Galea?'

'You saw him?'

'I did, but thought he hadn't seen me. He's in trouble, the same as I am.'

'Was it you with Alan at the island?'

'Up the top, like a couple of teenagers on heat. There was nothing wrong with what we were doing.'

'Did you kill him?'

'Why? I wanted him to make a decent woman of me. I had no reason to want him dead. I left him up there as I made my way down a set of metal stairs at the rear of the place and got away before anyone else saw me. That's the truth.'

Natalie wanted to believe the woman, but, as with the others, the truth did not come easily. She couldn't believe Alice Minchin any more than she could believe Melinda Greenworthy. Haddock had a similar problem with Claude Liddie, who saw plenty but kept the most contentious to himself.

'Tell me more about Melinda,' Natalie said. Even if Alice was unreliable, she knew of Alan Greenworthy and his unusual relationship with his wife. And if Melinda had been in contact with her husband regularly, why hadn't she visited him? Why hadn't he visited her? He hadn't been out of the country for five years, and there was no record of Melinda Greenworthy entering the country, although she could have used her maiden name. Even so, more needed to be known about the woman. She was mysterious but no more so than her husband.

'I'm not sure there is a lot more to tell. Alan went overseas and did not keep in contact, which didn't surprise me, and then he was at my door, asking if he could come in. This was before I sold myself and lived in a gilded cage. He was quieter than I remembered, with a soulful look as though he had seen a lot and experienced more. He wouldn't talk about it, only saying that he had married a Chinese woman and that it had been good for a while, and then it had soured. He would speak more to me than anyone else, almost certainly more than he would have spoken to her. But did he ever tell the full story or bottle up what he didn't want to remember?'

'What do you think?'

'I don't believe anyone understood that man's anguish, what was hidden in the deepest recesses of his mind.'

'Malevolent, cruel, into rough sex?' Natalie said. She was fishing, pushing the woman, wanting to understand the dead man and those who professed to care. She could not believe that Melinda did but was that prejudiced, the woman appearing at the opportune moment to claim her inheritance. And how had she known that the man was dead? On the internet, she could have found a copy of an Australian newspaper which would have reported the name, but that would have required conscious effort, or had she been notified by persons unknown that an obstacle had been removed?

Alice was the closest person to Alan Greenworthy, according to her, but could she be trusted? After all, she sold herself to men, pretended to care, to caress, to have sex with them, conversation if that was required. She played a part with the men; was she an actor with the police? A question that would need to be answered truthfully and without malice or intent to deceive.

The intercom buzzed, and Alice rushed to answer. She was no longer in control but a puppy on a leash. 'Yes, sweetheart. Give me five minutes to make myself pretty for you.' On the other end of the intercom: 'Ten minutes, no need for pretty. You know what I want.'

Flustered, Alice came back to where Natalie was sitting. 'I'm sorry, but he's here,' she said.

'And you need to pay the rent,' Natalie replied.

'Something like that.'

In the foyer, Natalie observed a man waiting near the elevator.

He looked as if he was a businessman, but he could have been a criminal, a drug runner, a wife-beater, or a saint. And if a sinner, what kind? Did he know of Alan Greenworthy? Was there a connection to be made?'

***

The remaining members of the Maligned Manglers had met, decided that they wanted to continue, and were actively looking for another person to replace their lead singer. Jeb Barton told Natalie that in the heavy metal community, a murdered band member gave them gravitas.

The Maligned Manglers were hardly the stuff of legends, although Alan Greenworthy might have been.

In Cambodia, the local police were working with the Australian police to investigate who Greenworthy was, where Melinda came from, her background, and if she was involved in illegal activities. A similar request had been made to the Hong Kong police, although there would be delays in their reply.

Would it affect Melinda's claim on Alan Greenworthy's estate if she had been involved in a crime? Victoria Adderley thought it would have no bearing, as the woman had not committed a crime in Australia, and her last time in the country had been four years before, the holiday in Cairns eventually confirmed.

Jeb Barton looked across the table at State Crime Command. He had come of his own volition. Natalie was concerned that he might ask her out, which she would decline.

'What is it, Jeb?' Natalie asked.

'You've found the woman that was with him?' Barton said.

'We have. She has admitted to it, not to his murder. Is there an issue?'

'And another woman was waiting for him?'

'How do you know this? It's not been reported.'

'I don't know about the woman with him, but I know who the other woman was. She was around the back of the stage, asking for him. Could she have killed him?'

'Her name?'

'Crystal Andersson. She was keen on him, even though he was ambivalent, unsure if she would have been up to a romp on the island. She could have been jealous. And hell hath no fury like a woman scorned.'

'Shakespeare.'

'William Congreve. I remember the quote from my school days. She was livid when he took off with another woman.'

'Another person who said they were not at the concert. Why haven't we been told this before?'

'Maybe you didn't ask the right questions.'

Natalie realised there was truth in what the man said. Another woman had slipped through the net on the island. If she had stormed off in a huff and taken the next ferry, she would have been home before the body had been discovered, and Greenworthy's death was a cumulation of events and persons leading to one outcome – murder.

'What else don't we know? What other questions should we have asked? Are you aware of his background, his time overseas, a wife?'

'None of us were.'

'None indicates that you've spoken to the other Manglers.'

'About keeping the band going, but yes, we spoke about Alan. How couldn't we? With him murdered, we are in demand. Macabre, not sure I like it.'

'You do,' Natalie said. 'You are the same as Minsky and Gomolka. Frustrated musicians, disappointed with your lives, wanting to be somebody. Jeb, apologies for my bluntness, but you are middle management.'

'That's true, and Alan had it all, and it didn't make him happy.'

'Enough to play in a band and not care about employment. Sorry, that's a flippant answer. He was wealthy, and a wife and two other women professed love for him. And you alone, with no girlfriend. It must have irked.'

'It did. I'm Mr Average, lost in a group of four on the stage. Even Minsky had more success than me with the women, but I would have taken Crystal in an instance.'

'Love?'

'I thought she was a good person, but now, could she be a murderer?'

'We've no proof. Did you know about his wife?'

'No, but he wouldn't have told me. Do you reckon there is something about him that is important?'

'We do. We believe we know the woman he was with on the island, but that's on her admission. No proof that it was her or that Crystal would have known where they had gone.'

'Not sure if I am a liar? Or could I be someone else, pretending to be middle management when I'm dynamic and resourceful?'

'Jeb, you are middle management. Be proud of it, accept the reality, find a nice girl, not someone who hankered after another.'

Natalie thought it was the kindest thing to say to the man but realised that Barton, like Haddock, had reached the pinnacle of his career, and for them, it was a case of holding on and accepting the inevitable.

***

Claude Liddie had seen the flowers placed on the spot where Greenworthy had died. There was no indication of the person who had put them there.

He had not told Haddock the last time they had spoken, not because he intended to be obstructive but because he had a secret. It was a secret he had guarded, which gave him little concern but would take him from caretaker to suspect. In his defence, he would say that it had been demanding since his wife died. He had thought of moving from the island and living in a small apartment, but he had seen some and knew that on the island, his backyard was the expanse of the place, the engineering workshops, the prison ruins, the ghosts of the past. Not that he believed in apparitions, but his wife had been a student of the island's history and had contributed significantly to what was known of the place. She knew where the people had suffered, their names and crimes, and those who had died at the hands of the overseers or through disease and neglect.

To him, the island was his wife, and if he was no longer a caretaker, through infirmity or enforced retirement, he was sure that a place would be found on the island for him to stay and to see out his remaining years.

Even so, the loneliness weighed on him, and he had often walked around at night, knowing where not to tread, to be as quiet as a mouse, to watch those in the tents and what they were doing, to look in the windows of the guest houses, to see amorous couples.

He missed a woman's affection, her arms around him, the banter of a loving husband and wife. She had died of cancer in her early fifties. And now, he was sixty-three, and time was against him, not that he would consider another, but looking did no harm. But he knew the police would not agree, and if they knew that he had seen Greenworthy and the woman on that grass, they would have questions he could not answer. However, he could not ignore the flowers. He had no option but to phone Inspector Haddock.

Haddock and Natalie looked at the flowers. They had taken a ferry to the island and would take a water taxi back to the mainland if they were to stay long. The island was not far from the mainland, and Natalie was sure she could have swum the distance, but those incarcerated never tried, apart from Fred Ward and Frederick Bitten in 1863. Ward then went on to a career as Captain Thunderbolt, a notorious bushranger, before his luck ran out in 1870 when he was shot by a police constable in Northern New South Wales

'A woman,' Liddie said.

'You saw her?' Haddock asked, conscious that the caretaker had been drinking.

'During the day, a few people up here. Most stay down below, rarely venturing up here, but this is where the history is.'

'That's not an answer,' Natalie said. 'Either you saw someone lay the flowers, or you didn't.'

'I did not. I don't often come over here. I'm unsure of the ground. The silos are not in good condition. Some have been opened to the elements due to the workshops down below. A geological engineer reckoned it was safe to walk there, but I'm not sure. And besides, nothing to look at over there; just make sure it's neat and tidy, no need to walk on it.'

'And make sure no bodies are there,' Haddock said flippantly.

Haddock walked away, leaving Natalie with Liddie. Natalie couldn't be sure why he had, but it allowed her to use feminine guile with the man.

'Unnatural, out here on your own,' Natalie said. She had taken a photo of the flowers, not as evidence, as they would have had to be put in an evidence bag, but for reference. She thought it a nice touch, whether due to sadness, guilt, or both.

Three women contended for the man's attention, but only one had married him. The other two had waited in the wings, taking what they could from him. But what was it with him that the women wanted? Wealth was a reason, but Greenworthy had lived as a pauper. Charisma, but he rarely spoke? Or was it the need to mother the man? Natalie had seen the body and had to admit that he was attractive, but a dead body gives no indication of anything other than man's mortality. At the murder site, he had a glow; on the pathologist's table, it was just discarded bone and skin.

'You get used to it,' Liddie said.

'Over the years, you must have seen plenty of change?'

'I remember when they used to refit submarines here when the workshops down below were in use. Even so, not many came up here. I have no idea why; my wife thought up here was the place to be. A lovely woman, and I miss her, but we all die, some before our time.'

'I don't believe that you didn't see something. A caretaker, eyes in the back of your head, and you would hear persons late at night if they were up here.

'Sometimes, there are cicadas; they make a noise. Other times, I get those staying on the island walking around. A few drunks up here, and I caution them that it is easy to fall off the edge if they aren't careful.'

In the distance, a ferry was coming alongside the wharf. Natalie borrowed Liddie's binoculars. It was two in the afternoon, and she did not expect to see anyone she knew, surprised when she did.

Leaving Liddie and telling Haddock to keep out of the way, she hurried down to where the ferry docked.

'Why?' Natalie asked as she drew up alongside the woman on the road to where Greenworthy had died.

'Sergeant, I didn't expect to see you here,' Crystal Andersson said.

'Flowers for Alan?'

'Someone must. Have you met his wife?'

'We have. Did you know about her?'

'I didn't.'

Natalie realised that the concerned persons were in communication. Barton knew of the wife, as did Alice, and it had now been reported in the media that the woman was in Sydney and engaging contractors to renovate the house. Natalie thought she was a bloodsucker, preying on a vulnerable man in Cambodia. But that was not a crime, nor was claiming the place for her own, only the speed at which she had secured it.

'You were angry on the day, angry enough to murder?'

'Jeb Barton told you,' Crystal said. 'Angry enough to have struck him, but I didn't know it was Alice.'

'How do you know it is now?'

'She phoned me. We knew of each other, and we both cared for him. I liked her, regardless of what she did. She worried about him the same as I did, but I never knew he had a wife; I was shocked when I heard. What is she? A gold digger, or did she care for him?'

'We're unsure. How long do you intend to come out here?'

'Who will mourn him? Alice and I will. Jeb will come to his funeral, so will Igor and Gus, a few fans, some from the other bands, but it will only be me and Alice who cared for the man.'

'His wife?'

'Separated, living in other countries, hardly love.'

Natalie had to agree, but what Crystal showed, and Alice admitted to, was that love? Was Melinda the ministering angel or the she-devil?

Crystal knelt atop the island and laid the flowers close to the others. She then clasped her hands together and prayed. It was moving, the woman wiping away tears as she got up and moved away. Natalie did not follow her. A woman could have been the murderer as much as a man, but until Melinda Greenworthy's part in the saga was clarified, the investigation could not progress.

Natalie found Haddock over the other side of the island, close to where the boats of the well-heeled or the seriously in debt were stored.

'Crystal,' she said.

'Was she here?'

'She reckons someone must mourn. Also, she is in contact with Alice, broken hearts in concert.'

'We should assume she is genuine. Unlike Alice or Melinda, we know of no vices, and Crystal comes from a stable family. What do you reckon of Melinda?' Haddock asked.

'I don't. Too easy, her returning on his death, making herself at home, lady of the manor, lording it over whoever. Any updates on who and what she is?'

'Not yet. It might be best to ask her.'

'And receive a pack of lies,' Natalie said. 'What are you doing over here?'

'I need to scout the island, get a perspective on the place, and determine if the murder was premeditated. Committed in anger, or was the killer calm and calculating? It could be tied up with Greenworthy's time overseas and his wife. Cambodia is an unusual place to get married, and why wasn't she in Australia with him? He's got money, even if he doesn't want to spend it. She could have taken it and done what she wanted, but she remains overseas, doing what? Have we asked?'

'Not confirmed.'

'Then better if we do and soon. We can't expect much help from the police in Cambodia, and probably not a lot better in Hong Kong. No longer controlled by the British, in the firm hand of the Chinese government in Beijing.'

Chapter 8

Four days later, correspondence was received from the police in Hong Kong. Although it revealed that Melinda Greenworthy, nee Huang, had no criminal convictions, there was more. The first and potentially most damning point was that Greenworthy was not her first husband.

That honour, which Natalie thought was a dubious claim from Inspector Haddock, went to a fifty-six-year-old Hong Kong national, and the man, wealthy, had died after an altercation with another man in the street one night when the husband had been drunk and argumentative. A copy of the police report was included, which confirmed that the man was known to them for belligerency and that death by persons unknown had been recorded. And then, three years and two months later, Melinda Huang married again, this time to a fifty-nine-year-old university lecturer. A marriage which lasted thirteen months until he suffered a massive heart attack due to stress and overwork. And that due to the man's age and poor health, and his inability to relax, obsessed as he was with academic research, the heart attack had been fatal.

Natalie could see a pattern, a clever approach to wealth creation. Marry men with money, but not obscene amounts. Men who were low-flyers, not showing off their money, but who had underlying issues that could be played on, exacerbated, and then, either by accident, violence, or natural causes, died, the widow claiming the inheritance.

The only problem Haddock could see was that Greenworthy had not been in his fifties but almost two decades younger than the youngest of the two other men at his death.

Had Melinda made an error with her last husband? Had she misjudged him? She must have known of the wealth, and she did have a joint account which she could draw on, although not full access to his money, not even legal title of the house, not that it stopped her renovating the place, a crew of workmen there every day from seven in the morning until five in the evening.

Had the woman married her last husband for love, or was he one in a string of men? There was no way the woman could be grilled for crimes she had not committed or even been suspected of, and certainly not in Australia, a country with no crimes against her. Natalie was inclined to believe there was guilt, but that was a hunch, a woman's intuition, and there was no way the police could barge into her house, demanding that she talk to them.

The woman had not been in the country at the time of Alan Greenworthy's death, although that was not definite. She travelled with two passports, one in her maiden name and another in her married name. A third passport would not have been difficult to arrange, but that would have been criminal, and Natalie didn't believe the woman would do anything that could bring focus on her. Death of the first husband due to an altercation on the street, the second due to a heart attack, but the third death was murder, and no amount of spin would alter that fact.

Alice Minchin had admitted being the woman with Alan Greenworthy, Crystal Andersson visited the murder site regularly, and Melinda Greenworthy showed no emotion, which might have been suspicious, apart from the fact she had not seen her husband for several years. Where had she been? What was she doing in Hong Kong? Why stay married if there was no intent to live together?

Melinda Greenworthy was thirty-six years of age, no longer a young woman playing the field, a string of lovers, but, as Natalie suspected, a cold-hearted bitch who had been pleased when her husbands had died. However, Alan had been in excellent health; overwork would never be a condition he would suffer. No heart attack for him, and he was a pacifist by nature and by action. The only way for her to rid herself of him was by murder, and that had occurred.

Natalie could not see the reason to let events unfold slowly. It was for her to push back and confront the woman, to see if there beat a heart of ice or fire behind the impassive exterior, of love or hate. Were there emotions trapped deep in the woman? They would not be revealed in an interview room at a police station, a controlled environment where the police needed to abide by specific rules.

How was one question; where was another. Would she, as a police sergeant, be compromising the murder investigation? Natalie knew she possibly could be. Even so, she was determined to find out the truth, aware that the Hong Kong police had given what they could and that the police in Cambodia would not.

The two women met at a neutral location. The gloves were off for Natalie who was in a combative mood. If Melinda was innocent of all crimes and not the murderer, then it was necessary to look further. Could it be one of the band? Jeb Barton had seen Alice; the others hadn't.

Melinda arrived dressed in designer clothes. She was driving a late-model Audi, whereas the frugal Alan had driven a fifteen-year-old Hyundai, bruised, battered, and in poor condition.

'New car?' Natalie said.

'Almost. No point having money if you don't spend it,' Melinda replied. It was an inflammatory comment. If, as was known, she had received the bulk of the wealth of two previous husbands, she would have plenty to show for it, and Alan Greenworthy's money was the icing on the cake, but not the cake.

They sat at a restaurant close to the harbour bridge. Natalie ordered fish, and Melinda, petite and slim, chose a salad.

'We've checked on you with the Hong Kong police and made representation to the police in Cambodia,' Natalie said.

'It's what I would have done,' Melinda replied as she sipped a South Australian Riesling.

'You've had experience with police investigations before?'

'My previous husbands, but you know that, don't you?'

74

'Both were older than you; you received most of their wealth when they died.'

'And their debts. Was that mentioned?'

Natalie had to admit it wasn't, but was that an oversight, or was the woman lying?

'You are the one who gained by your husband's death. You are the logical person to have murdered him. We must be suspicious of you.'

'Must? That's a strong word.'

Natalie had almost accused the woman of murder, but Melinda Greenworthy sat calmly, eating her salad and sipping wine.

'Your first husband dies in a fight, your second of stress. No attempt to implicate you.'

'Why should there be?'

Either the woman was innocent of involvement or a skilled actor without a conscience, but that would require a psychologist to analyse. Something that would not happen unless there was evidence linking the woman to the murder. Immigration was checking to see if any other names that Melinda used were recorded as entering the country during the last three years, a chance for her to reconnoitre and to decide on a fate for her husband. Natalie was inclined to think not, which meant that if Melinda had not killed the man, someone else had. An assassin did not come cheap, but why? Greenworthy had been wealthy. Enough not to have worked another day in his life, not even if he spent at a prodigious rate, as Melinda appeared to be doing.

'Your previous husbands? Did Alan know?'

'Why would I tell him?'

'No secrets between husband and wife. I would have thought it was important.'

'You might, I didn't, nor would Alan. My previous life was behind me; maybe I wanted to start anew with a clean slate. Are you sure this is not a witch hunt? The wicked wife who has flown in to take advantage of her husband's death. I haven't, no more to say.'

'You don't seem concerned.'

'I'm not. This is Australia; evidence will not be fabricated, and nothing will be found against me. I will spend Alan's money as I see fit, see it as his legacy, giving to a deserving cause, to me.'

None of which sounded convincing to Natalie. The woman was lying through her teeth, probably did it all the time, barely cognisant of the truth. Was she an evil woman? Or was she opportunistic, preying on vulnerable men, using her female wiles to seduce and wed, and then, at an appropriate juncture, get rid of them, take their assets, and move on to the next man?

Natalie knew that moral crimes were not prosecutable, but had the woman bitten off more than she could chew this time? Her previous husbands had been older, more susceptible to ill health and death, and more likely to have a fatal accident, but Alan Greenworthy was young and in good physical condition.

Further investigation was needed into who Melinda was and what Alan Greenworthy had been doing in Cambodia, meeting a Hong Kong national and marrying her, only for them not to live together, although supposedly maintaining contact. Natalie wasn't sure if she would get it from the woman, but she would continue trying to verify what she had been told. But that would require a trip overseas.

It was a double-edged sword: a woman who would lie and government departments who would obfuscate.

'Why your husband was murdered is important. There are two scenarios: a jealous lover, or he died for a reason that can only come from you,' Natalie said. She was frustrated with the woman, anxious not to show it, but aware she was. A man dies, but his wife appears not to be upset.

'A whirlwind romance,' Melinda said. 'I had just broken from a previous lover, thought that a trip to Cambodia would do me some good, visited Angkor Wat, took in the culture, and bought souvenirs. I had not expected to meet Alan, but on the rebound, we fell into each other's arms.'

'Melinda, it will come out eventually. You are a serial wife; fall into the arms of one, make sure you have got sufficient of their money, and then move on to the next. I'm not accusing you of a crime, but you could have known your previous husbands weren't long for this world. An altercation in the street, a man close to sixty in poor health.'

'He was. I had tired of him, but I did not kill him.'

'And the next husband, a few years younger, had a heart attack. He was in his fifties, not the usual age for a heart attack, but feasible. Aggressive lovemaking, fatty foods, stress, all factors; none are crimes, but attenuating reasons for a weak heart.'

'Sergeant, your imagination does you credit. Firstly, my first husband was a drunk. It was not mentioned at his inquest, as the police were determined to ensure the man who had hit him was not convicted, to make out my husband was the provocateur. Not unknown in Australia, placing emphasis on what was important to a conviction, downplaying or concealing what was not.'

Natalie sensed there was more to the woman than she was saying. Her answers were crafted, her body language was correct, and her English was perfect, with not a trace of a Chinese accent when she spoke. Was it a facade the woman wanted her to see? Was she Alice Minchin, personified in the body of an Asian woman. Natalie felt the need to probe.

'Too glib,' Natalie said. 'You sound plausible, but I'm not convinced. You appear soon after Alan dies. Nobody knows about you, apart from a few, but no one has ever met you. Who told you he was dead? It might be news in Australia, but not in Hong Kong or the mainland.

'I received a phone call.'

'From whom?'

'Alan's lawyer.'

***

Natalie and Haddock were aware of a lawyer and met with the man, received the usual line about confidentiality, his function being to look after his client's interests. 'And yes, I knew of a wife in Hong Kong, a tangled web from what I could see. But then, I don't believe I would be incorrect in stating that Alan was an unusual man, unlike his father, who was ebullient, larger than life, driven by success, sometimes at the cost of his family.'

The lawyer's speech had verged on the indiscreet, but the police were used to persons, when questioned and guiltless, saying too much or too little, fluffing their rehearsed speeches.

Besides, the police knew that Alan Greenworthy was an oddball, gregarious with his band, reclusive when not, admired and loved by two women, and that he had slept with both. Professed to one his intent to marry her, the most unlikely mate of the two due to her lifestyle. The other, demure and sweet, the loved daughter of an upper-middle-class family, waited for him and was willing to give the love he needed. And then, Melinda. She didn't have the attributes of the other two other than being attractive. There was a cunning about her, back in Sydney soon after her husband's death, eager to dive into his money, to renovate and redecorate his house, to treat herself to a new car and to hit the shops in a big way.

Melinda Greenworthy remained the primary suspect, but her alibi was solid. Not only did her passport confirm her arrival date in Australia, but on Facebook, a photo of her standing by the water's edge in Hong Kong, the date irrefutable.

If she hadn't wielded the knife, had someone else on her say-so, or had that person been paid to do so? Natalie had to believe that life was cheaper in Cambodia and that paying someone to kill another would not be expensive. A flight to Sydney, a couple of nights in a low-cost motel west of the city. The music concert had been advertised, the dead man's presence was confirmed, and Melinda, along with his band and the groupies who hung backstage for his favour, would have known. Yet Alice had admitted to being the woman with him on that windy and exposed place high up on Cockatoo Island.

Natalie had to curb her willingness to condemn Melinda, the person she liked least. To her, the woman represented the worst of womankind: married to a man, not living with him, not divorcing. But was that about timing, in that Alan Greenworthy had died young, or was his death engineered. After all, there were two other husbands, both dead and now a third.

Natalie speculated whether the woman was an intelligence operative, but that would be hard to prove. Two previous husbands, good covers for her, expendable when no longer required. She believed the mainland China government would be capable of the deception and the removal, but why the interest in an antisocial Australian, and why Cambodia? Was Melinda a woman who rarely experienced strong emotional ties to another person, or was she cold and calculating, sociopathic by nature?

'Did you love Alan?' Natalie asked.

'I did, or I thought I did. Sergeant, I am opportunistic. I married my first two husbands for stability and prestige. You live in Sydney. You have never experienced an empty belly, a father who was absent most of the time, a mother who drudged, cleaning houses for those who could afford the pittance to have someone work for them. I resolved not to have that life, educated myself, learnt to speak with a refined accent, to marry for my benefit, not to live the life my mother had.'

An eloquent speech, Natalie had to admit, but was it crafted as though the woman was reading the police sergeant, pre-empting her questions.

'Thought?' Natalie reminded Melinda.

'I wanted stability, a conventional relationship with a man. I thought I had found it with Alan.'

'But you hadn't.'

'In Cambodia, as with the band, he was agreeable, sociable, and caring.'

'And in Australia, you found a different person?'

'Don't ask me why. It would take a professional to diagnose. I moved in with him at the house. After a month, I found that the man I had loved in Cambodia was not the same person in Australia. In Cambodia, wanting a good time, loving and affectionate. But, in Australia... you've seen the house. He drove an old car, was antisocial, introvert, a miser. Am I telling you anything about the man you don't know already?'

Natalie could not dispute the woman's evaluation of Alan Greenworthy. 'No,' she reluctantly said.

Melinda had gone from guilty to possibly innocent, although Natalie wasn't willing to concede that the woman was guiltless of other crimes. That depended on others and their part in the saga.

Melinda's phone rang. 'Got to go,' she said.

'Important.'

'You'd not understand.'

Natalie did. The woman had another man. The question remained whether she'd had the man before her husband died or after and whether he was implicated. That would have to wait. Haddock had messaged. Two words: *Cockatoo Island.*

Short, cryptic messages meant one of two things. Another murder or there had been a development.

Chapter 9

Claude Liddle stood tall and proud. Haddock looked down from where he was standing.

'Didn't see it myself,' Liddie said. 'Never gave it a thought.'

Haddock looked at Natalie. 'Simple error. It should not have happened. If it hadn't been for Claude, we would have been chasing our tails for weeks,' he said. 'Melinda Greenworthy, any more insights?'

'Some, not sure if I was fed a lie or not, almost impossible to confirm. We'll not get much more from the Hong Kong police. And we can't be sure they're not protecting their backs; orders from the mainland. Forget Cambodia: there is no chance of the truth. According to Melinda, Alan was the life and soul of the party over there, a miserable miserly recalcitrant in Australia.'

'Rings true,' Haddock said.

Of the seventeen convict-cut bottle-shaped rock silos, each capable of holding five thousand bushels of grain, carved out of the sandstone on the island, three remained intact, the others destroyed by subsequent building construction. Initially, wheat was stored in them as they were weevil-free. Later, they were used for water storage, but now one of them, close to where the murder had occurred, contained evidence. The entrance had been covered by a metal grille when Greenworthy died, but now, after Liddle had shone a torch down into the silo, it had been removed. A woman, her face was masked, hung from a rope close to the bottom of the silo.

'A bit more,' she shouted.

Natalie looked at where the woman was, shuddered at the inhumanity of convicts being lowered into the silos to laboriously carve away at the sandstone and then send it up in small buckets to the surface. More than one convict had died during their construction.

'Got it,' a voice hollered from down below.

'Nobody looked,' Liddie said.

'An unfortunate oversight,' one of the crime scene investigators said.

Haddock thought it was more than that; it was incompetence. Natalie, more sympathetic, was concerned with the woman in the silo. 'You better bring her up,' she said.

'Ready?' a CSI shouted down the hole.

The woman was hoisted up, a relief to Natalie, who would not admit, especially not to Haddock, that she suffered from claustrophobia, the legacy of locking herself in a barn at her parent's farm as a child, staying there in the dark until her parents had returned four hours later.

At the top, the CSI handed over an evidence bag. 'Needs to go to Forensics,' she said.

'Not until we know what it is,' Natalie said.

Natalie, Haddock, and the CSIs moved to Liddie's cottage, the man glad of the company.

With due process and ensuring no contamination of the evidence, the honour of opening the evidence bag was entrusted to the person who had been in the silo. 'It must have slipped out of his pocket,' she said.

Or put down there as a red herring, Natalie thought. She knew it was time to accept the promotion and that she had outgrown Inspector Haddock. It was she who saw the inconsistencies, the intrigue, the obfuscation. And if Liddie had found it, had he placed it there. And why? Who had instructed him? Were they involving themselves in something they hadn't expected? Reds under the bed, foreign intelligence operatives, hired assassins.

Natalie realised she was being fanciful; the evidence had not been revealed yet. But she had spent a disturbing two hours with a woman of intrigue, a woman with a history, and not all of it was good.

'Are we certain it's not rubbish that a visitor had stuffed down there?' Haddock asked.

'Unlikely,' another CSI said, 'and there's a date.'

'Not just a date, but one day before the murder,' Natalie said.

The evidence was a boarding pass. Qantas, Hong Kong to Sydney. It had Melinda Greenworthy's maiden name on it.

'It looks like you've got your murderer,' Liddie said.

Haddock thought the evidence was concrete; Natalie wasn't so sure. There was something fishy about the new evidence and Claude Liddie's exuberance. Regardless, Melinda Greenworthy would be brought to State Crime Command in Parramatta. No longer an informal chat but serious questions with serious answers, a legal representative if required.

***

Melinda Greenworthy, when confronted by Natalie at her house – Natalie thought it wise to advise her in advance of what was to happen – went into verbal overdrive.

'I hoped for a reconciliation, booked an earlier flight, and changed my mind at the airport. I was flustered. Three marriages, and the third was finite, not necessarily from me, but from Alan. He wasn't returning my calls. I had to do something.'

Natalie wasn't buying any of it. Melinda Greenworthy was not a woman to get flustered or confused, but an exceptionally well-balanced woman who had seen off two husbands, and the flight a day before the third had died at the hands of a yet unknown individual was more than circumstantial. This was fact, not a conspiracy, and the woman was central to the investigation. Whether she was the murderer or not was unclear, but the evidence pointed in her direction.

'Regardless, a police vehicle will pick you up and transport you to Parramatta,' Natalie said. 'Time enough for you to call your lawyer if you have one.'

'I do. Alan's.'

Melinda was on the phone in another room with her lawyer. Natalie was able to understand, as the conversation was in English. A second call, this time in Chinese. Natalie couldn't understand but was more interested in who was on the other end of the phone.

The suspicion that Melinda was more than she said appeared to be validated, but what she was, Natalie was not willing to speculate, concerned that it might be a job for ASIO, Australia's security organisation. She hoped it wasn't, as that would mean the murder investigation would be taken away from Homicide, given to others, or buried.

'I can go with you,' the woman said on her return.

'I have somewhere to go; best if you go in the police car I've sent for. If required, it can pick up your lawyer on the way. Who were you speaking to in Chinese?'

'It doesn't matter, personal,' Melinda said, taking a seat and pouring herself a glass of wine. 'One for you? You look as though you could use it.'

'Later, maybe. Make sure you inform your lawyer of the facts. We'll update him at Parramatta, access to all information.'

Natalie wasn't sure now why she had visited the house. She could have phoned, but that was impersonal, and she still doubted the woman's guilt. A police officer's instincts were that the pieces were falling into place too easily. She was convinced the woman had been in the country when her husband died, but where and with whom? Was it the Chinese person on the end of the phone? Was he a friend, a lover, a potential new honeypot to woo and wed? If the woman was as bad as Natalie thought she might be, did she have the hallmarks of a sociopathic disposition, if not personality? But could her story about her childhood be true, the deprivation, the cruelty, the malevolence wrought on her? Had it distorted her mind, made her incapable of guilt or conscience, only aware of self?

Questions to answer, but how come Liddie had found the ticket? Was that the first time he had shone a torch down through the grille on the top of the silo? From the years he had been on

Cockatoo Island, he knew every nook and cranny, every creak of a nighttime in the disused and decaying engineering workshops, and the wind in the trees. Undoubtedly, he perved on the campers in the tents on the island and saw more than he should have. An old silo would have held little attraction unless he had seen something. And when had the boarding pass been placed in the silo? By whom? Could it be Liddie, a man alone, desperate for excitement in his life, or was it for money, the chance to leave the island?

Liddie had become a man of interest. Initially regarded as benign and lonely after his wife's death, he was a man who no longer wanted to be on the island but could not live elsewhere. But now, time had passed him by, and the chance to break free was no longer an option. And then, there on the island, tourists, some camping in the tents set up for rental, and the old overseers' cottages renovated and for renting. Persons drinking too much, behaving frivolously, lovemaking on a grassy knoll of a night, and Liddie familiar with the island.

Also, the man had a predilection for whisky. Haddock had commented to Natalie that the man was a low-functioning alcoholic, capable of his job, but the world outside of the island with its traffic and its noise would baffle him, as would having to deal with renting a place to live, buying a car, filling in forms, and the general hubbub away from the island.

Liddie had admitted that much to Haddock during one of their drinking sessions. Haddock, unusual in that he was not a drinker, a curse of too many police officers, but when the need suited the purpose, he would drink one for one with whoever. That had been de rigueur in a prior murder enquiry, getting drunk with Josh Costello in the hotel in Parramatta, and then the man had been murdered. Liddie was still alive, but he could be a murderer.

At one in the afternoon on a Tuesday afternoon, with an overcast sky and the likelihood of rain, Melinda Greenworthy, nee Huang, arrived at State Crime Command in Parramatta. Alongside her in the interview room was a man in his late sixties with greying hair and a pallid complexion. He was wearing a suit with a blue tie. 'Frank Addison,' he said as he shook hands with Natalie and Haddock.

Natalie felt the firm handshake, observed the confident manner, and saw the steely eyes. This was not a man to trifle with. He was also the man that Alan Greenworthy's father had entrusted to oversee his financial legacy.

Haddock dealt with the formalities and outlined the investigation so far. Once he had finished, Natalie laid out the situation regarding Melinda Greenworthy. 'We are aware of Mrs Greenworthy's legal title to her late husband's assets,' she commenced.

'I've read the case file,' Addison said. 'I suggest you get to why my client is here. What you have seems perilously thin.'

To the police officers, it was not thin but thick, damning evidence that the woman had arrived in Australia before her husband's death. Addison, it appeared, intended to bully his way through the interview.

Natalie continued. 'Mrs Greenworthy arrived in Australia, not on the date she said, but one day before her husband's death. How the boarding pass to confirm this came to be in a grain silo at Cockatoo Island is unknown. That will form a major part of our investigation. If it was Alan who slid it through the grille as he was dying, that indicates that he knew his wife was in Australia, a logical assumption if she was staying at his house. It seems illogical why he would be carrying a boarding pass. If he didn't know his wife was in Australia, that would indicate that the person who murdered him would have brought the boarding pass to the island to frame Mrs Greenworthy.'

Haddock interjected, 'Another question is why Claude Liddie decided to shine a torch into the silo.'

'Someone paid him,' Melinda Greenworthy said.

Natalie noticed Addison's hand on the woman's arm, a clear signal to button her lip and to let him deal with the police officers.

'It's a relevant point,' Addison said. 'We contend that the boarding pass is a fake and that it was planted to incriminate my client, who has become a wealthy woman due to her husband's tragic death.'

'And the prime suspect,' Haddock said. 'Mrs Greenworthy, regardless of what Mr Addison has just said, you admitted to Sergeant Campbell that you intended to take the earlier flight and had a boarding pass but did not. Your response to this would be appreciated.'

'What I said to Sergeant Campbell is correct. My reasons for coming were varied. I'm not sure why I intended to come.'

Addison did not respond but looked over at his client, realising that she had fallen into the trap set by Natalie.

'Why?' Natalie asked. 'Was it to kill him, or did you know someone else would. We've found no proof that you didn't board the flight, and your arrival in Sydney has been confirmed. You were in Sydney when your husband was murdered. Were you at his house?'

'My house.'

'Answer the question,' Haddock said. 'Were you at his house, and if so, why?'

'He was my husband. Isn't that enough?'

'Not after four years, by your admission. No.'

'I was not at the house.'

'Where were you?'

'I stayed with Alice Minchin.'

'At the penthouse?'

'Yes. If she was entertaining, I would either go out or stay in my room.'

'Alice Minchin has admitted that she was the woman with him at Cockatoo Island that night,' Natalie said. 'Are you confirming this?'

'I wasn't there, but she told me she was. I had no reason to disbelieve her.'

'Nor for you two being friends. You were married to the man. She wanted to marry him, which would have required him to divorce you. Considering that you and Alan had lived apart for several years, it would have been a formality.'

'Except I would have challenged the divorce.'

'On what grounds?'

'On what Alan had been doing in Cambodia.'

'I believe my client has not a comprehensive grasp of English,' Addison said. 'I would ask that her last comment be struck from the record.'

Addison's response was unusual, and regardless of his client's comprehension of the language, whatever was said would remain on the record.

Melinda's lawyer was civil, not criminal, and she would have been advised to have prepared herself better for the interview, and there was no question that she had not understood perfectly. It did not wash in a police station, not with Haddock or Natalie.

'It's recorded,' Haddock said. 'Two questions. Why discuss it with Alice? And what was Alan Greenworthy doing in Cambodia? We realise that it was not sightseeing, or could it be the girlie bars, getting drunk and making a fool of himself, except he meets his future wife, falls in love, gets laid, and then gets married. What are you, Melinda Greenworthy, and no more platitudes about you being a simple housewife, not after the death of three husbands? Trying for four? This Chinese man Sergeant Campbell heard you talking to.'

'How did she know it was a man?' Melinda replied, scratching the palm of one hand with the nails from the other.

'I could hear a voice, not clearly, but certainly a man,' Natalie replied, aware that Haddock was giving her the lead.

Addison was out of his depth. Natalie could only feel pity for him, who, according to all that she had heard about him, was a good man. Alan Greenworthy's father had trusted him implicitly and had set in place processes and counterchecks to ensure his son, who the father would have known had issues, be looked after, free of the day-to-day humdrum of running a business. But what was that business? Was it something to do with Cambodia? And where did Melinda come into it? A harmless floozy or a conniving bitch? In Australia, she was pleasant, but she had the money, no more grafting to pay the rent, and control had fallen to her. Addison appeared to be on her side, but why?

'I spoke to Frank, and then I phoned a friend in Australia, told him where I was, and that I would need to report to the police to answer questions about Alan's death.'

'This friend, personal or professional? Three years away from your husband, young and attractive, you must have found solace in the arms of another.'

'I had, although judging from what I know of you, you haven't,' Melinda replied.

Haddock thought the woman was biting, getting aggravated and losing her cool. It was time to raise the heat.

Natalie led off. 'You come to Australia to meet with Alice Minchin, an escort. Is that what you are?'

'It's how I met Alan.'

'A girlie bar?' Haddock asked.

Natalie was bemused by Haddock's reference to the bars that lined the back streets in parts of Asia.

'High-class, not that I was as consistent as she is with her favours. They were in and out on rotation in the few days I stayed with her.

'High-class in Cambodia, not what the average red-blooded Western male would associate with the country. Or were you low-rental, putting on a show in a bar, blow jobs on demand?'

Haddock was baiting the woman, attempting to break through the carefully crafted façade. Although she was playing a dangerous game, the woman was intelligent, cunning, and nobody's fool. This was Australia; bribes and threats would not work, whereas, in Hong Kong, she would have the mainland government in her corner if in their employ. But why, and would she reveal the truth?

'Talk to Alice, ask her why I needed to talk to her. I didn't kill Alan, but I wanted out. I did not intend to leave as a pauper. In Hong Kong, he had supported me, not sure why, but he was an unusual person, as you well know.'

'What will she tell us?' Natalie asked.

'You've met her. What did she say about him?'

'She had known Alan for a long time and wanted to marry him. Respectable, the adoring wife, a couple of children, the whole box and dice.'

'He had asked her. Don't ask me why, but he told me two months back. We discussed the divorce: old-fashioned chivalry on his side and financial practicalities on mine. And yes, I engineered him into marrying me. I was not turning tricks in a bar. I wasn't selling myself, but I knew Western men are easy prey. Most of those in Cambodia couldn't find a woman in a pub in England or wherever they had come from. Most of them were degenerate drunks and druggies, worked menial jobs, had enough money for a fortnight in Cambodia, plenty of cheap sex and cheap drugs. And there was Alan, visiting the tourist sites. I met him in a restaurant, got chatting, and found out that we got on, and that I was available, and he was wealthy. It was mutual; our marriage was not made in heaven or in the eyes of God, but two people looking for something.

'However, looking and wanting are not the same as needing. He wouldn't leave Australia, and I wouldn't live here. An impasse, and then along comes Alice.

'She's a whore, but good-hearted. She would have done right by him, and I wished him well when he told me, but I knew I would be disadvantaged. I had married twice for money and security, but I had been genuine when I married Alan, although the relationship inevitably soured. The man that Sergeant Campbell heard on the phone is the man I intend to marry and for love.'

Natalie thought it an eloquent speech. She also knew it was a fabrication. Frank Addison did not sit alongside his client out of loyalty to her but because there was still something unsaid – the truth.

'Was it Alice with Alan at Cockatoo Island?'

'Yes.'

Chapter 10

Haddock turned to Addison, who had said little during the interview. 'Mr Addison, what allegiance do you have to Melinda Greenworthy, other than she's agreed to your costs?'

'The good name of Greenworthy,' Addison replied.

'What name?' Natalie asked. 'We've never heard of it, not mentioned in the who's who of the higher echelons of Australian society.'

'Wealth is not with those who flaunt it but those who don't.'

'Alan Greenworthy certainly didn't. How is the wealth generated? Why do you act ethically? Or do you? Alan would not have known, but Melinda's smarter. She would have asked to see the financial records, and Alice is no slouch. Maybe she's a more appropriate person for Alan to have married, but without a woman, Alan would be easier to manage.'

'Old money. Real estate, acquired over decades. More than fifty properties around Australia, houses, units, shopping centres. All are purchased under a company name. I have no reason to cheat, scheme, or defraud the Greenworthys, father, son, and wife, current or future. Besides, anyone marrying Alan would have been subject to a legal agreement not to interfere or ask, although there would have been sufficient money to indulge any fancy. Melinda understands that. I doubt if Alice Minchin would. As Melinda has mentioned, Alice is a loose woman, and whereas you have seen one persona, there is another, more calculating.'

'What about Crystal Andersson? A sensible woman, no issues with her?'

'No issues at all, except Alan would not want her. He had no need for a subservient, dutiful wife. He needed a strong person to lead him. His father satisfied that requirement while he was alive. I have for the last few years, and Melinda could have, and so could Alice. Personally, I would prefer Alice, as Melinda comes with baggage.'

'What baggage?' Melinda asked. She had brought the man to represent her, but now he acted as if he were her prosecutor.

'A man in Hong Kong. His name is Chong.'

'How do you know this?'

'It is my job to. I'm saying this for your benefit. Allow me to finish.'

Melinda went quiet.

'When Alan informed me that he had married in Cambodia and given me the details, I employed the services of a person skilled in investigative work in China and Hong Kong. This was someone I knew by reputation and could be trusted. Over two weeks, he kept me informed. He told me about Melinda's previous husbands, her profession as a prostitute on occasion, and the mistress of a man when she was younger. He also confirmed that her childhood had been difficult, and she had used her obvious assets to her advantage. She was intelligent, had been to university, obtained a degree, and that elocution lessons had perfected her English. By all standards, she is a capable woman worthy of respect; however—'

'However?' Natalie said.

'There is a dark side to Melinda. She did marry twice before, both husbands dying before their time. One was an alcoholic and got into an altercation; the other was a workaholic. The deaths were attributable to those causes, and the inquests did raise the matter of a younger wife. There is no indication of wrongdoing on her part, and she acted as the wife to the two men, a little joy for both. The children of the first man acted as character witnesses for her, and the second family sent a letter stating that Melinda was a person of good character. She was absolved of any blame and inherited most, if not all, of the two men's wealth. Neither were as wealthy as Alan, and I believe she married him partly out of affection but mainly for financial return.'

'Not much of a reference,' Haddock said.

'Melinda is an astute woman, and whereas I did have reservations, she would have served Alan's interests well, but he was disturbed. His father had known it, so had his mother, and had tried to resolve what ailed the man, but it was in his genetic makeup, melancholy, depression, solitude, interspersed by moments of lucidity. He got that through playing in a band and marrying Melinda. He might have achieved close to that with Alice, but it would fluctuate. Although I know her well from childhood, and she would be the right person for him, I would ensure that.'

'How do you know Alice?' Natalie asked, curious about what Addison had said.

'She is my daughter from my first marriage. I do not speak about it, given her current profession.'

'Her marrying Alan would have given you de facto control of his money,' Haddock said.

'I had that control already. I have never cheated the father or the son. Old-fashioned values, Christian values, something you don't hear spoken much of these days. If Alice had married Alan and had children, the Greenworthy legacy would have continued.'

'But with Melinda, a different outcome?' Natalie quizzed.

'As I believe I've outlined. I believe that I have quantified my part in this investigation. My reports on Melinda in Hong Kong are available, as well as her movements in Australia.'

'You've had me followed?' Melinda shouted.

Seeing a client and their lawyer arguing in an interview room was rare. Natalie had never seen it, although Haddock had once before, a wife-beater and his lawyer, the man's brother-in-law. That time, it had almost come to blows, a couple of officers restraining the man accused of putting his wife in hospital with a severe concussion and two broken ribs.

'I did. You were a complication. Alice was committed to Alan. If Alan hadn't phoned, you would not have been in Australia. However, my diligence is to your advantage.'

Addison looked away from his client and over to the other side of the desk. 'Melinda was in Alice's penthouse on the night that Alan died. She did not leave.'

'Your investigator will testify to that?' Natalie asked.

'She will.'

'And Alice?'

'I was not having her watched. She probably did go to the island to meet with Alan. She might have had the boarding pass.'

'She might have killed him? You realise what you are saying?'

'That I might be condemning my daughter while giving Melinda an alibi.'

Natalie knew it wasn't cast iron, but it had strength; Alice Minchin could have taken the boarding pass and left it at the murder site. It still didn't explain how Liddie came to find it.

'Why?'

'I can't protect the guilty, regardless of family loyalty.'

'Does Alice know you're her father?'

'She does.'

'And what will she say when we inform her of what you have done today?'

'She will understand.'

Melinda Greenworthy leant over to Frank Addison and kissed him on the cheek. 'Thank you,' she said.

*****

Back-to-back interviews in Homicide were not the norm; Haddock did not like them, not enough time to digest what one person had said and to use it in an interview with another.

Natalie felt they had no option, that the investigation needed to be hard-hitting and fast-moving, and that Melinda was more intelligent than she portrayed, and immediacy was required.

Unbeknown to Melinda, Claude Liddie had been brought to the station. He would either verify, hedge his bets, or lie. He was a caged man, yet he didn't know it yet.

The officers' concern was that Alice Minchin was protecting someone and that someone was her father. Claude Liddie appeared to be the key to resolving the impasse. A police launch transported him off the island to a waiting police car at a nearby marina. From there, a trip out to State Crime Command. On arrival, the man was perplexed, out of his comfort zone, which suited Haddock and Natalie.

He sat quietly and mumbled when Natalie and Haddock entered the room.

Legal aid had been provided, although the person supplied looked young, disinterested, and wet behind the ears, unlikely to be helpful to the client and more likely to be a nuisance with inane points of law.

Haddock had no intention of letting Liddie not answer questions due to an intrusive legal aid, who, even before the proceedings had started, wanted to argue the evidence put forward, not aware that his client, if not careful, might be spending time in a police station's cell.

Liddie had confessed to Haddock that the mainland held fears for him: too long on an island, which, apart from the tourists during the day and those spending the night, there was a serenity that the mainland did not have.

'The boarding pass you found is crucial evidence,' Haddock said. 'We've been told it was put through the grille and into the silo two days after the murder. We can't be sure about that, uncertain if we've been told the truth.'

'I wouldn't know,' Liddie said. 'I found it, that's all.'

'But how?' Natalie asked. 'It's in a silo, a small entrance at the top, only just wide enough for a man to fit through, covered by a metal grille. Why look?'

'Curious, I suppose. It was a murder, and there was no evidence. You say you know who the woman was but not the murderer. Maybe I thought I'd do some snooping.'

'No couples canoodling?' Haddock said, baiting the man with the knowledge that he snooped on couples in the campsite below.

'Not me,' Liddie said. 'I might have seen something up where the murder was. I have seen others up there before. I'm not a peeping tom, and don't you forget it.'

Natalie thought Haddock had overstepped the mark. There were no marks against Liddie, and he had been cooperative, although the question needed answering. 'Why did you look in the silo? It's dark in there; I needed a good torch to see to the bottom. You must get rainwater down there occasionally, and insects?'

'Sometimes. Originally, they contained grain. The opening would have been solid, no chance of intrusion, but now it's a grille, and sometimes I look.'

'Or are paid?' Haddock interjected.

'Not paid. Sure, I go stir-crazy, especially after my wife died, but I don't take bribes or condone murder at any cost. The paperwork I've had to fill in since then, and now, there are those in authority who want to remove me from the island. I've nowhere to go, nowhere I want.'

'Travelled far in your life?' Natalie asked.

'Once, a cruise up around Fiji and New Caledonia, but only for ten days. Apart from that, the island suited us, the supermarket on a Saturday, took the ferry.'

'It doesn't hold up,' Haddock said. 'A clue is left at the crime scene, but it's not evidence if it's not discovered. We have a person who says they put it there, but no explanation as to how it was found.'

'Okay, you win. Two days after the murder, the area is still taped off, but I'm concerned that I didn't see much that night. Sure, I can remember silhouettes, a cloudless night, and a couple having sex, but I didn't take much notice. It's not the first time I've told you that. My memory's not as sharp. Maybe it's age, maybe it's something more. Was there something I missed? I couldn't be sure. I saw someone kneeling by the grille. I kept quiet.'

'This was two days after the murder?'

'It was dark, and I wasn't sure if it was a man or a woman.'

Too little, too late for Haddock. Liddie was stalling, uncertain of himself. His job was on the line, the cottage on the hill, the uncomplicated lifestyle, and it was this murder that would condemn him.

'If the person put the pass through the grille, which makes no sense, the CSIs would have been thorough. It is unlikely that a piece of paper would have escaped their notice, or you're lying. Did someone phone you, although that doesn't make sense. After all, phoning would tell you if it was male or female, and you'd be crazy to take a bribe to find the evidence.'

A resigned look on Liddie's face; the game was up, and it was time to come clean. He poured himself a glass of water from the pitcher on the table, took a swig, and cleared his throat.

'I'm close to retirement age, and those I report to reckon I'm past it. They're right, of course, and the murder has put a focus on the island. I was below their radar, especially after my wife died, but that's a few years back. Six months ago, they approached me about taking a financial package and leaving, but where to? My wife's sister is in Queensland; no love lost there, and she would not want me around. I was hoping for a few more years on the island, but with the murder, they want me out. Yes, I saw the person and the boarding pass. The person was clever, didn't put it on the ground, but in a bush. It could have been missed, blown there by the wind.'

'The person who put it there was confident you would find it.'

Liddie was spouting verbiage, attempting to deflect the conversation. Natalie realised that shock tactics were needed. 'Mr Liddie, Claude,' she said, 'your job is on the line. The murder has brought focus on you, your failing health, and your memory loss. Was your wife handling the administration, sending in the reports, and organising if needed? And you were the face of the island.'

'It's true. She was more capable than me, but she loved the island as much as I did. Neither of us wanted to leave, ever, wanted to be buried there.'

'Which she was.'

'Her ashes were cast into the sea near the island, that's true.'

'Then why are you interfering in a murder investigation, altering evidence?'

'I knew there would be renewed focus if more evidence was found. I realised that if I took the boarding pass, and yes, I had looked at it and read that the dead man had a Chinese wife, and the flight on the pass was from Hong Kong to Sydney.'

'And you had seen more than you told us?'

'It's true, what Inspector Haddock said. Lonely, I sometimes see more than I should. I knew it wasn't a Chinese woman with the dead man, that much I could tell.'

'In the dark?'

'Up there, your eyes adjust. I could make out the profile, the two on the ground. The woman was not Chinese; something about her.'

'Later, you found the pass and put it into the silo. Why?'

'I suppose I've committed a crime. Instant dismissal when they find out.'

'Not instant,' Haddock said. 'You're a crucial witness. Any more to tell us while you unburden your soul?'

'Isn't that enough?'

Chapter 11

The relationship between Alice Minchin and Frank Addison confounded the police, although clarification from either would have to wait for another day. For now, Haddock had a family drama to deal with. Whereas he was still living in Parramatta, he visited his wife and daughter every week, sometimes once, sometimes twice, but when there was a murder, he often didn't make it, and when he did, he was incommunicative, absorbed by the crime, the evidence, the people interviewed, the dead person.

'She's your daughter,' Haddock's wife bellowed when he walked in the door. He had had a hard day and tried his best, but life intervened. He was responsible for his daughter and wife; even though they were separated, they had not divorced. Haddock knew the problem was their daughter. She was sixteen, her first failed romance behind her, the love of her life bragging to his mates at school about how she was an easy lay. She felt distraught and cheapened, and her mother wanted counselling for her, another cost on the meagre salary of a police inspector. He could not afford it. Haddock argued that she was a teenager and would grow out of it. He wanted to say that life is not a movie, sweet music, and loving relationships; life is hard, and he was trying his best, as were their daughter and his wife.

He put his arms around his wife, 'It'll be fine,' finding that he enjoyed the experience, wanting more, but aware now was not the time.

The two sat at the kitchen table. Haddock ate steak and chips; his wife ate a salad. 'Trying to lose weight,' she said.

Haddock had heard that for most of their married life. He couldn't see anything wrong with his wife; on the contrary, he liked her the way she was. 'Give it two weeks,' he said. 'If she's no better, we'll see if we can get counselling.'

He spent the night in the spare room. The investigation troubled him, and when his daughter had come home that night, he had not spoken to her other than a cursory 'Hello'.

In the morning, they had spoken. 'Dad, it's alright. I was a fool, a silly child. Mum worries, but I bet she was as bad as me.'

Haddock knew she had been. Three months pregnant when they got married. However, that was the past, and their daughter's mother had matured, as had the father. Not necessarily for the better in his case, given the occasional night with Theresa de Klerk. He knew he should break it off with her, but wasn't sure he could. Enter the door of Theresa's apartment, and there would be a bottle of wine, a hearty meal, and a double bed with a willing partner. Enter the family home, and it was strife.

He left the house at nine in the morning, which was late for Haddock. His wife had walked him out to the car and kissed him. 'Thanks,' she said.

He didn't know why she had kissed him but appreciated the moment of tenderness.

Forty-five minutes later, Frank Addison sat across from him and Natalie, a follow-up from the previous session with the man. Addison wasn't implicated yet, but Natalie was suspicious. He had made a statement of great significance, namely being Alice Minchin's father.

Both persons were integral to the murder of Alan Greenworthy. One intended to marry him; the other had been his lawyer, accountant, and business manager.

Yet, interviewed separately, Alice referred to her father disparagingly, not once mentioning that she was his daughter. Frank Addison had stated that Alice knew he was her father, and there was proof he had been married to her mother until three months before her birth.

'Did you visit Alice in her penthouse?' Natalie asked.

'No. I knew what she had become. Her mother had been wild; no reason to believe Alice would be any different.'

Natalie didn't think Alice Minchin was wild, just misguided in her choice of profession. 'Prostitution, your former wife?'

'Liberal with her favours. We were married for a couple of years. We thought it was love, but it wasn't. Infatuation, hard to tell from the real thing.'

'And now you're the model of propriety,' Haddock said sneeringly.

'Age tempers the ardour, Inspector,' Addison replied. Natalie could see that he was irked by her inspector's aside but was unwilling to respond. Natalie had to admit that the man was controlled, not easily given to rash behaviour, an admirable characteristic for a lawyer and a money manager, and a handy talent when contemplating murder.

'Why did your daughter not once refer to you as her father in the conversations that we've had with her?' Natalie asked.

'She does not regard me as her true father. I was not there when she was born, nor was I involved in her upbringing. Our relationship is dispassionate. I was the biological seed, but her stepfather took responsibility for her and did an admirable job.'

'Your daughter prostitutes. Why, if she had a good upbringing?' Natalie asked.

'I believe, Sergeant, you could direct that question at others as to why their children, given a good upbringing, education, friends, and moral grounding, end up on the street shooting drugs and wasting their lives. Alice took the easy way, not with drugs, but with men.'

'Does it worry you?'

'The emotional tie is weak. I care and ensure she doesn't get into trouble she cannot handle, but if she sells herself, I cannot stop her. There's no point in being the responsible father now that she's an adult. It might have been different if I had stayed with her mother, but that's not how life works.'

Haddock had to agree. He had grown up in a working-class area on the city's western outskirts. As a youth, he was a street hoodlum, getting into fights with other hoodlums, winning most, and in his early twenties, he had matured, gone to university, married, fathered a child, and joined the police force. Gazza Kelly, whom he had known on the street as a youth and hadn't seen again until recently, when Sasha Cornell's body had been found, hadn't changed; he had skirted serious crime but eventually admitted to the woman's murder and was now behind bars. Two men with similar backgrounds, yet each had taken a different road in life.

Regardless of her parentage, Alice Minchin had ended up as a high-class escort, a concubine to those who could afford her, wanting a man she could have had if he had lived. But it had been evident in a previous interview that Frank Addison favoured Melinda Greenworthy over his daughter.

The truth was hidden behind a veil. The police officers needed to look through to the other side.

'It was clear that you favoured Melinda when we met with her at State Crime Command,' Natalie said.

'She was my client, and Alan is dead. She inherits, not Alice. If Alan had lived, Melinda would have divorced Alan, and he would have married Alice. But he didn't. The dynamics have changed.'

'To whose advantage?'

'To Melinda's. I believe that's obvious. Melinda will be interfering, and she's no slouch. Understands how to add two and two—'

'And to see that you are feathering your nest. We know you are and that Alan's father knew, and Alan didn't care or didn't understand. What was wrong with the man? What's the medical condition? It must be diagnoseable.'

'His parents spent a lot of money, the best people in their field. It's not a disease but a psychological trait. It can be improved, but that needs the patient willing, and Alan wasn't. Another environment and he changes, as you saw at the concert, and apparently in Cambodia.'

'Would he have been better to leave that depressingly shabby house and go and live somewhere else?'

'He would have, but he wasn't causing any harm and not annoying the neighbours. I couldn't force him, nor would I. In his bubble, he was content. My promise to his father was to ensure that he came to no harm.'

Frank Addison was smart enough to have killed Greenworthy, but killing him before his daughter had married made no sense, or could he have switched allegiances before Alan died? Was that the reason for his daughter's dismissive reference to her father? Was there an underlying animosity? Alan hadn't been dead long, and Alice had shown no emotional distress at the passing of a man she had supposedly loved.

The only person who showed genuine emotion was Crystal Andersson, the woman he might have married if not for Alice.

Too many variables. Too many unknowns. Natalie could see the investigation stagnating, and Claude Liddie had tampered with evidence for his benefit. Who else had lied and cheated? The answer was obvious: everyone.

'Who pays for the penthouse? You must know.'

'I'm not sure it's important.'

'It's Clive Morton, and you know it. We've based our investigation on either Alice or Melinda, but it could have been you if Alan was reluctant to divorce Melinda. Did he love her, see something in her that he didn't see in Alice? And what about this fancy man? Does he live in Sydney? What if the arrangement suited him, Alice in the penthouse, at his beck and call. It strokes a man's ego, having a bought woman.'

'Not mine, not with my daughter.'

Frank Addison had married Alice's mother but divorced within two years. Subsequently, he had married two more women, neither of whom had had children with him, and he now lived on his own in a four-bedroom, two-storey house in Vaucluse, in the Eastern Suburbs, a view up the harbour from the upper floor. In contrast, the Greenworthy house was large but unimposing and decaying even before Alan's father died.

Wealth was usually reflected in a person's lifestyle, especially in the socially conscious Eastern Suburbs of Sydney.

Addison had the house, if not the best in the area, to announce to the world that he was wealthy, while the Greenworthys, both elder and younger, did not. And now, Melinda Greenworthy was rectifying that situation, renovations underway, spending a lot of money, money she still didn't have, not until the murder enquiry was completed and the necessary paperwork filed by Addison.

Even so, who owned the penthouse was relevant. Melinda had said that the men were in and out on rotation, but Alice was high-class, a kept woman. No man spending that much money would want his woman pawed by others. It was a flaw in her and Haddock's investigation they had missed. A flaw that would need to be rectified. Melinda had lied, and the man Natalie had seen in the foyer when she visited the penthouse might have been Alice's benefactor. She remembered a man in his fifties with greying hair, wearing a navy suit, white shirt, and a blue tie. Attractive, on recollection, and obviously wealthy. But who or what was he? Was he a jealous man, a criminal? Was his money honestly earned or crime, old or new? He would need to be interviewed, although Alice had said he regarded his privacy as sacrosanct. That would not be enough to deter two determined police officers.

***

Proof that Alice was Frank Addison's daughter was confirmed, along with a report from Sue Morgan, a private investigator employed by Addison to keep tabs on his daughter.

A police car had been to the penthouse with instructions to bring the woman in for questioning, but she wasn't there, hadn't been seen for two days, and her phone wasn't answering. Natalie assumed a client; Haddock thought it suspicious. She was eventually located in a suburb close to where she lived, her phone turned off, a chance to escape the drama.

If guilty, she might have taken off somewhere quiet and remote, somewhere with weak extradition treaties with Australia, although that seemed more the legend of fiction than reality. It needed money to stay hidden and to bribe those who would protect you, and Alice Minchin had no history of subterfuge. Her profession was known to those she regarded as friends: her mother, who worried, and her father, who had implicated her in murder.

'Miss Minchin, we know from Melinda Greenworthy that she was with you at your penthouse before Alan's murder. Is that correct?' Haddock asked

'It is,' the woman replied. She was dressed casually, wearing a loose-fitting blouse, a pair of blue jeans, and trainers. Her hair hung down the back of her neck, and she was constantly fiddling with it, brushing it away from her face. This was not the woman that Natalie had met in the penthouse. She had been immaculate there, awaiting the penthouse owner, ready to ply him with loving attention.

'Was Melinda in the apartment when I was there?' Natalie asked.

'She was not. After Alan's death, she moved out. I don't know where she went, nor do I care.'

'Why? Bosom buddies, a vested interest, an official handover, is that how you saw it? And what about her statement that Alan had intended to marry you?'

'Not buddies, as you put it. Alan intended to marry me, and he knew his condition was worsening. His mother had traces of it, and it was genetic. In another few years, he might be incapacitated, not physically, but mentally, unable to face the outside world. His father hadn't suffered from it, and with me and any children, the percentage probability was that they wouldn't be affected.'

'But you couldn't be certain, or is it a defective gene? Is modern technology able to diagnose the unborn baby?'

'If it was affected, a decision would need to be made.'

'Abortion?' Haddock said.

Alice Minchin was talking, as had Melinda Greenworthy. Whether it was the truth was unknown and would need verification. He felt that the love triangle pointed towards the murderer. Natalie, more circumspect, would not countenance that, not yet.

'That's not why I'm here, is it?' Alice said.

'It's not. Why did you lie?' Natalie asked. She had been willing to believe that the woman was a good person, even if her profession was not. But now, in the air-conditioned interview room, austere but functional, she needed verifiable answers. So far, apart from the dead man, there had been a lot of possibilities but very little provable. Was Alice the woman at Cockatoo Island? Or could it have been Melinda? And if it was, why lie? Where was the gain?

'You were intent on marrying Alan, is that correct?' Natalie asked.

'Always. I trusted him.'

'How? The man had issues but played in a heavy metal band; apart from that and the groupies, he would have been classified as reclusive, miserly, and antisocial. Traits which might be genetic but may be personality-driven. Traits that a child may inherit.'

'It was a risk I was willing to take, but Alan had married Melinda. She is… well, I'm sure you've figured that out. I sell my body; she takes their soul and drives them to an early death. Not so easy with Alan, but he died anyway.'

'Was it you with the boarding pass at the island?'

'I spent time with Melinda, knowing she would play hardball, half the assets, and that her lawyer, the sanctimonious Frank Addison, would side with her. I met him a week before Melinda appeared and explained the situation, and he wanted to ensure Melinda received suitable recompense and that Alan would be protected. I wasn't certain I could trust him.'

'We've met him,' Natalie said. She didn't want to state the connection between Alice Minchin and Frank Addison. It was for the woman to confirm and DNA testing to prove.

'And you could tell that Alan was siding with Melinda? Can you be certain of this? Is this when you decided to murder him?'

'Never. I loved him.'

'You said that it was you with him at the murder site. Do you hold to that?' Haddock asked.

'I do. I knew he would have found another if I wasn't there. There was always Crystal Andersson. If I were to walk away from my life, he would have to walk away from his and seek counselling. His father had been cold, his mother more interested in her friends, when it was their son where they should have been focussed. I doubted he would ever be whole and remain at home most of the time, but he would be more communicative and willing to interact.

Frank Addison had been cheating Alan and his father over the years, but his father knew. There was plenty of money, and Addison made more than enough to compensate. But with Alan, he had become more aggressive and started taking risks. Alan didn't care or know, incapable of comprehending. You've seen how he lived. On the street if he didn't have a house. However, there would be a lot more money for Frank Addison with Melinda, a partnership made in heaven, and Alan, pliable and docile.

'I was the fly in the ointment, and Alan was listening to me, almost like trying to convince a child.'

'Your message was sweet and loving, compensating for his cold upbringing. Whereas Melinda was assertive.'

'This was being decided by three persons; the fourth was merely the figurehead, the person to sign the cheques,' Haddock said.

'It was. Alan would have gone along with Melinda and Frank Addison or me. I intended it to be me. I went to Cockatoo Island and made love to Alan, where he died. I didn't kill him. I put that boarding pass there two days later. I didn't kill him, believe me.'

The admission that the woman had been responsible for the boarding pass at the murder site was not expected, although it was clear that only three people could have placed it there. The first would have been Alan, but apparently, he didn't know his wife was in the country; the second, Melinda, but if she had been on the island, that would place suspicion on her; and the third, Alice, who admitted to it.

Natalie sat back in her chair, unsure where the interview was heading. 'When did you place the boarding pass there?' She needed to be sure that she had heard correctly.

'I believe I said two days later.'

Natalie could see the person to gain the most from Alan Greenworthy's death was his wife, although there was another issue of concern – Frank Addison. Where did he fit into the crime? On one hand, he was Alice's father, but then, if she had killed Alan to ensure that Melinda inherited, what did that make him? Hardly the loving father, but had he ever been that, or was he merely an adjunct?

'Could Frank Addison have placed the boarding pass out at Cockatoo Island?'

'I did. I've admitted to it.'

'Unless you're protecting him. Was Alan's wealth important to you? Or was it the stability you wanted, aware that you would be financially secure whatever happened? And if so, why whore?'

'I told you. I would stop, although I would miss the lifestyle. Besides, all good things come to an end.'

Natalie couldn't see how whoring was a good thing, and her once-favourable opinion of the woman had been tarnished.

Chapter 12

Haddock wrapped up the interview and walked out of the building. Natalie knew where: a short walk from State Crime Command, an assignation with Theresa. The man was incorrigible; she despaired for him.

'We need to know, Alice,' Natalie said. The two women had bought food in the station's cafeteria and found a small meeting room near Homicide. A cordiality existed, an opportunity for the woman to talk off the record.

'I can't. You must know that.'

An informal chat, act as a friend, Natalie had suggested it to Haddock, disappointed in her inspector, further confirmation that the man was waning, his enthusiasm for murder overshadowed by a blousy woman in her forties.

'Clive Morton, we know the name.'

'Not from me. Ask me anything else. I know he's not involved; why would he be? He hasn't asked me to marry him or be exclusive, even though he's paying for the penthouse.'

'He pays enough for you. The penthouse can't be cheap. Why doesn't he insist on exclusivity? Did he know about Alan? You've known the family for a long time.'

'I loved Alan, even when we were young. His condition has worsened.'

'But why? Psychological? Was it curable? You said he would only get worse. Before his father died, were you sleeping with him? You're easy with your favours. Did he pay you?'

'Once. When I was nineteen, I spent a weekend with my father and the Greenworthys in a shared house in the Hunter Valley. A chance to visit the vineyards and to sample wines.'

'The first time you've mentioned your father,' Natalie said. 'Why?'

'Our relationship is strained.'

'From when you were nineteen?'

'He caught me in bed with Alan's father, called me all the names you can imagine, plus a few you can't.'

'I can,' Natalie said. 'Was there a scene?'

'My father criticised me, not Alan.'

'Elaborate.'

Natalie sensed that the subject was still a raw emotion with a woman who now sold her body for profit. Could that be the reason? Natalie knew that most who sold themselves had an issue from their youth. Was this Alice's? She didn't smoke or take drugs, and she was educated. And so far, there had been no mention of violence in her life, but now, the father of the man she had wanted to marry sleeping with her at nineteen. Did that bring into question why? The daughter of his friend, young and innocent, or was she? And what about the father?'

'I was nineteen, not a virgin, lost that at fifteen, a boy at school. Nothing special, just a quickie, but I wasn't promiscuous, no more than most. You must have been the same.'

Natalie didn't reply, although if she had, it would be to say that, yes, she went through that phase, and thankfully, it hadn't lasted long, much to the relief of her parents.

'Was it voluntary, you're sleeping with Alan's father?'

'It was the first time and the last. Everyone was out of the house. It was just me and his father in the house. I didn't want to go, not feeling well, and Alan's father wasn't into wine tasting and preferred to stay at the house and read. Not that I could blame him; I'm not much of a drinker.'

'He took advantage?'

'Sort of. He was an attractive man, charismatic, and easy to talk to. I had known him since I was eight when my father started to work for him. They were alike, mine and Alan's. You've met my father, sensed the allure.'

Natalie had met Alice's father but had not seen what she had. To her, he was a typical lawyer, standoffish, interested in protecting Melinda Greenworthy, the fly-in from Hong Kong, who was the beneficiary of the Greenworthy estate. Although, if a divorce settlement had been driven through between Alan and

Melinda, it would have been Alice if she had married Alan. It was complex and becoming more so, Natalie thought. Intrigue within intrigue.

'We're not talking rape here, are we?'

'No. I was over the age of consent, and I knew he fancied me, always looking at me in that way. The two of us, the house empty for a few hours. He gave me a whisky and poured one for himself. He's asking me about my future, what I had planned.'

'Which wasn't prostitution.'

'Hardly. I thought I might become a lawyer, intended to get a law degree.'

'Your relationship with your parents?'

'My mother could be awkward, always complaining about the state of my room, but apart from that, she was fine. My relationship with my father was difficult. He came back early. It happened; I literally fell into bed with Alan's father.'

Natalie knew that was the woman's excuse. Regardless, the father arrived home unexpectedly, finding his daughter and friend in a compromising position, and there had been fireworks.

'What did your mother say when told?'

'Nothing, not sure she ever knew. My father caught Alan's father with his trousers around his ankles, and I'm straddled on top of him. Sure, he exploded, but at me, not him. Said nothing, pulled me off, slapped me hard, called me all the words you can imagine, and flung me out of the house. I had to hitchhike back to Sydney, couch-surfed for a month, and then, desperate for money, sold myself. Not that I wanted to, but I was nineteen, a law degree to get through and to pay for, as my father refused to.'

'Did you get the degree?' Natalie asked.

'Eventually, but I paid for it myself. Working in a café wouldn't pay enough, and I didn't have the hours to devote to regular work. On my back, it paid the bills and got me through. I always intended to quit once I got the degree, but you know.'

Natalie did. 'Easy money, instead of sixty-plus hours a week with a law firm.'

'As a junior, the promise of a partnership, an office in the corner, and a company car.'

'You tried it?'

'I'm not a whore. Maybe my father mistreated me, but he never chastised Alan's father, members of the same club.'

'Club?'

'My father and Melinda Greenworthy. Haven't you figured it out? You must have seen the body language. She's sleeping with him, probably the same modus operandi she used with her first two husbands. Not with Alan, too young and fit, had to use a knife on him, but my father, marry him, then she's got the Greenworthys' money and then my inheritance. No justice, is there?'

'Only reality. How do you know she killed Alan?'

'Stands to reason, doesn't it? She knew I would marry Alan, but there would be more money for her if Alan died. She's negotiating the divorce with my father and sees him as viable. He's still young enough to have his head turned by a pretty face and a svelte body, old enough for her to wear him out with excessive bedroom antics.'

Natalie had to agree that Alice's reasoning was sound, although there was no proof. Melinda or Frank Addison needed to confirm that they were involved, or else she would need to find out for herself. For that, she required surveillance.

***

Natalie and Haddock sat in Addison's office, the two of them ready for the confrontation. Frank Addison knew his way around the law and how far the police could push before evidence was inadmissible, and he had a way with words and was capable of controlling the conversation.

The office was bare and drab. A copy of his law degree on one wall, framed and ageing: Sydney University, honours, 1976. Along another wall, a bookshelf full of legal books and weighty tomes. There was a smell about the room, musty and tobacco. At the back of his house, a sprawling but pleasant four-bedroom, two-storey building, the office had been his primary place of business for almost forty years.

'You've been speaking to my daughter,' Addison said as he opened a drawer and took out a box of cigars. 'My house, my rules,' he said.

Natalie wanted to object, but the man was right. In the world outside, political correctness and rules, but he could do whatever he wanted in his place.

'One for you, Inspector?' Addison said as he held the box over the desk.

'Not me,' Haddock replied.

The office was warm, and the window at the rear closed. 'You won't object if I open the window,' Natalie said.

'Not at all. I know the smell is offensive, but a man has got to have some vices, and if he can't have them in his house, then where?'

'Fair comment,' Haddock said. 'Doesn't alter the fact that we have certain information that needs to be clarified.'

'My relationship with my daughter is complex,' Addison said as he sucked on his cigar.

'Due to her and Alan's father?' Natalie asked, a handkerchief in one hand, ready to bring it to her face if the smell worsened.

'Did I catch them in bed? Is that it?'

'It is. What's the truth?'

I knew what she was, but it was my daughter. I'll not say she was innocent; no doubt she had amused some of the lads at her school, but she had a budding career in front of her. She thought I should have confronted the man, but I didn't. Not that I wasn't angry with him, but I knew he wouldn't change, no regrets for what he had done. My daughter needed a swift kick up the rear end, or if not, a sharp reminder that she had overstepped the mark. It was me who found them. What if it had been Alan or his mother? Can you imagine what would have happened?'

'No,' Natalie said cynically, 'but we expect you to tell us.'

'Alan's mother was a difficult woman. She knew what her husband was and tolerated it as long as he supported her and her son. She was devoted to Alan but rarely showed it, ambivalent towards her husband. But it was my daughter in bed with the man. She would have forced Alan's father to sever the relationship that I had with him. But she never understood that I was integral in creating the wealth. It would have been an untenable situation.'

'You knew what was likely to happen when you left the house that day for the wine tasting,' Haddock said.

'Alice was beautiful and adored the father as much as the son. One was shy and retiring, plagued by inner demons; the other was open, gregarious, and available. I made excuses and returned to the house; my fears were proven. I protected my daughter and chastised her. It was her that I loved, not him.'

'It backfired?'

'Alice didn't see it that way and moved out of the house, went to university, and financed it herself.'

'With prostitution,' Natalie said.

'I wanted to pay, but she wouldn't let me. I thought I had done the right thing, but obviously I hadn't. No regrets in your life?' Addison said.

Haddock would have said the affair with Theresa de Klerk; Natalie remembered her reaction to her live-in boyfriend after he had slept with a work colleague. She was alone and lonely, not even a cat or a budgerigar for company. But this wasn't about them, but Alan Greenworthy and his death.

'It's your regrets that interest us,' Natalie said. 'She finished the degree, tried working in a legal office for a while, then found that selling herself was more profitable than being a lawyer.'

'Not the whole truth. As a junior, she worked for a lawyer and had an affair with him, destroying his marriage. No doubt she didn't tell you that. Ask her. She's a good person, but she's easy with her favours. Like father, like daughter.'

'Has she forgiven you?'

'Our relationship is civil; besides, she's an adult, not a promiscuous nineteen-year-old.'

'And unlikely to forgive you now that you are sleeping with Melinda Greenworthy. It's true, isn't it? Natalie said.

'Alice cannot marry Alan now. Melinda will get the inheritance.'

'And you believe your charm will work with her?' Haddock asked.

'Birds of a feather. She knows where the strength is. Melinda cares not one iota for me, and I'm not one of her foolish husbands. I know what she is, what I am. She's beautiful, and I have the key to the golden chest. I know where the assets are and where the money is deposited. And what did you expect me to do when she came on to me? Reject her?'

Natalie's Puritan morality might have said yes, but Frank Addison's answer was plausible. But was it the truth? It would require Melinda to answer that question, and the veracity of whatever she said had to be regarded with suspicion.

Chapter 13

Crystal Andersson sat in the office at her father's engineering firm. She was back to her usual cheerful self. That was until Jeb Barton phoned and asked her to meet with him that evening. She would have refused, not ready to date again, and certainly not Barton, whom she thought was lacking in drive and physically unattractive, but he had said it was important, something to do with Alan.

Although why she had loved Alan, she thought after the phone call had ended, made no sense. He had no drive, was charismatic when playing with the band, otherwise reclusive and antisocial, only met with her occasionally, and stated that he was fond of her, but the emotion of love was not his to give, not to her or anyone else. Then she discovered that Alice Minchin, a high-class whore, intended to marry him.

The two met at a pub not far from the engineering firm. It was seven in the evening, and Barton was dressed casually. Crystal had come straight from work and wore her office clothes, a navy skirt, a white blouse, and sensible flat-soled shoes. There was no kiss on the cheek, only a brief handshake. Crystal saw that the man was not as unattractive as she had thought, only having met him when the band played. There, he had adopted grunge but was now clean and tidy, with a parting in his hair, clean-shaven and smelling of aftershave.

'You look different,' Alice said as Jeb handed her a dry sherry. He held a beer in his hand.

'You're still as attractive,' Jeb said. 'That is a comment, not a flirtation. Please don't misconstrue why we're meeting.'

Crystal didn't but knew that give the man an inch, and he would take a mile. Her reason for the meeting was professional, not personal. She had loved Alan, but he was dead, and she wanted to know why and who had murdered him. Her intentions were honourable. She wasn't one hundred per cent sure if Barton's were, and if he wasn't quick with a reason for their meeting, she would throw her drink over him and walk out the door.

It had only been in the last week that she had felt able to think of Alan without becoming emotional, and another man using his death as a means of sidling up to her on the rebound wasn't going to work.

'Five minutes.' She realised she was impolite but didn't care, having played puppy to Alan while he dallied with Alice, Melinda, and whoever else. She had known her love had been irrational and that the man didn't deserve it, but she had loved him from the moment she had first set eyes on him, up on the stage, belting out lyrics that made no sense.

It wasn't her kind of music, and she had only gone because a group of her friends, conservative and demure, wanted to walk on the wild side, the excitement of something daring.

Crystal was smitten when the Maligned Manglers came on stage. Before them, a couple of other acts, including one group who could not keep in tune and kept forgetting the lyrics, compensated by one demonstrating how not to play a guitar solo and the drummer who walked off in a huff. But then, six months later, they were top of the heavy metal charts, headlining in Australia and the USA. The second group kept in tune but was not heard again when the lead singer crowd surfed into the audience and was hauled off to the hospital after he hit the concrete floor hard.

She had to admit that Alan's group were good, and even though she didn't like the music, the crowd did, especially a woman he disappeared with after the gig. Even then, she had wished it was her, but not with her friends present and almost certainly not with her gentle morality. One-night stands were not her thing, and to her friends, especially Marg, who enjoyed them and didn't care who knew, Crystal was an innocent child.

There had been a man, or more correctly, a boy pretending to be a man, who had taken her virginity at seventeen but it had been outside the pub they frequented on a Saturday night. She had drunk more than she should have, aware of the probable outcome. A virgin at seventeen, it had seemed banal to her and ridiculous to her friends, who derided her for her standoffish manner.

'Get it over with,' they would say. 'No point in missing out, and what have your parents got to do with it? They belong to another generation.'

They were right, Crystal knew, but she wanted romance, not a spotty individual who would only brag about it and then blast it out on social media that Crystal Andersson was a slut.

At least, she had to give credit to Tim, shorter than her, unshaven, and with a wispy beard that was going nowhere. He was clean and casually dressed. Outside the pub, the kissing moved on to wandering hands, her feeling excited, him with a hard-on. The deed was over quickly, and they were back in the pub, no one the wiser, apart from Marg, who had seen what had happened. 'Good on you,' she said. 'Welcome to the twenty-first century.'

Crystal hadn't felt that she had changed from child to adult, only that she felt dirty, and the sex had been unprotected. What if she became pregnant? What if she had caught a disease?

Tim, whom she had considered a cut above the rest that night at the pub, never told anyone, and they never dated, only smiled at each other the next time they met.

After that, two other men, both of whom had been decent; one she had loved and considered moving in with, but the romance withered. Only with Alan Greenworthy did the passion remain, to be sated only thrice over eighteen months. The first, at a concert, around the back of the stage, but she wasn't into casual sex, yet somehow hadn't felt guilt over her actions. The second, a weekend away, where he had spoken little, preferring to remain in his self-imposed shell. They had made love twice that weekend, and Crystal had been delighted. Alan even thanked her for their time together. The third, two days before he died, when he had told her that he intended to marry Alice, and whereas he was fond of her, she needed a man to look after her, something he was incapable of, whereas Alice would take control and nurse him through the dark times. Crystal was sure there was another reason. She would listen to Jeb Barton before deciding what to do. Whether she should contact the police with her suspicions or remain silent.

Barton ordered a hamburger; Crystal didn't eat. Her figure came at a cost. Her mother told her to put on weight. Her father just hugged her when the subject came up.

'What are we here for?' Crystal asked.

'I remembered something,' Barton replied, averting his eyes. He had asked her to the pub to discuss Alan, but he had always fancied her from afar, and her presence, so close, yet so far, troubled him. He regarded himself as solid and upright and held a middle management role with Ryde Council. Attributes that should attract a woman to his side, but never the woman he wanted, which was Crystal. On one occasion, he had seen her with Alan backstage, a crack in a partition, where he had seen the two cavorting. Even Gus Gomolka and Igor Minsky, the two other band members, had better success than him with the ladies, although Gomolka was uncouth and Minsky had his head up his arse with his intellectual babble about the purity of heavy metal and how it could be incorporated into classical music. Gomolka, credit where it was due, was competent with a guitar, but his guttural accent and unpleasant look apparently appealed to the groupies more than Barton did. Even Minsky, when he wasn't writing music, would take the occasional woman, but he, Jeb Barton, decent and upright, found he was often the odd man out.

'At Cockatoo Island?'

'Did you know his wife?' Barton asked. He was on his third drink; Crystal was on her first. He felt a stirring in his groin, knew he wanted her, but regarded her as out of his league. She had benefited from a private school education, a wealthy family, and a five-bedroom house with a swimming pool. His education had been government-funded and not academically rigorous. Home as a child and in his teens had been a three-bedroom fibro on the fringes of the area where she lived, the wrong side of the track, working class, although he wasn't sure what that meant and always believed it to be derogatory.

'No. I knew about Alice, something to do with their childhood and growing up together, an inseparable bond, but what was she? Easy with her favours, any man for a price.' Crystal knew she was being vindictive. The woman hadn't done anything to her, pleasant if they spoke, which was rare, a phone call now and then, meeting once, to discuss Alan's worsening condition.

'And what a price. Do you know how much?'

'I don't. Have you paid? It might have upset Alan if he had known. You were jealous of him, weren't you?'

'I was, still am. Two beautiful women fawning over him, another he married. I'm not sure if the band will survive.'

Barton knew mentioning the band was dumb.

'Hell to the band, get to the point,' Crystal said.

'I saw Melinda Greenworthy the day before he died.'

'Where? Is it relevant? And now she's screwing an old man?'

Jeb Barton could see it acutely. He had been keeping tabs on the leading players in the saga, and so had Crystal.

''How do you know this? Are you keeping a watch on Melinda?'

''How did you see her?'

'I went to see Alan to check that everything was ready for the concert. I saw a car parked across the road. I didn't pay any attention to it, but forty-five minutes later, it was still there, a Chinese woman in the driver's seat. I looked over at her, and she averted her eyes. It could have only been his wife.'

'Did Alan know?'

'He didn't mention it, but then, Alan would have kept it to himself. The police probably don't know either.'

'How do I know about Melinda and the old man? Is that what you want to ask? Do you think I'm snooping?'

'Crystal, you are. But why? You've nothing to gain, apart from becoming a suspect if the police find out.'

'Which they won't. You won't tell them, will you?' The voice was calm and seductive, allowing Barton to hope.

'I won't, but why? I saw Melinda by chance. You obviously saw her and the old man due to your snooping. Why? What's in it for you? Alice has a tentative claim due to her childhood friendship, and Melinda, as his widow, has a legal claim, the strongest of all. You have nothing.'

'I do. Alan's heir.'

Barton gulped down his drink and walked over to the bar. 'Another one, better make it a double whisky.' In shock, an instant deflation. It was an unforeseen complication; if it was Alan's, she would have a claim on the estate, not for all the money, but sufficient to raise the unborn child.

Barton sat down. 'It complicates,' he said.

'Why would you get pregnant?'

'You know the answer.'

Jeb Barton did. Crystal wanted the man, and she had known of Melinda. How was unimportant for the moment. A pregnant woman, a divorced Alan, the man would have honoured his obligation to the unborn child and married the mother, pushing Alice to one side. There was a side to Crystal Andersson, a woman he wanted, but who was she? The devil incarnate, trapping a disturbed man into marriage, or was the pregnancy the unfortunate consequence of an unrequited love?

'I didn't intend it,' Crystal said. 'It was before he died. We met out west and spent the night in a motel. I could tell Alan was troubled, but I wanted him, don't you see?'

Barton had wanted Crystal, but now he was not sure. Could she be the murderer? She had everything to gain, nothing to lose, apart from Alan. But she would not have known she was pregnant one week before his death. Or else…

'What will you do? Tell the police? You could keep quiet, I suppose.'

'For how long? Three, four months. Sergeant Campbell will see the difference in me, the belly expanding, the firm breasts, the changeable moods.'

'Your parents?'

'Not yet. My mother will throw a fit, my father will blow hot and cold for a few days, and accuse me of everything under the sun. Eventually, they will accept.'

'And pay?'

'I don't want their money. I wanted Alan, but I can't have him now. Or can I? I can have the memory and his child.'

'Is that sufficient?'

'No, but it's the best there is. I didn't want him dead. The police will understand.'

Barton thought the sergeant might, but the hardened and cynical inspector would not. 'What now?' he said.

He would drive her home to ensure she was safe. Though he no longer had her on a pedestal, she was still the same beautiful woman, even if she was carrying another man's child. He thought of the possibilities, their raising the child, not caring that he was not the father. He smiled at the thought, realising that Crystal was looking at him, a smirk on her face.

'I don't want a bastard. If you're interested.'

'I am,' Barton said.

Crystal smiled again, but Barton wasn't sure if it was a smile of joy or amusement that she had suckered an infatuated fool. A person who would provide an alibi if needed.

He considered the situation and realised that he would do what she wanted, only if…

That was resolved later that evening, near to where her parents lived. In the back seat of his car, the two made love. The vindictive and the infatuated, the temptress and the fool, the beguiling and the beguiled.

Outside the car, as Barton drove away, Crystal bent over in the road and vomited, bringing up her drink, the salad she had eaten, and the smell of the man she had seduced. She regarded what she had done with abhorrence and knew that Barton was correct. The police would not believe her to be a good person.

She could see lights at her house and realised that her parents would question her night out. She wasn't in the mood to talk to them, ashamed of herself, although reluctantly excited that it wasn't only Melinda Greenworthy and Alice Minchin who could twist men around their fingers and get them to perjure themselves. She had now joined their ranks. Her car was in the driveway. She got in and drove away, making a phone call on the hands-free. 'Sorry if it's late, but can we meet?'

Natalie, always on duty, even in the early morning, answered in the affirmative. 'When?'

'Now. I know who the murderer is.'

***

Jeb Barton was arrested at 5:14 a.m. and taken to State Crime Command in Parramatta. Confused, he barely registered his surroundings in the interview room. He had gone to bed elated after making love to Crystal. But now, as he calmed down after the arrest, the indignity of the handcuffs, and the enforced relocation to the police station, he had time to reflect. Was this Crystal's plan – to seduce and play him for the fool? Had she had him arrested to deflect suspicion from her? The events leading up to his arrest swirled in his mind as to why and for what purpose. He couldn't believe her to be the murderer, but being pregnant by Alan was another factor to consider.

Haddock had been made aware of the two women meeting, a phone call from Natalie soon after Crystal had phoned her. Initially angry, interrupting a night with Theresa de Klerk, casual sex without the complication of a troublesome daughter to discuss and a wife who was still giving him the cold shoulder. He knew it was wrong, but it was addictive, and he couldn't give it up, not yet; maybe next month, maybe never, depending on how the situation played out with his family.

Natalie had known where he was, but if Crystal was meeting to discuss who the murderer was, then he needed to be alerted to the situation.

Natalie had lived in Neutral Bay when she first came to Sydney. Upmarket, expensive, and cosmopolitan, she had enjoyed the village feel of the place on a Saturday if she was free, less often than she had expected. Kings Cross Police Station had been a baptism of fire, and the chauvinism there had annoyed her.

A studio apartment two blocks down from the shopping area on Military Road, cold in winter, hot in summer. The only plus was that it had been cheap and she had stayed there for eight months. She knew Maisy's Eatery would be open until three in the morning, a godsend for the hours a police officer worked, equidistant for her and Crystal.

They met just after two in the morning. Crystal ordered a Wagyu beef burger with fries. Aware that creating a sense of alarm and shock was in order, scoffing down a burger and fries would create the intended effect.

Natalie sipped at a coffee.

Crystal took a bite of her burger, stuffed a handful of fries in her mouth, took out a handkerchief and held it to her eyes. 'He raped me,' she said.

Somewhat taken aback, Natalie felt empathy with the woman. It had nearly happened to her once at Kings Cross Police Station until she had kneed the man, and a fellow officer, an inspector, had grabbed him and flung him across the room. They had become lovers for a while, the knight in shining armour and the damsel in distress, but in the end, the ardour had waned, and then he accepted a transfer and promotion to Chief Inspector.

'Who?' Natalie said as she put an arm around the clearly distressed woman.

'Jeb Barton.'

'It's a crime.'

'Provable,' she said. 'I have the bruises. A medical examination will confirm that it was him.'

Natalie thought the woman was clinical in her speech. Raped women, and she had met a few, were invariably in shock, then denial, and then believing they had egged the man on, but Crystal wasn't any of those, and as for the handkerchief, Natalie hadn't seen a tear, only a woman who had scoffed down a burger and fries in record time.

A police surgeon lived close to the café. Natalie phoned her. 'Twenty-five minutes, my house. You know the address. How long since the rape?'

Natalie looked over at Crystal. 'How long?'

'I phoned you five minutes after I got free. Sixty minutes.'

Natalie relayed the information.

'Any other issues to consider? Bruising, bite marks, restraints?'

'Bruising,' Crystal said.

Natalie realised that under normal circumstances, Crystal, even if slight in stature, would have been able to hold off the mild-mannered and inoffensive Barton. But rape was not a normal circumstance, and a man in heat, enamoured of the female after a few drinks, possessed strength, and the female would retreat into submissive mode very quickly, detach from reality, unable to remember details afterwards as the shock came. But Crystal was cognisant and sure of her facts. Natalie didn't like her body language: measured, as though she was acting. However, subject to the doctor's confirmation, it was rape, and the man would be hauled into the police station. And, once the doctor's report was in and Crystal had made a statement, charges would be laid.

'He rapes you, but murder? Are you saying he murdered Alan Greenworthy?'

'I met him. We had a few drinks and a meal to discuss Alan's death. Jeb was curious and thought he was an amateur detective, and maybe he did know more, but he didn't know one thing: once Melinda was out of the way, Alan would have married me.'

'He wanted Alice.'

'Want is not the same as would. I told Jeb, I'll tell you. I'm pregnant with Alan's child. He would have married me, and then he died.'

'Who else knows this?' Natalie asked, shocked by what she had just been told.

The examination by Dr Eugenia Karvan confirmed that Crystal was pregnant and that there were signs of bruising, but it was inconclusive that they had been caused by a man beating her or holding her down. However, the doctor confirmed that the woman had had sexual intercourse within the last two hours. Rape was not confirmed, but Crystal's meeting with Jeb indicated a development.

Haddock and Natalie knew Jeb Barton, and Natalie also knew that Crystal had told her once before that she didn't like Barton, yet they meet, share drinks and a meal, and then he drives her home, all the makings of a romantic night out. Only Crystal didn't tell it that way; she didn't tell much other than the rape and that she was pregnant.

To Natalie, a motive for Crystal to want Alan dead if he intended to marry Alice, and that if she couldn't have him, no one else would. But if she had known she was pregnant, a reason to want him alive. The dates were tight. Two days either way before a pregnancy test would have told her.

One hour after the examination, Crystal was at home, anxious parents worried about where their daughter had been. 'Out, friends, nothing to worry about. Off to bed, bye.'

The temptress had laid the trap well, but was it good enough? With the inspector, it was foolproof, but then he was a fool. Taller than her, he had come in close, looked down at her cleavage, and imagined what lay beneath, the firm breasts and the curve of her arse. She had experienced it before and used it to advantage with Barton.

But had she been wrong in calling the sergeant to tell her of the rape. The woman was not much older than her, but with a police officer's instincts, a member of her sex, immune to cleavage, breasts, and hidden delights. Had her story been convincing, would they pin the murder on Barton?

Chapter 14

Frightened, bewildered, and unsure of himself, Jeb Barton sat in the interview room. A hearty breakfast had been brought to him by a burly constable, who pushed against him as he left the room. Barton knew that rapists and child molesters were regarded as the lowest of the low; better to be a murderer than involved in a sex crime.

He had been told of the charge levelled against him by the two officers who took him to Parramatta. Confused, he believed that Crystal had been genuine when they had made love, and there was the hope that he could be the child's father, the mother's husband.

'You're aware of the charge?' Haddock said after he had gone through the preliminaries in the interview room. Barton had declined legal aid. 'Anything you say…?'

He wasn't sure what to say, didn't understand what had happened. He saw himself as condemned; the breakfast, his meal of choice before the hangman's noose. Emotions raced through him. He had had sex with Crystal, a fantasy of his, since the first time he had seen Alan with her.

He had wondered then if she was the person she portrayed: attractive and well-spoken. Screwing backstage was not the behaviour of a respectable woman. And then, if she screwed him and then screamed rape to the police, what did that make her? What was she? Could she have murdered Alan? But that made no sense, not if she was pregnant. He had gone home from their tryst, believing that his life was on the up. Promotion with the council beckoned, or possibly a senior position in her father's company. Husband of the daughter and father of the latest addition to the Andersson family bloodline.

'I am,' Barton said, brought back to reality.

On the other side of the table, Sergeant Campbell. He had to admit she was attractive, but nothing compared to Crystal.

He had put her on a pedestal, but had the woman smashed him on the head with it? Or was there something else? Was this a challenge for him to keep quiet? Had she murdered Alan? Would she murder again? Questions for which he had no answer. Whatever, he had to defend himself but not condemn her.

'Crystal Andersson has accused you of rape,' Natalie said.

'It was consensual,' Barton replied. 'Why would she do that? I thought we had an agreement.'

'What was that agreement?'

Natalie wasn't condemning, nor was Haddock, after Natalie had spoken to him before the interview; that there were inconsistencies, and Crystal's body language was not that of a violently raped woman, pretending there were tears when there were not, shuffling in her seat while her feet stayed firmly planted on the ground and not moving.

'She told me about Alan's child and that she didn't want it to be born a bastard.'

'An old-fashioned attitude,' Natalie said.

'I believed I could be the child's father; no one would ever know.'

'Except the child has claim on the Greenworthy estate. DNA will prove if it is Alan Greenworthy's.'

'Level with us,' Haddock said. 'The evening from start to finish. The two of you met in a pub, a few drinks, a meal, and you drove her home.'

'I phoned her, told her I knew who the murderer was. She agreed to meet. I intended to behave, not to get too close or show my affection.'

'But you couldn't resist. Is that why you raped her? She got drunk, and you drove her home.'

'No, it wasn't like that.'

'Start from the beginning,' Natalie said.

'I told her who the murderer was. She agreed to meet with me. She was the only person I could tell, and I knew she was interested in finding out. I didn't know about the pregnancy, not then. She told me why she couldn't have murdered Alan and that if he had lived, he would have married her instead of Alice.'

'Which makes sense.'

'I knew she had been snooping around; I told her I had seen Alan's wife in a car outside his house. She was sitting in it when I went in to meet with Alan and again when I came out.'

'Dates, time,' Haddock said.

'One day before he died. Early morning. She might have gone in the house after I left, but I doubt it. I drove past the end of the street later, and she was still there.'

'And that makes her the murderer?'

'It's suspicious.'

'It's rape, although Melinda outside the house is concerning.'

'How could I have raped her? In the back seat? How did she get there? Do you think I dragged her from the passenger seat in the front to the back?'

Another inconsistency in Crystal's statement. The car was at Barton's house, and a crime scene investigator had confirmed that there were indications that sexual intercourse had occurred in the last twelve hours: semen and sweat marks on the back seat. Whether violent or passionate could not be determined. Natalie thought the latter and that Crystal might be using rape as a defence mechanism to deflect blame from her. Firstly, by having sex with someone she had no feelings for, and secondly, rape was an easy accusation but harder to disprove, and Barton would choose to protect her honour than throw her to the wolves.

'Why did she have sex with you?' Natalie asked.

'Like-minded persons, would that suffice?' Barton said. It would not.

'We knew of her love for Alan. How the man was so successful with women mystified me.'

It might have mystified Haddock, but Natalie knew why. Alan Greenworthy was the puppy with a sore leg, the bird with a broken wing, someone to love, to mother, someone who would respond to licks and a wagging tail in the case of a dog, a squawk in the case of a bird, marriage in the case of a woman. And he would always need to be mothered, smothered with love, the child who never grew old.

'You've not answered the question,' Haddock reminded Barton.

'I hoped that Crystal would see me as a substitute. Someone she could rely on. I wanted a future with her, on the rebound, I suppose. And if she hadn't been pregnant, would Alan have chosen her? Probably not.'

'Because of Alice?' Natalie said. She realised that Barton was giving viable answers and his body language was appropriate. Haddock was not so sure.

'I met her once,' Barton said. 'I was introduced, and apart from her profession, she was attractive. Even so, I preferred Crystal; but I could hope, and then, with hope comes the possibility, and then she accuses me of rape. No justice for the good, is there?'

'There isn't,' Natalie agreed. 'Even so, we can't dismiss the accusation against you based on your testimony. What Crystal told us is fundamentally correct. She is pregnant. You had sexual intercourse with her. That is proven. You must appreciate our sensitivity in such matters.'

'Is Melinda Greenworthy the murderer?'

'There is the possibility, but not the proof. We know she was in Sydney two days before Alan's murder. Outside Alan's house does not make her a murderer. You must be a suspect.'

'How? I would not have harmed Alan, not even a fly. Okay, maybe a fly, but I'm a pacifist, the type of guy who gets sand kicked in his face at the beach by a bully, head in the urinal at school.'

'Did that happen?'

'The school I went to. Until—'

'Until what?'

'Nothing,' Barton said, 'just talking.'

'It might be best if you tell us, or we'll need to find your schoolmates and ask them,' Haddock said.

'It's on my record; you must know what I'm referring to. I was fourteen.'

'As a minor, your crime would have been expunged from the record. We could make a formal request and find out.'

'Fourteen, short for my age, skinny, nothing to look at. Bart Andropov, the school bully, used to pick on me, push me over when he saw me, and steal my lunch and any money in my pocket. He had a couple of offsiders who would back him up, jeer at me, stick me in the waste paper basket, whatever.'

'And you got revenge?'

'Last day of term. My mother was outside the school, picking me up. I can see Andropov up the road teasing a couple of girls. I get in the car, put it into gear and drive at him. He's on the road, playing the fool. I hit him, not fast, not enough to kill, enough to break his ankle. Hauled before juvenile court, three months in the workhouse, and then back home, a different school.'

'Andropov?'

'Never heard any more of him. He wasn't too bright, more brawn than brain. Labouring somewhere, might be in prison, dead for all I care.'

Natalie and Haddock sat back in unison. There was a dark side to Barton, a man capable of violence if riled, of premeditated murder if the circumstance demanded, and Alan marrying Crystal would have been that circumstance if he had known that she was pregnant. But how? She hadn't known, not when Alan had died, or had she? And if she did, how did Barton know?

'Rape is a crime of violence,' Natalie said, 'and by your admission you are capable of violence.'

'I was fourteen, the victim of a school bully. Crystal never did anything against me, didn't tease or bully me.'

'Her crime was ignoring you. Isn't that the same as Andropov, her regarding you as no more than dirt beneath her feet?'

'I loved her.'

'Infatuation is a powerful force, and then the chance to have sex with her when she was most vulnerable. Is it you who are lying? We can't prove rape, nor can we absolve you of the crime. And why is Melinda the murderer? What further evidence can you offer, or was it a lure to spend time with Crystal?'

Natalie was convinced it wasn't rape but uncertain why the woman had placed herself in a potentially compromising position. Previously the least likely of the three – Alice Minchin, Melinda Greenworthy, and Crystal Andersson – Crystal was now considered the most likely to have killed him, but that meant she had not known she was pregnant. The date of conception was important; the date when she had proof of the pregnancy was critical.

There was another consideration, which would not be proved until the child that Crystal Andersson was carrying was born. Was it Alan's child? The woman's testimony on anything she said now must be considered suspect. And if not Alan's child, then whose? Had she gotten pregnant to secure Alan as a husband, sidelining Alice, playing on Alan's sense of decency and fair play?

Questions integral to the investigation would rely on the testimony of a woman who could not be trusted. The bruising on the woman's body could have occurred before the rape or during it, as the two had sex in the car's back seat.

There was no alternative but to release Barton on his surety that he would remain in Sydney and avoid the claimant.

Natalie doubted a charge would ever be laid, although she requested Jeb Barton's file and the crime he had committed against Bart Andropov. It would not make the case any firmer against Barton but would give greater insight into the man's thought process and inclination to violence if provoked.

***

For two days, both officers remained in Homicide at Parramatta. Facts needed to be verified, and consideration given to the evidence so far, which on reflection was contradictory, dependent on the person giving the statement and the faith placed in the veracity of what was said. Crystal Andersson had gone from sweet and innocent to malignant and devious, and Jeb Barton had gone from decent and harmless to rapist and violent, the latter proven after Natalie received proof that Andropov had suffered a broken ankle. Natalie had phoned the man, no longer in Sydney, but in Perth, Western Australia, a five-hour flight from Sydney if she wanted to meet him.

'I forgave him a long time. Barton was right. I was a bully; he was the only person who stood up to me. Never saw him again, only at juvenile court. I did not say much, couldn't condemn him,' the Reverend Bart Andropov said.

Haddock spent time on reports and one night at the family home, a cordial welcome by his daughter, a brusque reception from his wife, realising that he should have changed his shirt, Theresa's lipstick on the collar. Apart from that, news that their daughter's school reported improved behaviour and that her academic results were above average.

Commander Payne kept his distance; no politicians or Supreme Court judges were pressing him for action with this murder, and no former prime ministers were attempting to protect their reputation. In Legal, Victoria Adderley confirmed to Natalie that she and Payne were having an inter-departmental fling but asked her to keep it secret, which she would have, except that the bush telegraph was working well and everyone in the building knew.

Theresa de Klerk had taken to acknowledging Natalie's presence in the building and was courteous, each asking the other how they were, pleasantries about the weather, nothing mentioned of Theresa's ongoing fling with Haddock, which Natalie thought had the signs of ending, judging by the reduced number of love bites on his neck, discretely hidden by his shirt collar, more visible if he loosened his tie and undid the top bottom of his shirt late in the day when inspector and sergeant got to sit down and natter about life in general and murder in particular.

***

Three persons met on the other side of town at the Greenworthy house. Melinda, who had called them together, Frank Addison, and Alice Minchin, who had used her stepfather's surname after her parents had divorced. It wasn't a name she liked, and she regarded the stepfather with disinterest. He had treated her mother well, although he had a habit of getting too close to Alice, especially during her teens, as though the title of stepfather implied certain privileges.

Frank sat between the two women, contenders for a dead man's affection – a battle Melinda had fought and won. There was another reason to meet, to discuss a development.

'You're not pregnant, are you?' Melinda asked Alice.

'Should I be?'

'It would help.'

Frank looked at his daughter, remembered the bundle of joy that had bounced on his knee as a child, and saw the woman she had become: beautiful, seductive, a whore. If he had stayed with her mother, he thought, would she have been different, a professional woman, married with children.

It was a foolish thought, he knew. Life wasn't ruled by certainties. There were crossroads in every life: turn left or right, stay married or divorced, stay a virgin until marriage or play the field. And besides, his daughter had a body for love; no man could resist her, and if she was amorous by disposition, a nurturing family home wouldn't have made a difference. Although it might have prevented her from selling her body for money – or would it? The wrong man, a couple of kids, she could have been on the street or in a brothel turning tricks rather than in a penthouse funded by Clive Morton.

'Melinda, you called this meeting,' Frank reminded her, looking at her and remembering the previous night.

'Jeb Barton phoned, wants a piece of the action.'

'A piece of you,' Alice said scathingly.

'He's already had Crystal Andersson, why not you? The man's trouble and reckons he's in the box seat, playing us off against each other.'

'Why?'

'A good question. Do you realise that at least five people could be a murderer? It could be one of us three. We've all got reasons to have wanted Alan dead, apart from you, Alice, if you intended to marry him.'

'If you would have agreed to the divorce settlement,' Frank reminded her.

'And now, you're sleeping with my father,' Alice said. 'Is that part of your plan? Is that why we're here now? Looking for my blessing, not that you're likely to receive it.'

'I would have agreed to the divorce eventually. Alan wasn't involved in the final settlement details; your father was. I didn't sleep with him before Alan's death. I am now, but not for the reasons you assume.'

'Then why?'

'Protection, and I prefer my men mature. Alan was an aberration on my part and on his, as well. We both knew that soon after we married.'

'You've not explained why you're here,' Alice reminded Melinda. In front of the three, on a coffee table, three glasses, a bottle of wine, Australian, Barossa Valley, South Australia.

Frank Addison poured three glasses, handed one to Melinda, another to Alice, and took one for himself. 'Facts, Melinda. We must assume that we're not the murderers, agreed?'

'Agreed,' Alice said. 'I would have married him. No reason to want him dead. Melinda's gained because of his death, but I'll give her the benefit of not believing she's responsible. However, Father...' Addison knew that was a bad sign; she never called him father unless there was anger or a demand. '... you gained regardless of whether he lived or died.'

'I wanted you to marry him, and your children would have secured the fortune.'

'None of us had a reason to kill him,' Melinda said. 'I had already seen off two husbands, and Alan and your father would have come to a deal. There was no reason to involve the police by killing him, and they are relentless. Are we in agreement?'

Frank nodded, and Alice smiled, a sign of acquiescence. Now was not the time to argue. The heat was on; secrets which were best left hidden would be revealed.

'Crystal Andersson accused Jeb Barton of rape,' Melinda said.

'How do you know this?'

'He phoned me, attempted to bribe me.'

'Why? How?'

'He knows something. I don't know what. "Dynamite",' he said.

'And you believe him? Have you met him?' Alice asked. She drank her wine and realised it was not cheap but would have cost more than a hundred dollars.

'You have?'

'Once, near the Opera House. Alan introduced me, but we spent no more than forty minutes with him. Polite, ineffectual, didn't seem interested in me.'

'Not everyone is.' A catty remark from Melinda. Frank let it pass. Get two women together, and there was bound to be baiting.

'And you say he raped Crystal Andersson, skin and bones?'

'He was accused, claims it was consensual, wants money to defend himself if it goes pear-shaped, his words, not mine.'

'Do we believe the rape?' Frank asked.

'Not on her say-so. She wanted Alan, would have made the perfect wife, dutiful, a good mother.'

'So would you, Alice. And the Andersson woman claims she is pregnant by Alan. She would have pressed the advantage.'

'If the woman's pregnant, how? Or should I say when? He hadn't seen her for a couple of months. That's what he told me, and I believed him.'

'But it was you on the island, on your back, legs open, going hell for leather,' Melinda fired back.

'And you were in Australia. Yours is the motive.'

'Ladies, focus on Barton. I agree that Alice and I would not have gained from Alan's death. Nor would Barton, from what I can see. I suggest you report this to the police. We don't want to become involved in underhand payouts, especially when none of us is guilty of crime.'

Three hours and forty minutes later, long enough for Natalie to have driven to the house, to listen to Melinda recount her conversation with Barton, for the man to be read his rights at the council offices where he worked, and to be put in the backseat of a marked police car and driven to Parramatta.

Chapter 15

Jeb Barton sat quietly as the facts were laid before him. The rape accusation from Crystal Andersson, the bribery or, as Melinda had phrased it, the request for financial assistance.

'We discounted the rape initially,' Haddock said, 'even your breaking of Andropov's ankle while still a juvenile. The benefit of the doubt from us, and now we have you phoning Melinda Greenworthy, asking for money. Why would she give it to you?'

Barton stood, although he had been told before the interview to remain seated and on his side of the table.

'I, Jeb Barton, admit to the murder of Alan Greenworthy,' he said. He then sat down and uttered no other word, only to write on paper. He outlined how he became jealous of Greenworthy, the time spent with Crystal Andersson, the woman he loved, and that he had seen him steal off with Alice up to the top of the island and then her leaving, overjoyed as the man confirmed that he would marry her once he was rid of Melinda. And Greenworthy lying there, aware that Crystal still wanted him, and knowing that she would wriggle herself into his affections, married or not, and she would be lost to him.

Natalie read it back to Barton, ensuring that he understood what he had just signed.

Charged with the murder of Alan Greenworthy, Barton was led down to the holding cells beneath the station. Murder, a confession freely given, would not allow bail, but remand in Long Bay prison, close to Botany Bay.

The interview and confession had taken twenty-five minutes. Haddock leant back on his chair and looked over at his sergeant. 'What just happened?' he said.

'He might have killed Greenworthy, but it doesn't hold up. Even though she accused him of rape, he's protecting Crystal and has something on Melinda Greenworthy. The demand for money is not proof of wrongdoing on her part.'

'Find out what it is,' Haddock said. 'He's confessed, but we can't offer evidence to confirm, or can we?'

'Claude Liddie?'

'The man who sees all, knows all, keeps his mouth shut, and doesn't want to be evicted from a cushy job, wife or no wife.'

Clutching at straws, Natalie thought, but what option did they have. They had to act on the confession, regardless of the evidence or lack thereof. Alice had been with Greenworthy on the island, but Melinda's boarding pass was found there later; Alice admitted that she had put it there, and Liddie might have seen it in a bush or the silo. The man had tampered with evidence. Barton had confessed to a murder. Crystal Andersson had claimed that she had been raped, and Melinda Greenworthy had been guilty of subterfuge, not revealing that she had arrived in Australia earlier than she initially claimed. So far, there had been no crimes levelled at Frank Addison, other than the crime of bad taste by sleeping with his daughter's nemesis, Melinda, although after the death of her husband, apparently. A fact that needed clarification.

Haddock headed out to Cockatoo Island. Natalie made her way to Addison's office.

'Clive Morton,' Addison said. His office, dated and worn, had a lived-in feel to it. He had welcomed Natalie in, giving her a coffee from an espresso machine in the corner, noisy as it percolated and then heated the milk, the froth on top of the coffee. Natalie didn't think it tasted better than the ground coffee she purchased at the supermarket. This time, he did not smoke a cigar.

'That was my first question,' Natalie replied. 'Here is the hard one. Who or what is Melinda Greenworthy, and why are you having sex with her? She's a manipulator, having seen off two husbands, another murdered. Men and Melinda, oil and water. She will spit you out when she is finished with you or fuck you to death. Sorry about the vernacular, but polite doesn't seem to wash with you people.'

'What people?' Addison replied, mildly annoyed by the presumptuous sergeant, who was more attractive than Melinda but not as beautiful as his daughter. For him, Melinda was fun while he strung her along.

'You've heard of the golden goose?' Addison continued, careful not to be angry after provocation.

'I have.'

'A fairy tale, but not so with Greenworthy senior or junior. I was, still am, the holder of the golden key. Alan's father trusted me, and Alan, you know what he was like.'

'Never met him, unless as a corpse counts. He could not have been as bad as people made out, or was it an affectation on his part, the simple rich idiot?'

'Morose, deep thinker, hidden depths to the man. Rich he was, simple he was not, only he didn't apply himself to the business, no interest. His life took a different direction.'

'Why now, why open up on Alan now?'

'Twists and turns. That fool Barton has complicated the situation, and that silly woman Crystal has got herself pregnant and laid a claim against Alan's estate.'

'Which will be honoured?'

'If proven, a provision will be made, but why? Why accuse a man of rape and claim it's Alan's child?'

'Is it?'

'It might be. We'll need nine months, probably eight and a half, before it can be confirmed. That's how it goes, medically, isn't it?'

'It might be possible, but that would require Crystal's permission. I doubt if she would want to potentially harm the unborn child.'

'Who or what is she?' Addison said. 'I know what I am. I know what Melinda is. I know what my daughter is. We're all flawed, but the previous vestal virgin, Andersson, who is she? And what about Barton? I met him once, an insignificant little man. Rape? He couldn't blow the skin off a rice pudding.'

'We're not convinced of the rape. However, he has confessed to the murder. We don't believe that either. But more importantly, why ask for money from Melinda? Does he have leverage against her? And if he does, what was to be gained by her phoning me?'

'Maybe you should ask her?'

'I will, but you're in close, having sex with her. You're not a fool; you know how the world rotates. Her phoning me goes in her favour, but why?'

'Because I advised her to. It's a murder investigation, not corporate fraud, not skull and bones, undercover, foreign agencies. Melinda's smarter than we all reckon, and she thinks that wiggling her arse and giving comfort to a man old enough to be her father affords her a degree of protection.'

'Does it?'

'To some extent, but this might be more involved than any of us know, especially the police who look for evidence and the guilty when the first might not be there and the second might be smarter than any of us believe.'

'Are you saying it might be a third party who killed Alan?'

'Theorising. This emphasis on his attraction to women is hard to understand. His father had it, and so did I. We used it when we could. The reason my marriage to Alice's mother broke down. Unemotional and distant, Alan's mother didn't care as long as it didn't interfere with her socialising, her group of friends, or her credit card.'

Everyone had a secret, Natalie knew, but not everyone was guilty of murder and protecting their interests. Frank Addison wanted the money, Crystal Andersson wanted Alan, and Jeb wanted the woman he couldn't have, who had accused him of rape. Natalie could see him in love with an illusion, the pure and sweet Crystal, but her pregnancy and denouncing him convinced Natalie that the man confessed because he believed the woman had committed the murder.

Nothing made sense, plenty of motives forming, more than enough people to charge with the crime, but where was the evidence? Did it lie with a caretaker who drank more than he should and looked in tents?

***

Claude Liddie ducked and dived, but Haddock was relentless, not that it stopped the men downing three shots of whisky apiece.

'Can't help you if you won't help us,' Haddock said.

They sat on the back veranda of the small cottage, away from the prying eyes of the island visitors who made it up the gentle incline of the road or the steep metal stairs affixed to three sides of the elevated rise in the centre of the island.

'We've had a confession.'

'I heard about it,' Liddie replied. 'One of the band. More than a few years in prison for that.'

'Only we don't believe he did it, no proof.'

'Do you need proof? Easy conviction, a confession.'

'If he holds to the confession, a good defence lawyer might argue there is no crime without proof. But that will only occur if the man retracts his confession and asks for a lawyer to defend him.'

'Can he refuse a defending lawyer? It wouldn't make sense,' Liddie said.

'The judge might enforce it, but if Barton maintains that he acted alone, out of jealousy for Greenworthy, love for one of his women, then a conviction might be recorded. Claude, you're not telling us the full story; nobody is. You're skating on thin ice, and if I tell them about your perving of those staying overnight or for a weekend in the tents below, out on your ear.'

'I've been given three months as it is. They've employed a security company. Foolish if you ask me, but they aren't. There is no point pretending I'm happy about it, and if there hadn't been a murder, I might have got another year, possibly eighteen months. I can't see myself lasting long on the mainland.'

Haddock had heard the sob tale before; he was immune to the man's plight, of no interest to him. Life was what you made of it, his father used to say, although Haddock knew he hadn't made much of his: a broken marriage, a casual lay in Parramatta with Theresa de Klerk, a career that was at its pinnacle, the chance of substantive promotion beyond him, work till retirement, superannuation to maintain him into old age, hopefully with his wife by his side.

It was something he had not reflected on before. He was forty-eight but looked older, his expanding belly reflecting his lifestyle: too many snatched meals in pubs or fast-food outlets, although he hadn't smoked a cigarette for seventeen months. Ignominious obscurity, confined to an out-of-the-way station when his skills in solving murders diminished, and even now, police investigations were the domain of the computer savvy. He could manage an internet search and check through the databases and reports of previous crimes, but he was far from an expert, a one-finger typist, whereas his sergeant typed at forty words a minute.

'I was doing my job,' Liddie added. 'We've had assaults out here, drunken fights, even a rape. It took the police forever to get here, and then, where's the proof. The woman had been screaming blue murder, and then she retracts the claim, makes me look like a real idiot.'

'Claude, don't spin a tale. I've been around, seen things, done things. You are what you are or were. When your wife was here, maybe you didn't do it too often, or if you did, from what you've told us of her, she would have known when you were up to mischief. Drugged up, staggering around, the occasional woman, somewhere dark and lonely. You must have taken advantage. It's human nature, isn't it?'

Liddie downed his glass, poured himself another, and attempted to top up Haddock's, who moved the glass to one side. He had the man on the ropes, and he wasn't going to damage his line of enquiry by getting drunk, as Liddie was.

'I've seen things,' Liddie admitted.

'On the island?'

Haddock had his phone on record. It might not be admissible as evidence, what Liddie was about to say, but that was the least of the inspector's concerns. The mainland, which Liddie gave the impression as being over the horizon, was only three hundred metres away, less than the distance Haddock would have swum on a Saturday morning at Bondi Beach in his youth, but now he couldn't have managed fifty. A fitness regime, he thought, once this murder is solved.

If she had been privy to the man's thoughts, Natalie would have said, you won't. But he was on the island, in the company of Claude Liddie, another person at the pinnacle of their career but of retiring age. Haddock had another twelve years if he took compulsory retirement at sixty. Another few years, if he worked for a security company, although patrolling shopping centres and offices didn't appeal. Not much of a future, he thought, allowing himself to be lulled by the quietness of the island, understanding that Liddie, lonely nights without his wife, her presence in every part of the island, in every room of the cottage, could have gone half-mad with despair and melancholy.

'Before I married, I was in the navy, a submariner. That was how this job came about. Our boat was in for a refit on the island, and it was time for me to consider a position as a civilian. My time was up; I had no job to go to other than back to the land, three generations of growing cereal crops. I didn't want to be the fourth, although the offer was there: enough money to live well and more than enough work to break my back. I wanted to be near the water and saw the advert for a caretaker here. Newly married, I applied, showed a passion for the island, knew its history and the position was mine. We were happy here, visits to the mainland for supplies every weekend, treating ourselves to McDonald's, going to a movie, and then back here.'

'You're avoiding the things you saw,' Haddock said.

By now, Liddie was downing the whisky at an accelerated pace. Soon, he would be incapacitated. Was Liddie slowly going crazy on the island? Had the man's wife noticed? What had she done about it? How did she die? Her death certificate had said cancer. Haddock realised that Liddie would be deemed sane, even

144

if solitary and lonely, and with a fascination for couples making out.

'In the navy, foreign ports, girlie bars, that sort of thing,' Liddie said.

The man was stalling, and Haddock reckoned he had ten minutes before he passed out. Time was of the essence; the time was now.

'Cockatoo Island. Not overseas or on your summer holidays. It's this island I'm interested in.'

Liddie sat down and placed his drink on the table, almost spilling it as he did. He was swaying, close to the end. He spoke. 'I saw someone else spying on the dead man and the woman.'

'And you chose not to tell us this before?'

'I was threatened.'

'When? How? By whom? It's not going to be in your favour if you prevaricate.'

'I'll tell you what I saw, and it wasn't that dark, more than silhouettes. Alan Greenworthy and Alice. I'm sure of that, but not far away, another woman, Chinese.'

'We know who she is. Are you confirming that it was the man's wife?'

'It was her.'

'She spoke to you?'

'She said that it was her husband and one of his women. That she was involved in a fractious divorce, and she didn't want it complicated by anyone knowing of her presence.'

'Logical on her part, stupid on yours. Paid you to keep quiet?'

'She told me that it would weaken her position if it was known that she was there. She didn't kill him.'

'Certain?'

'One hundred per cent. I walked down to the ferry with her and saw her leave. He was alive when we left, dead when I returned.'

'You delayed reporting his death?'

'I was confused. The woman begged me to be discreet.'

'But it's murder, not a fine for speeding. Don't you understand the seriousness of what you've done?'

'Now, I do. Back then, I was confused. She was delightful; you would not understand.'

'How much? The woman has a history of old men. She didn't catch the ferry, so what's the truth. We know where she is, and she'll talk in time.'

'Three months, after all I did for them, out on my ear. I can't afford anywhere near the harbour, and she said she would help. Next day, there's a package for me, a post office on the mainland, inside twenty thousand dollars and a note.'

'What did it say, this note?'

'Thanks, nothing more.'

Haddock wondered what it was with Melinda Greenworthy that made her desirable to older men. What was it that allowed her to sleep with them?

'You were paid to keep quiet. Where was she when you reported the murder?'

'In one of the cottages on the island. I took her to the mainland later.'

'Sex and money, not a bad night's work. Proud of yourself?' Haddock said. 'Lied, hindered a murder enquiry. It's a criminal offence. I'm charging you.'

Although, Liddie hadn't heard what Haddock had just said. He was comatose, the effects of too much alcohol and the strain of the confession.

Haddock phoned Natalie, who informed Melinda Greenworthy. One hour later, a police car picked her up and took her to State Crime Command.

As for Liddie, Haddock left the man where he was, walked down to the ferry, and took it to Parramatta.

***

Dark clouds hovered over Parramatta, the threat of rain. Haddock could feel a coldness and closed the buttons on his suit jacket and hunched his shoulders. Liddie's confession was unexpected, but the officer's sixth sense had always convinced him that Liddie was holding back.

Melinda Greenworthy arrived at State Crime Command with Frank Addison, now confirmed as her lover. Although not guilty of any crime, the man had a sheepish look.

Liddie's confession showed that Melinda used sex as others used their skills, qualifications, and minds. The woman had proven herself to be a hussy, a slut, a whore, worse than Alice, who admitted what she was.

As the four sat in the interview room, a police launch arrived at Cockatoo Island. Two constables from Homicide made the trek up to the top of the island, locating the caretaker's cottage from a tourist map freely distributed at the ferry wharf. It showed all the points of interest: the silos where Greenworthy had died, the engineering workshops when the island had been a ship repair facility, and the cottage where Melinda Greenworthy had hidden.

They knocked on the door of Liddie's cottage three times before the more agile of the two constables scaled the wooden fence at the back of the cottage, slipping on the wet grass and landing on his rear end. The other constable, his head over the fence, laughed. The men's task was routine: bring in a man who would not resist, although he might moan at the indignity.

Time away from the office, rather than staring at a laptop screen, writing reports, following up leads, phoning persons, and gossiping in the corridor, appealed to the man now standing in the rear garden of the cottage, looking at the veranda where Inspector Haddock and Claude Liddie had sat.

'The inspector said the man was drunk,' the first constable, strapping, bulky, and who played rugby at the weekend, said.

The shorter of the two officers knocked on the back door, shouted a couple of times, and turned the handle. It wasn't locked. The cottage was deathly quiet.

In the kitchen, on the floor, lay the body of Claude Liddie.

Natalie looked down at her phone, on silent, vibrating in her handbag. *Claude Liddie dead*, the message said.

Nudging Haddock, who was ready to begin questioning, she called him outside, a constable entering the interview room in their stead.

'What is it?' Haddock asked.

Natalie showed him the message. It was an unexpected development. Haddock believed that the man's consumption of alcohol, coupled with his mental state due to his dismissal, the death of his wife, and probable health concerns, meant that the death would be medical.

Natalie, who had not had the benefit of a drinking session with Liddie, glad that her breath didn't stink as Haddock's did, wasn't so sure. Melinda Greenworthy brought trouble with her wherever she went, and paying twenty thousand pounds with a bonus was not the actions of a disgruntled wife intent on divorce. The marriage was over; the woman had said that on several occasions, and if her soon-to-be former husband wanted to fornicate with his intended on an island, what did it matter?

In Haddock's office, on speaker phone, he and Natalie spoke to the two constables at Liddie's cottage.

'Nothing suspicious,' they said.

'You've called Crime Scene?'

'Spoke to their head. We know the routine.'

Natalie remembered the older, more experienced officers who treated her as a rank amateur when she started as a junior constable. Even after she had graduated top of her class at the police training college. She thought the constables had done the right thing, but even she had to question them.

However, there was more for Liddie to reveal, but he was dead, not more than one hour after Haddock had left him in quiet repose.

In the interview room, Melinda and Frank Addison listened as Haddock outlined the situation and told them that due to the death of Claude Liddie, the interview would be rescheduled until later in the day.

'Tell us when, and we'll return,' Addison said.

'Unfortunately, given the testimony which Liddie would have given, and which I have a recording of, your client will remain in the station.'

'A formal charge?'

'Make yourselves comfortable either in a spare office or the cells. The choice is yours.'

'Always willing to help the police,' Melinda said. Natalie could see the look on her face as she said it. Who was this woman? Natalie thought. There were hidden depths not yet revealed. Had they been chasing down the wrong path? Was it love and marriage that had caused Alan Greenworthy to be murdered, or was it something else, something more sinister? Her suspicions would have to wait. The police launch that had dropped the two constables at Cockatoo Island was waiting for them at Parramatta Wharf. The body was still warm; time was of the essence.

Chapter 16

At Parramatta, Melinda sat calmly while Frank Addison stewed, worried that Melinda was trouble with a capital 'T'. They had slept together one week after Alan's death, and he appreciated her company and affection. He had not slept with a woman for three years before Melinda, not because they weren't available, but because he had grown used to the solitary life, finding solace in a book or a bottle of brandy. And now, a woman who brought out the passion in him and made him feel alive. But he worried whether a woman who could give so much love could also give death. Her history was not good. He had known that from Alan when the divorce had been mentioned.

Access to the top of the island was restricted to the police and authorised personnel, to the consternation of those day tripping, interested in early Australiana, wanting to see the prison cells and where the warders had lived.

'He staggered in here,' one of the CSIs said. A pleasant woman in her forties, of Indian heritage, second generation, both officers had confidence in her.

'He was drunk, very drunk,' Haddock said, hopeful that the man hadn't died as a result of the alcohol that he had consumed with him.

The CSI defused his concerns. 'It's murder,' she said.

Outside, in the garden at the rear, the three stood, having left the crime scene to two CSIs, a crime scene photographer, and one of the two constables, who aspired to promotion, and a murder was a valuable learning experience.

'Suffocation,' the CSI said.

'How?' Natalie asked.

'Exceedingly drunk, if the bottle of whisky is any indication. From behind, a cushion over the face. We have a cushion; it looks as though it might have been used. Forensics and Pathology will confirm.'

Haddock didn't mention that he had drunk at least a third of the bottle. There was no point in riling the beast, not at the island. He would leave that to Payne, who had been on the phone.

There was no need to stay longer. The two had seen the murder scene, and they walked down the road back to the ferry.

Natalie said it first, although Haddock had realised it as well. 'It can't have been Melinda Greenworthy or Frank Addison.'

What was it with the woman? Both knew that she was integral to solving the murder. Yet again, Natalie harboured a doubt but hadn't said it aloud. What if it wasn't emotional but something more sinister. Whatever it was, Melinda Greenworthy was the key.

***

There was to be no bonhomie as Haddock walked into Commander Payne's office.

Payne, formerly from a bush station, where a loud mouth and being bombastic was required, had initially brought that approach to Parramatta. Politically incorrect for the first year, inappropriate verballing of lacklustre performers, and transferring others out of the station on a week's notice, he had ridden roughshod over those who served under him.

Haddock had disliked the man intensely, but closer involvement during four murders in the Eastern Suburbs, and then dealing with the bullying Bernie Cornell, politicians, and judges, even his superiors, with Payne holding them back and supporting him and Natalie, had proven the man's mettle.

Payne was a man who blew hot and cold. Haddock was prepared.

'Inspector, what have you got to say for yourself? You were drinking with the man, and now he's dead. Have you considered the situation?'

'I have. Liddie was holding back; I could sense it. Embittered, three months to leave. He sees everything but says nothing, apart from dribs and drabs. Alcohol was the only way to get through to him. I made the only decision possible. I got drunk with him, and then he revealed more. Probably not all, but enough to haul in Melinda Greenworthy and give her the third degree. She's one tough cookie.'

'Not fortune, I hope. It's not a time for a Chinese joke. Take a seat, give it to me straight. You could be up on a disciplinary for this, and I can't protect you if I'm kept in the dark.'

Haddock knew the rollocking was over, and the man would protect him, whatever the cost. For fifteen minutes, Haddock went over the case, those they were suspicious of, those who had a motive, even if obscure, the pregnant woman, the prostitute, her father, and especially the dead man's wife.

'Do you think she murdered Greenworthy?' Payne asked.

Haddock sucked on a mint; Natalie had bought the strongest she could find for him. Payne drank tea. Two men, equal not in rank but in experience, discussing the case, looking for another angle. Open and frank, the way Haddock liked it. He had never gone for the 'Yes, sir, three bags full, sir' routine.

Forty minutes later, Haddock left Payne's office, the man slapping him on the back and shaking his hand. 'God only knows what you and your sergeant have put me through,' Payne said.

Outside Homicide, Natalie asked how it had gone.

'Better than expected,' Haddock replied. 'Are they ready?'

'As quiet as lambs, but beware of the wolf in sheep's clothing.'

'Melinda?'

'Precisely. We can't trust one word she says, only one certainty we can be sure about.'

'She couldn't have killed Liddie, nor could Addison. Cast-iron alibis, the best there is, at State Crime Command or in the backseat of a police car.'

'Which suggests another person, and how did that person know that Liddie was spilling the beans?'

'Not from me. The two constables, out at the island?'

'Still there. I've asked them to get hold of any surveillance camera footage, and I've been on to Sydney Ferries for footage from one hour before you arrived on the island and one hour after Liddie's death. Needle in a haystack, more video than any ten CCTV officers can hope to view, and even if they could, who are they looking for? It must be a third party, someone we don't know.'

Natalie could see Melinda seething, yet the woman continued to smile, reaffirming that she was there to help the police. Addison, in his sixties, had slept while they waited. There was enough to hold Melinda for twenty-four hours, forty-eight if required, while investigations continued. But Haddock knew they would need more than forty-eight, and what investigations? The woman did not kill Liddie, but could she have been behind the killing? Would she admit to it? Not for one moment.

'You paid Claude Liddie twenty thousand dollars,' Haddock said.

'Did I? Not to my recollection, and why? I've had Crystal Andersson making a claim due to a child that Alan's supposedly fathered. She got short shrift; why would I give it to a minor functionary, a caretaker on the island. What is he?'

'The person who saw you there.'

'Proof?' Addison asked.

That was the problem; there was none. It would be impossible to prove, and the judge and jury would need to accept Barton's confession in a trial. The man was at Long Bay prison, isolated from the general population: murderers, rapists, perverts and petty criminals. Haddock had checked, ensuring that the ineffectual man, the supposed rapist of Crystal and confessed murderer of Alan, would not become a playmate for one of the inmates.

'You paid Liddie money to keep quiet that you were at the island and that he had seen you. He also told us where you hid and had sex with him. Come easy to you? Selling your body?'

'A sad old man, why would I do that?'

'We've checked the room, taking samples from it, hair, stains on the bedding. You, along with others, gave us a sample of your DNA. There will be enough proof if you were in the room.'

Natalie didn't know that had occurred and hoped Haddock wasn't eliciting a confession from the woman by devious means. In a trial, evidence would need to be produced, and if it wasn't, it weakened the prosecution's case. Using a ruse to obtain a confession was fraught with the possibility of being classified as inadmissible.

'I deny it,' Melinda said.

'Where's the proof?' Addison said. The man's skin was pallid, and his breathing was irregular. Natalie feared for him, and now he had the added responsibility of defending a woman guilty of a crime, even if not of murder, and sleeping with her. Natalie was sure Alan's marriage had been a sham. And that Melinda Greenworthy did not give herself to men for sexual satisfaction but used it as a manipulative tool. And who is the more easily deceived? An ageing male with waning libido, a fresh flush of testosterone with a pretty and younger woman.

Natalie imagined the woman's skills were commensurate with those of Alice.

'Nobody mentioned he was sad,' Natalie said. 'And how do you know he was old?'

'He must be making up stories about me. I'm the wronged person here, a dead husband. We might have reconciled.'

Haddock could see that she had been prompted by Addison. Play the victim, deflect away from you. Push the onus of blame onto the police, and whatever you do, be very careful in what you say. Haddock imagined the conversation between Melinda and Addison might have been over the pillow.

'We know you didn't kill Liddie,' Natalie said. 'However, it doesn't exclude someone else. Inspector Haddock might have seen someone spying on him at the island.'

It was what she said, but it wasn't what she believed. The inspector had been drunk, his faculties compromised. A rollocking from Payne was one thing, but what if the murderer had been listening in, and it was subsequently revealed in a trial that a serving officer had created a situation which had led to the man's murder. Natalie didn't want to think about it, too preposterous to be true, but …'

She picked up a phone and sent a message: Focus on Cockatoo Island. I've given you the name of a contact. Jimmy Rogers, a scruffy individual, knows his stuff.

A would-be paramour, a man who had made his intentions towards Natalie known, only to be rejected, humbly accepting the umpire's verdict, was still the best man for the job. If someone was prowling around the island, he would be the person to find him or her. Natalie knew the focus on the murderer being a male was based on statistics, but both murders could have been committed by a woman.

The fence-straddling constable replied to her message. Will do, he said. Natalie was confident the man would and would do it well.

The interview wasn't going well. The woman was guilty of more than one crime, but which ones? Where was the unassailable proof? There was no point in arresting her for a misdemeanour or withholding evidence.

'The money has been found,' Haddock said. This time, he had spoken the truth. Another CSI at the cottage had found a hidden hole in the wall behind a wardrobe in the second bedroom. The wardrobe had been pulled to one side, revealing, apart from spiders and dead cockroaches, two cloth bags. Inside one, the twenty thousand dollars, in another, one hundred and thirty-three thousand dollars. The twenty was from Melinda. The police had no access to her bank accounts, and she was unlikely to hand them over, or had someone given her the money?

'What about the Chinese man you spoke to at your house when I was there?' Natalie said.

'A friend, no crime in that.' Sarcasm. Melinda Greenworthy was starting to feel comfortable. She had come to the station without complaint; she might leave with one in mind, a letter from Addison, cease and desist unless there is provable evidence.

'Mr Addison,' Haddock said to the lawyer. 'Your daughter whores. Does that worry you?'

'What do you expect me to say? I'm happy about it. I wasn't there as she was growing up, did my best, which wasn't good enough under the circumstances. Fatherhood is fraught with difficulties; any father would tell you that.'

Haddock didn't need telling, he knew. 'And now, you are involved with a woman whose past is dubious. Do you know all of it? Has your client used sex for financial gain or for leverage.'

Natalie realised that Haddock was raising the tempo, getting Melinda Greenworthy to lose her composure and react.

Instead, the woman looked over at Haddock, placing a hand on Addison not to speak. 'Inspector Haddock, you might think you're a cut above the rest, but in Cambodia, it's not words that the police use, but violence and intimidation.'

'You've experienced this?'

'Alan has.'

'Not now, Melinda,' Addison said.

'It is now. I didn't kill Alan; I didn't kill an old man who watched Alan and Alice screwing.'

'Then who did?'

'Alice possibly, but she had nothing to gain. Crystal Andersson, out of jealousy, if she knew he was going to marry another. Mistiming on her part if she's carrying his child.'

'Could she be?'

'No reason to doubt her. No doubt Frank will make an accommodation for the child, ensure it is brought up well, and given a decent education, but that implies no guarantees. Alice is a testament to that. She might have believed in the happy family dream, but that was impossible with Alan, broken in body and soul. He would not be there for her, and she embraces men too readily. Gets paid for it, but with her, the sex is not mercenary but vital.'

'The same with her mother,' Addison said. 'I wasn't a retiring soul, took advantage if offered, but her mother, my wife, couldn't resist men. Caught her with Alan's father once.'

'Like mother, like daughter,' Natalie said.

'This is not about them. This is about Alan,' Melinda said. 'A dark chapter in his life, in mine.'

'Cambodia?' Haddock ventured, something he had suspected but could not confirm. He thought nobody could be as twisted as Alan Greenworthy by dint of their birth and upbringing. Severe psychological changes had occurred. And now it looked as if the person who could reveal the story was willing to talk. But was that as a defence for her part in the death, or was she innocent?

'Why now?' Natalie asked, her thought process in unison with her inspector. It had been sergeant and inspector for too long, but now Commander Payne was adamant. 'Held off too long, need to promote you,' he had said to her the last time they had met. 'Inspector, Homicide, best I can do.'

'Inspector Haddock?' Natalie said.

'Work as a team. Haddock has seniority, but the two of you are thick as thieves. Are you sure you are not—'

'Commander, wash your mouth,' Natalie had answered back. This was the first sign of overt familiarity he had shown since she had transferred to Parramatta. Did it mean that the promotion was conditional? If it was, she didn't want it.

She had wondered what had allowed Theresa de Klerk to resume her position in the station, given that she had used her computing skills to hack into other people's computers in the building. Was she…?'

Perish the thought. Theresa was in her forties and putting on weight. Victoria Adderley was in her thirties, and she had confided that Payne's marriage was on the rocks, and she was going to move in with the superintendent, a cosy love nest in Parramatta. Natalie had advised against it, aware of the implications, dragged into a battle royale between husband and wife, and that no good would come of it. However, it was pointless. The woman was determined.

Before they had met regularly and spoken about work and play, why Natalie couldn't find a boyfriend, and how Victoria had more than her fair share. Highly competent as a lawyer, Victoria was foolish with love. It was a one-way street to oblivion, and when the relationship with Payne soured, inevitable given the age difference and complicated by his children, what then? The two couldn't remain in the building, unable to avoid each other, the butt of jokes. Regardless, Victoria was determined.

'Needed to know, just in case,' Payne had said. 'My apologies if I offended.'

'No offence taken.'

Chapter 17

In the interview room, Melinda fiddled with her skirt and took lipstick from her handbag, which she then applied.

After what seemed an eternity. 'Psychological scars.'

'And?' Natalie felt the need to comment. 'Does your lawyer know?'

'He does, now.'

'An inkling before, but no details. Melinda told me more in the last few days, but it's not the full story, and it's unlikely she will reveal it all today. What Alan did is worthy of commendation,' Addison said.

Haddock tapped a pen on the table, Natalie remained silent, and Addison looked at his client, who stared up at the ceiling. No one spoke. It was Melinda who broke the ice.

'I didn't know Alan as a child, although I've read his profile. Frank can contradict me if I'm in error. Alan had issues, even as a child. Solitary, bullied at school, academically gifted, but never had the chance to show it. He was ideal.'

Addison said nothing.

Melinda continued. 'He was in Cambodia, seeing the sights, visiting the bars, no different to others. Into drugs as a teenager, heavier drugs in Cambodia.'

'Hardly commendable.' Haddock had to make a comment.

'You've heard of the Golden Triangle?'

'We have,' Natalie replied for her and her inspector. 'Opium.'

'Processed into heroin, buy it for a fraction in Phnom Penh.'

'Which Alan did.'

'He was in the country for over two years, initially as a tourist, then an addict, and finally, a drug mule.'

'Using his Australian passport, a false lining in his suitcase, condoms full of heroin up the rectum. Criminal, long time in prison if caught.'

'He never was. Not that the authorities were dumb, but because they had turned a blind eye, and nothing as crass as strapping them to his body or hiding them in a suitcase, not even concealed in a jar of coffee. Alan was smarter than that.'

'Still criminal. Where do you come into this?'

'I did what I do best. I seduced him.'

'Paid to whore?' Haddock said.

The woman was procrastinating. If there was something to say, then damn well say it. No shillyshallying, no attempting to explain your guilt. How many times in a trial had he heard the lame excuses: a sick child, family to support, an abused childhood – he might consider that valid if the child was female, connotations of sexual abuse. And now, Melinda Greenworthy was attempting to explain why she had been a prostitute, gyrating on a pole in a seedy bar, turning tricks around the back.

'Sergeant, you asked about the Chinese man on the phone. I'm now at liberty to tell you who he is. His name is Inspector Chong, and he works for the Narcotics Bureau of Hong Kong.'

'We contacted the Hong Kong police and requested information. Who were you? What were you? That's how we learnt about your two husbands, who had both died under explainable circumstances. Was that a fabrication?'

'In essence, it was; in detail, it wasn't. I was an addict in Hong Kong, selling myself to pay for the addiction. Inspector Chong is a family friend who brought me back from the brink. Addiction is not something we choose, and why someone would start taking drugs defies logic. But we are not logical, but of flesh and bone, vulnerable, susceptible, stupid.'

'A man?' Natalie asked.

'Young and foolish, in love. It was he who introduced me to heroin. It was Inspector Chong who saved me. I owe the man my life.'

'After your salvation? We need confirmation that what you are telling us is true.'

Frank Addison pushed an envelope across the table. 'You will find all that you want inside,' he said.

'Seduction has become an art form,' Natalie said. 'Your lawyer, easy pickings, or keeping your hand in?'

'Neither. For five years, I was addicted, sleeping where I could. My condition deteriorated. I was underweight and looked older than my years; another few years and I would have been dead. Inspector Chong grabbed me off the street, put me in a clinic, paid all the bills, and asked me to work with him.'

'Why? A family friend, why would he have done that?'

'He didn't pay, nor did my parents. I was ideal for what the Narcotics Bureau required. Someone who knew the terrain, those selling the drugs, and those importing.'

'A spaced-out junkie?'

'Spaced out, junkie, the epithets fit. Also intelligent. I knew what I was, unable to break the vicious cycle, but I observed. I saw things that the Narcotics Bureau didn't. I had been down by the docks, saw shipments coming in, saw people and remembered them. Inspector Chong asked me to look at photos they had on their database. I recognised three, knew where I had seen them, what they had done. None of them realised that a street whore could be anything other than a slag, good for a blow job or a screw or a fist in the chest.'

'That occurred?' Natalie asked.

'It did and more. I was impervious, able to take the humiliation and the degradation. Alice doesn't have an addictive personality. I do. She has succeeded in her chosen profession; I have in mine.'

'Cleaned up, you whored for the police?' Haddock asked.

'I wasn't police, not officially. Undercover, Inspector Chong looking out for me. I went back to work, starved myself to look like I was at the end of the line.'

'And you were willing to do this?'

'I had seen what went on, what happened to the addicted, the abuse meted out. Think of it as my civic duty, giving back to society, to Inspector Chong.'

'And your parents,' Haddock said, thinking of his daughter, confident that her life would not unfold as Melinda Greenworthy's had.

'As you say. After eight months, two of the three largest drug importation gangs were effectively closed down. The third had political connections in Beijing and was untouchable. But I had become visible, and certain people were suspicious. One day, I'm on the street; the next, I'm chained to the wall in a dingy basement, having the life beaten out of me. Half-dead. The inspector, on a tip-off, found out where I was and rescued me. End of my time whoring on the streets in Hong Kong.'

'You don't appear to carry scars,' Natalie said.

'I do, on my body. Mentally, I am strong; physically, I am resilient. I recuperated, put on weight, and changed my appearance. No one would have recognised the worthless hag on the street, the hag they had raped and beaten with a chain in that basement.'

'Cambodia?'

'The husbands first,' Melinda said.

'It's your story.'

'Hong Kong national, independently wealthy. Not the full story. I couldn't go back to the street, nor did I want to. His wealth came from financing the drug importation for the third gang. Unofficially, the Narcotics Bureau had been told to back off, but Inspector Chong wouldn't buy into that. The man, scrupulously honest, knew that if he couldn't take on the gang, there was no harm in a little fishing around. He asked me if I was interested; I was. Drugs are addictive, so is undercover work, getting people to do what they don't want, to listen in to conversations and feed it back to the police, to see the man brought down.'

162

'Is being raped and beaten with a chain addictive?' Natalie asked. 'You had been lucky the first time; it wasn't likely to happen the next.'

'My training was vigorous, and I learnt to block the pain receptors. I knew the risk. I accepted it.'

Either Melinda Greenworthy was a brave woman or a liar. Natalie knew that the truth could be concealed, and if she had worked with the Narcotics Bureau in Hong Kong, then it was probable that she was not guilty of murder. For now, the woman would talk. The truth, whatever it was, was somewhere in what she was telling. Disseminating it from the verbiage would be a task for later.

'His death?' Haddock asked.

'An altercation, what I had told you before. There was no attempt to arrest the guilty man, unprovable anyway, and the border with the mainland was nearby. My function was to gain my husband's confidence, not to trap his killer.'

'By fucking him,' Haddock said, unable to resist the need to bait the woman.

'Fuck, screw, and whatever other names you want to use, Inspector. I wasn't the virgin bride; sexual intercourse was not an issue. My job was important. Importation was reduced by sixty per cent, indicating that someone knew something and was reporting it to someone unknown. I was the conduit; it was only a matter of time before I would be identified. And believe me, being raped and beaten didn't appeal.

'My husband could be argumentative, especially after a few drinks. Inspector Chong organised it, I don't know how, but there was a fight, and my husband was dead.'

'Did you love him?' Natalie asked.

'He was kind to me, but no. After his death, the drugs flowed again, with no hindrance from the Narcotics Bureau. The gang accepted that he had been the informant, creaming drugs and money off the top. I acted as the man's widow for almost a year, sobbed when needed, said little, and rarely socialised. I had his money, a condition of my marrying him. I might have been doing my bit for Inspector Chong, but no harm in taking money for myself, legally mine, considering that I had married him.'

'The next husband?'

'Academic, honest, and decent. There were no vices with him other than he committed to academia more than to me.'

'Why marry?'

'The same reason as the first. The university professor had a brother, not known by many, not spoken about by him. One was in Hong Kong, the other in Shanghai. They were close, a shared childhood. They had known poverty. One had embraced academia; the other had involved himself in casinos in Macau, women in mainland China, and drugs in Asia. Regardless, my second husband, when he had realised that my affection was real, confided that he loved his brother, regardless. He fed occasional information out of his trust and love for me, unaware that Inspector Chong and others were forming a profile, taking what I gave and filling in the blanks. Thirty-two women were saved from sex trafficking to Europe, and a casino in Macau was shut down.'

'Drugs into Hong Kong?'

'I never got that far. I'm not sure if my husband knew the details. His death was due to overwork and stress. He had not been slated for liquidation, no reason as he was not criminal, only by association.'

'Your body is a commodity,' Natalie said.

'Used for good, but yes, it is. Don't expect me to be coy about this, and the only reason the situation has changed is that there is intelligence that Alan's card had been marked. After training in Hong Kong, he returned to Cambodia with a different name, blonde instead of brown, sporting a beard, minor facial surgery, enough to fool the most observant.'

'I always wondered,' Addison said. 'He was a different person when he returned. I didn't recognise the change in his appearance, but a tattoo on his shoulder was gone, a mole on his face, and he was thinner than before.'

'Did he say anything to you about what Melinda's telling us?' Natalie asked.

'Not a word, although that wouldn't have been unusual. Self-contained, never spoke about himself, barely acknowledged you most times. Internal, his inner self. His father took him to a couple of psychiatrists when he was younger, who told him that the son would grow out of it, and he did as a teen. Not that most would notice, still blood out of a stone most times. And then, in his early twenties, he went overseas, backpacking to see the world, his father's money. He communicated every few months, said he was fine and had made a few friends, but that was for his mother's benefit. He probably hadn't, and then ten years after he left, he walked into the house, up to his bedroom, and put on music. Didn't come out for three days, a tray outside the door at mealtimes.

'Upset his parents?'

'His mother died while he was away, brain aneurysm. His father tried to contact Alan, but where? The funeral was a week later, and then Alan walked in, managed to say sorry about Mum, and that was it. Six months after the prodigal son returns, the father has a fatal heart attack.'

'And you're in control.'

'Effective control. Alan wasn't about to get involved, and he would stay in his room for weeks at a time, venturing as far as the kitchen when no one was around. I employed a housekeeper and a cook, kept the place clean, prepared food and put it into the fridge, reheated in a microwave. Why he had worsened, I didn't know, nobody did. Not until the last couple of days. And now, two police officers will know.'

Slowly, Melinda spoke of her time in Cambodia, of Alan's. Haddock became quieter as the story was told; Natalie felt tears in her eyes.

'Hong Kong wasn't safe for me, not that there had been threats. But it's a small place, geographically, and it was decided that I should get out of the country. Cambodia was chosen.'

'Why?'

'A drug lord who went by the name of Heng. Not his full name, but that was how everyone referred to him: politician, entrepreneur, businessman, trade anything from rare artefacts, ivory, herbal medicine, drugs.'

'And women?'

'Not trafficking. For some reason, the man treated women well, not that it didn't stop him from owning a dozen girlie bars, blow jobs on demand, and ping-pong balls on the stage. I don't have to draw you a picture, do I?'

Natalie looked over at Haddock and saw him look away. He knew, but she had to think about the ping-pong balls and realised it didn't involve two bats and a net.

'We were working with the Cambodian authorities, which I was wary of. Inspector Chong told me not to worry, do my job, and he'd get me out at the first sign of trouble, ensure I had a bolthole somewhere in the world, plastic surgery, and a cover story.'

'You trusted him?'

'With my life, literally. Besides, I had known him since I was young, and he never let me down, only misjudged his contacts in Cambodia.'

'And we contacted them,' Natalie said.

'As expected. I worked in a high-class brothel frequented by Heng. By April, I was installed as one of his women in a mansion on the city's outskirts.'

'An Arab sultan?'

'As opulent and decadent. All we did all day was loll around, dressed to the hilt, looking our most seductive, hoping we would be honoured by him screwing us.'

'Picked often?' Haddock asked.

'More than the others, but that was why I was there.'

'Undercover, dangerous if he found out.'

'Deadly, but he was a strange man. I was there for three months and then back in Phnom Penh with an apartment, a car, and money. No further demands from him.'

'Alan?'

'I met Alan in a bar, not a girlie bar, but an upmarket, classy joint. We start talking. He's showing the signs of addiction but is still coherent. We start to date. Sex was for a purpose; to use it for pleasure would take me time. He tells me about his family, addiction, and aimlessness. A lost soul. I suppose that's the allure. I told him about my life, omitting large chunks of it for obvious reasons. We move in together, and he weans himself off heroin. He had the occasional relapse, but he did well.

'Inspector Chong contacted me, wanting to know who he is and where he had learnt to speak Khmer, the local language, and Thai. It was remarkable. He had great language skills, learnt them easily.'

'He spoke French and German,' Addison said.

Melinda continued. 'The inspector had a job for him, something neither a Cambodian national nor Chinese ethnic could do. Culturally, the white man garners respect, and as he spoke the language, it would be easy for him, three weeks in and then out. Alan was interested and thought it would be fun, but he didn't understand the implications of what was being asked. Naïve. Cambodia is not Australia; the Golden Triangle is not Cambodia. It's an area of disparate people, good and bad, slit your throat without compunction. Anyway, he agrees, spends three months out of the way in Hong Kong, and learns Cantonese, close to fluent. Crash courses in the martial arts, drug trafficking, the major players, and what was required of him.'

'Which was?' Haddock asked. For a woman who had said little before, she was now saying plenty. But this was a woman skilled in deception and lies. If it was true, it was impressive. If it was false, it was great fiction worthy of a novel.

'Opium production is centred in Northern Thailand, some of Burma, an area in Laos, and a small area in China. Growing the poppies wasn't hard, but processing and transportation were. Token efforts in Burma, rigorous in Thailand, nominal in Laos, and who knows in China, had effectively curtailed exports. The Narcotics Bureau wanted someone neutral, unknown by all the players, to deal with the impasse, get the heroin to Cambodia, and for Heng and his cronies to make a financial killing.'

'Why Alan? Why not let the trade stop?' Natalie asked.

'The stoppages weren't solid. Bribery, corruption, and violence would open them again, but a major expansion needed a new route out, which meant parts of Thailand, but by missing the main population centres, there was a new set of individuals to bribe. Alan was the obvious choice, unknown, and you know the man, able to keep calm under duress, not to say something foolish, to watch, listen and learn. And once the new routes were established, send in undercover operatives, not mild-mannered like Alan, and slam the place shut, kill people, destroy crops, wholesale vanquishing of the perpetrators.'

'Heng?'

'Kill Heng, and everyone goes to ground.'

'Okay, we'll accept that you are innocent of the murder, although that might be premature. If half of your statement is true, violence goes both ways. You might have suffered and acted courageously, but is this relevant? Alan's in Australia, you're in Australia, subject to Australian law, not the law of the jungle, no need to sleep with men to get what you want. No need to risk your life or to commit murder.'

'True. My involvement with Frank is personal, not professional. We are working together, sleeping together, nothing more, no infatuation from either side, only practicality.'

'Agreed?' Haddock asked Addison.

'It is. I believe Melinda. She hasn't finished the story. The ending's a doozy and, frankly, disturbing.'

Natalie made a phone call. Five minutes later, four coffees and a large plate of savouries. 'As long as we're settling in for the long run,' she said.

Natalie continued. 'Alan travels north from Cambodia. He's got a history of drug importation into the UK and Australia. Fake, of course, but solid, and no one looks that closely in Asia. Violent and painful death is a deterrent, inhibiting the foolhardy and the chancers from getting involved. He makes contact, spends a couple of months getting to know the lie of the land, who's who, who's putting on a show, but is a minor player, and realises that the Mr Bigs don't show themselves. He's got a route planned and people willing to give it a go, but they need to know if he's above board or another foolish Westerner who thinks he's a cut above the rabble in Asia, another colonist. They subject him to psychological and physical torment.'

'Torture?' Natalie said.

'More than that, five weeks, no sleep, electrical, beatings, worse than I endured. But he doesn't crack, and then, after two weeks of recuperation, the best food, clean sheets, and a couple of Thai girls. Bad manners to refuse.

'The route is tested, and Heng starts receiving drugs into Cambodia. Enough bribes and the problems vanish. The man's pleased, but he's a politician, determined to stamp out the trade but making a profit from it.

'Alan's back with me, a man I can love. He's one of us, undercover and loving it, extrovert, full of himself.'

'And then?'

'We marry, no ceremony, discreetly. The American government is holding Cambodia to ransom. No more aid money unless the drug barons are out of business. It's a ruse; there's no way foreign aid will dry up, not with China looking to strengthen its hold on the country.

'Heng takes flight and disappears into the Triangle, a compound with heavy security, but he's not the respected man he once was. He researches, finds anomalies, and finds out we have been working against him.'

'We're marked persons. Inspector Chong plans to get us out of the country, change our appearance, and issue us new documentation and history.'

'It doesn't end there, does it?' Natalie said.

'No more with me, but Alan's caught, coming home at night from a club we were members of. Inspector Chong got him out, contacts he had in Cambodia. He's in a bad way, but he recovers. Much later, I'm back in Hong Kong, and he's in Australia. But Alan doesn't want to live that way anymore. He becomes the Alan Greenworthy everyone knew, moves into the old house, and joins a band.'

'And?' Natalie said.

'You don't get it,' Addison said. 'It's not over yet.'

'Explain.'

'And now, Alice lives in a penthouse owned by a man who is still involved. Clive Morton. Coincidence or the long arm of Heng or something else. Could it be what Alan did in Cambodia was the reason for his death? Was it a revenge killing for the damage he wrought?'

'It could be,' Haddock said.

'We suspected something was afoot. Heng is back from his retreat, making a big noise in Phnom Penh, claiming it for himself, striking a significant blow against the drug traffickers. If he can't make money from drugs, he can use it to gain political influence. The man's a leech who would suck the blood from a dying man. I fear that Alan might have died as a result.'

Chapter 18

Tackling Clive Morton required forethought. This was not an ordinary citizen, but old money, connections in the right places, membership of the right clubs, and plenty who would gravitate to his support if threatened. Natalie and Haddock had known the name for a week before Melinda mentioned it, and Natalie had passed the man in the foyer of the apartment block once.

Alice Minchin confirmed that Morton was her benefactor. To Haddock, it clarified why the man paying for her to be in the penthouse did not enforce exclusivity.

If Melinda Greenworthy's extensive explanation of what had happened in Cambodia was true, it was surprising that she was still alive.

Melinda's revelation, either a pack of lies or true, had caused a distraction from Alan Greenworthy's murder and now Claude Liddie's. The question was why Liddie, a minor player in the saga, had cried poor, even though there was sufficient money to live comfortably for several years – if the money was his. And now Melinda was claiming privileged treatment because she had been an undercover operative of the Narcotics Bureau, and Alan had been integral to curtailing drug activity out of the Golden Triangle.

Could his death be unrelated to the three women who had vied for his attention and due to his involvement with drug traffickers and villains of the worst kind? And what about the Narcotics Bureau? Corruption was not unknown in Asia, endemic in Cambodia. Could his death have been sanctioned? Too many variables, too many red herrings.

Victoria Adderley, State Crime Command lawyer, a friend of Natalie's, although not as strongly as before, given that she was moving in with Commander Payne, his marriage consigned to the rubbish bin. Even so, Natalie had to grant Victoria some slack; after all, the woman was invaluable to Homicide, and in previous cases, she'd been willing to go the extra mile and stand up in front of a Supreme Court judge and a former prime minister and present them with documents and subpoenas.

The three met in Haddock's office, not that he used it very often.

'Bush telegraph, is it true?' Haddock asked. Natalie had wised him up to the relationship between the commander and the lawyer. She felt that factual was better than innuendo.

'Not the only one,' Victoria responded, testy that another person had asked. 'Early days.'

'Be careful,' Natalie said. 'You're heading down a road with no end. Careers have been dashed due to inappropriate relationships.'

'You told him?'

'I told him the truth two days ago, not the gossip. We're on your side, regardless.'

Unease in the office, a woman embarrassed, another annoyed with her friend, an inspector who didn't want to know about another office romance.

'Clive Morton,' Haddock said. 'What do we know about him?'

'Real estate developer, born in London, came to Australia as a child. Middle-class upbringing in Newtown. No trouble with the police, apparently pays his taxes, or, at least, submits a return. Fifty-eight years of age, twice married, currently divorced, and has owned the penthouse for five years. No information if he had other women installed up there.'

'Could she have been there for special clients, persons he wanted entertaining?'

'I'm a lawyer,' Victoria said. 'I'm giving you the facts, easily obtained. The man doesn't give to charity or lend his name to good causes. Season ticket to the Opera House, goes overseas every few months, mainly to Europe, occasionally to the USA.'

'Cambodia?' Natalie asked.

'Immigration has records of Australian citizens leaving and entering Australia. What he does overseas and where he goes is unknown. You suspect him of involvement?'

'We might have been fed a pack of lies, and Morton might not be involved. Unsure who to believe, and approaching Morton without evidence is our word against his. Melinda Greenworthy's thrown us a wide ball and deflected us from the primary motives.'

'Which were?'

'A convoluted love triangle, only more than three involved, could be four or five. When she first arrived in Australia, Melinda stayed with Alice and might have met Morton. Who knows, she might have had sex with him, and if she had, he might have known who she was, and then she spins this story that Alan Greenworthy is the great hero, righting wrongs and suffering as a result. Unproven and will remain so. Even if it's true, where's the proof? Deflects from the homegrown potential murderers, bringing Morton into the equation. I've checked him; if not honest, as close as possible.'

'"If not honest". What does that mean?'

'The man lives a better life than his tax returns would suggest, but he's in property development, so there are plenty of legit write-offs. Nothing criminal, only pushing the envelope, and then he's got Alice up in the penthouse. What for? A woman on tap, but she's spreading the joy around.'

Natalie had to agree with Victoria on specific points, but she had raised something that had concerned her for a while. Was Morton having sex with Alice? Or was it something else?

Alice remained in the penthouse, Melinda continued with house renovations, and Addison busied himself with transferring the title to Melinda, spending time with her more often than he wanted. If he had been honest, he would have said that the woman was wearing him out, the reason he unexpectedly visited his daughter.

It was the first time he had visited her at the penthouse. Apart from the trade that she plied, he had to admit she couldn't have lived in a better place: a view of the harbour and the bridge, the ferries plying up and down, the charter cruises taking their passengers out on the harbour to drink, eat and whatever else they fancied. He knew that a few were floating brothels, not that he held an opinion of them, only that his daughter before she had found Morton, might have been one of those prancing naked around a boat.

He wanted to think well of his daughter and find the love a father should have for a child, but he could not. There was an ambivalence, a neutrality. Unable to love, unable to hate, a nagging feeling that one woman deserved more from him and another was using him for her own purpose. He had been told the story of Alan before meeting with the police, Melinda's second telling more vivid than the first. He wondered about the veracity of it, although certain aspects had the marks of truth.

Hadn't he seen the young and lonely Alan in the back garden of his house pushing himself physically, sweat pouring off him, as he climbed a tree, up and down, up and down, not caring that, at the top, one slip and he would land on the concrete below, possibly breaking a limb? The activity was obsessive; the fear was either not there or controlled. Another time, Alan's mother was frantic; her son was not home, and it was after ten in the evening. She was not a controlling or affectionate woman, but fear was apparent.

Addison had been in the house, a late-night meeting with Alan's father. He had witnessed the father's disinterest, the mother's worry, the argument that had ensued when the father had told the mother to stop worrying, to go to bed, as he was busy, and Frank wasn't there to listen to her moaning. The slap on his face, the mother storming out of the room.

'He's a strange one, is Alan,' the father had said, one side of his face still red from the flat hand of his wife striking hard.

Hadn't Addison said that maybe she had a point, only for the father to remind him that Alan wasn't like other children. 'Climbing rocks somewhere, pushing the body, overcoming adversity, fearless,' he had said.

'Could get himself killed,' Addison had retorted.

'He could, but he won't. The boy knows his limit, pushes beyond it, and backs off when it's impossible. Psychologically, he is a basket case but brave. His mother worries, but it's not motherly love, but guilt.'

'Guilt about what?'

'When he was young, she dropped him, landed on his head, touch and go at the hospital for several hours. In the end, they said there was no lasting brain damage, but you don't know, do you?'

Addison didn't know what made him remember the father's throwaway line. Other than sitting with Alice in the supposed love nest, it made him remember his disinterest when Alice, in her teens, stayed out late. Her parents had stayed cordial over the years, more for their child than any other reason. Her mother was concerned that she was sleeping around, using her body as a commodity, expecting her school assignments to be done by others, and then, at university, he had known that she had perfected the act.

Maybe Alice wouldn't have sold herself if he had been a better father. If Alan's mother had been more caring, their son might still be alive.

'What is it?' Alice asked. The two had been in the penthouse for over thirty minutes with barely any conversation.

'Melinda has a theory that Alan's death might have nothing to do with any of us. She was here with you. Why?'

'I wanted her husband; she wanted his money.'

'But it would be me who would resolve any impasse,' Addison said.

'Neither of us trusted you. How could we? What with Alan's condition and your control.'

'I never abused it, you know that. You would have wanted more visibility than Alan, and now Melinda will want to dive in deep and conduct an independent audit.'

'Has it been suggested?'

'Not yet, but it will be.'

'And you having sex with her, a ploy of yours? You don't expect a young woman to be seduced by your bedroom charm, discussions over the pillows?'

'To the contrary. She's demanding, more physical than I want, and inquisitive. She's in the box seat, the legal inheritor. The marriage is valid, can't be disputed, and without a will to the contrary, it's hers.'

Alice took a seat, poured a glass of wine and pushed it over to her father. 'Drink it; you'll need it,' she said.

Frank Addison hoped he wouldn't hear more intrigue or another conspiracy. Sitting there with his daughter, he felt calm, something he hadn't felt with her in a long time, if ever. Or, at least, since her childhood, when he would see her once or twice a week, take her to the beach, buy ice cream, stroll up and down the esplanade at Bondi, spoil her rotten before delivering her home later in the day. He had to admit that her stepfather was a good man and had ensured that Alice never forgot her father. A sentiment that had lasted to puberty, and then the two had rarely met. Using her body to pass exams and pay for her lifestyle. Another young woman, he wouldn't have cared. After all, he had slept with many women, some much younger than his daughter, but this was different.

Was it, he wondered, with his daughter? Did he feel the guilt? Did she for what she had become. And then, a reconciliation of sorts, a marriage with Alan, then he's dead, and Melinda's in control. Had he been used? He was sure of the answer, but by whom, when, and why.

'Alan knew that marrying me would bring stability to his life. He knew what he was but could not change, but it was Melinda he loved.'

'I figured that out,' Addison said, unsure if he should elucidate his reasoning. That would mean revealing what Melinda had told him at the house and then, in more detail, with the police. And there was an added complication: the penthouse owner was possibly implicated with crimes related to what Alan had suffered for in Cambodia.

For a moment, he feared for his daughter. Involved in something she did not understand.

'Was Melinda playing us both for fools?' Alice asked, filling her father's glass and filling another for herself.

'I don't know, and that's the truth. You've been told about Crystal Andersson, claiming she's pregnant by Alan?'

'I have. It's probably true. The only one of us who loved him.'

'You didn't?'

'How could I? I was fond of him.'

'According to Melinda, he was a different man in Cambodia, and it had been love, but in Australia, he reverted to type, needing excitement to bring him out of his self-imposed shell.'

'What kind of excitement? I thought he was up there sowing his oats, girl in every bar, shooting up heroin. Are you saying there is something else?'

'No, that was it,' Addison said, aware that if there was any truth, then Alice, he, and Melinda could be in danger from an avenging drug baron masquerading as an honest politician. And his man in Australia was paying for the dead man's future wife to live in the penthouse.

Could his daughter be involved, Addison considered, but that seemed fanciful. She was probably the only one who was innocent, given that he had been fiddling the books for years, and Melinda had bedded and seen off three husbands. Did she intend him to be the fourth, as he had given her more details of where the assets were than he had given to Alan Greenworthy's father?

Frank Addison was frightened for his daughter.

✳✳✳

Haddock had pushed for it; Jeb Barton had resisted. 'Can't hold him,' Haddock had said to Commander Payne the night before in Payne's office. 'He confessed, but there's no proof.'

'He confessed to protect Crystal Andersson, sees himself as her consort, but she's carrying Alan Greenworthy's child,'

Payne said. 'Barton's a simpleton who sees love when there isn't any. But the law's the law. He confessed. He stays in prison for now.'

Haddock could see the injustice of a lovesick fool in prison for a crime he had not committed, but Payne was right: the law was the law, and Barton had made his nest, now he would have to lie in it until another person was found to have committed the crime.

'Devious woman?' Payne said.

It was late in the evening in Payne's office. The chance to talk off the record, to let the ideas flow, to give the commander something to keep the wolves at bay – his expression as to what he thought of his superiors – and for Haddock to lay out the reasoning for his actions and the direction forward in the investigation.

'Not that we know of. Well-educated, good family environment, works for her father.'

'But infatuated with a screwball.'

'Screwball, hero, or misunderstood, can't tell. We're working with whatever has been given to us by others. Almost impossible to determine the truth.'

'Okay, what do you have that has a better than eighty per cent probability that it's true?'

'Crystal Andersson is pregnant, one hundred per cent.'

'The father?'

'Not until the child is born, and then only with the mother's consent, or else a court order.'

'If she wants financial support from the Greenworthy estate, it is in her interests to comply.'

'In her interests not to agree to a non-invasive prenatal paternity test, just in case. If she's two months pregnant, that's possible, comparing the DNA of the foetus found in the mother's bloodstream with that of the mother and the father.'

'Has she agreed?'

'She's not been asked, another month before it can be done. There is every reason to refuse if she's dishonest. The baby didn't come into question until after the murder. According to Sergeant Campbell, her parents don't know yet. Her mother is religious and won't take kindly to it, and her father will be angry. The only child, an indulgent upbringing, and then she's carrying the child of a murdered man who had significant psychological issues. Tainted bloodline, a troubled baby, a family that will have to support mother and child, unable to find another man, not while the child is young.'

'And Barton, are you sure about this? Rape? It could backfire.'

'We could bring his confession to trial, but that would be fraudulent. And based on Melinda Greenworthy's evidence, and what we know of Crystal Andersson, there's reason to believe her claim is false, and his confession is a fabrication.'

'Cambodia? Can't prove it?'

'Impossible. We know that Heng is an important man in Cambodia and that he vanished, apparently due to Alan Greenworthy's part in shutting down the burgeoning drug route from the Golden Triangle to Cambodia. But the man's back and he or someone aligned with him could have been behind the murder.'

'Melinda Greenworthy, one of Heng's women, could she be playing both sides? What if Heng had found out that she was working with the Narcotics Bureau in Hong Kong? Could he have forced her to turn double agent, allow Alan to succeed, and set up another route? There is a lot of jungle up there. And then, Melinda's in Greenworthy's bed and married to him. Visits Australia and moves in with Alice Minchin for a few days. Anything on Clive Morton?'

'Nothing, but that doesn't surprise us. If he's smart, he wouldn't be personally involved, dealing through middlemen, and maybe no one knows his name.'

'Except Melinda does?'

'If she's to be trusted. She could be playing off both sides against the other, aiming to be on the winning side. If she's not careful, she could be the next body.'

Usually, a meeting with Payne was upbeat, and those in the office after hours left more motivated than when they had entered. But not this time.

Haddock realised the investigation had rolled on too long and still had a few weeks left.

Chapter 19

Claude Liddie's body had been autopsied and identified by a representative of the organisation that intended to retire him and then by his sister-in-law, who had flown down from Queensland.

'That's him,' she had said. Natalie had been present at the viewing and observed the woman as she looked down at Liddie's face. An unattractive woman, she had scowled when Natalie picked her up from the airport. She intended to deal with the formalities and fly back. Natalie was not warm to her, the closest Liddie had to a relative, and she was not interested in how he had died or why.

'You didn't like him?' Natalie asked.

'My sister did. He was unambitious and let life drift by. She was better than him, could have done better.'

'Why marry him?'

'I don't know. She always had her face in a book as a child. She could have become a teacher and married someone better, but Claude, in his twenties, was an attractive man who wore his uniform with pride. She didn't look further than the visual.'

'And you?'

'I married a local man, the eldest son.'

'Rich, successful?'

'Left me with two children, married a local tart, peroxide blonde, you know the type, killed himself on a motorbike.'

Natalie didn't know the woman that her former husband had married, but she had met women like the sister-in-law before. Jealous of her sister and her successful marriage with Claude.

'Burial?' Natalie asked.

'I'll need to check. Did they have insurance? Probably not, knowing Claude. My sister did when she died. Came down for that, probably not for his.'

The man was to be buried with no ceremony, no one at his graveside to mourn. It was a tragic end to his life, unloved, uncherished, thrown to the wind. Yet someone had an opinion of him and had killed him.

Natalie was sure it was related to Alan Greenworthy's murder and that Melinda had paid him twenty thousand to keep quiet about her presence on the island, but where had the other one hundred and thirty-three thousand come from, and why had Liddie cried poor, when obviously he was not.

'We found a lot of money after he died,' Natalie said. 'Any thoughts about it?'

'My sister never cared for material assets or wealth. A timid woman but smart. My parents adored her.'

'And you?'

'I was a nobody, a plain woman with little education. Never read a book in my life, not since I left school. They were right, but I expected more from my parents.'

'Your children?'

'The eldest, she's a hairdresser, doing well for herself. My son, better if we don't talk about him.'

'We've checked,' Natalie said. 'In prison, robbery with menace. Your brother-in-law had made it clear he didn't want to go and live near you and your family. It seems he wasn't as stupid as you seem to credit him.'

'You've no right to talk to me like that.'

'I have. This is a murder investigation. Claude Liddie was murdered. We need to know why, and we never met your sister, only know what he told us about her. Where did one hundred and thirty-three thousand dollars come from?'

'I don't know. I've no money to waste, certainly not to give it to my sister and her husband.'

'It's got to be illegal,' Natalie said. She was baiting the woman, not believing she was guilty of a crime, but the investigation needed something. Reinterviewing the current list of persons of interest was drawing to a close. The investigation required impetus, something hidden in plain sight. It was unlikely that Liddie's sister-in-law would provide it, but Natalie felt she should press the point.

Natalie dropped the woman back at the airport and thanked her for coming. There was no more for her to answer, and Natalie was glad when she got out of the car.

Crystal Andersson had been approached and refused to agree to a medical procedure to determine the father. 'It might harm the child,' she had said. Natalie knew that it would not, but she could sympathise. If she was pregnant, she would have objected.

***

At Cockatoo Island, even though it was after seven in the evening, two crime scene investigators worked in the cottage. They had returned after Haddock had insisted. 'Check in the roof, the garden, anywhere you haven't been. It's a rabbit warren, and the engineering workshops are voluminous, full of oversized lathes and milling machines. You could hide a battleship there.'

Natalie and Haddock reasoned the one hundred and thirty-three thousand dollars came not from a bribe but criminal activity and could explain why Liddie had died.

The money had come as a surprise, and now it was known that Melinda had been on the island on the night of the murder.

Either Claude Liddie was the biggest fool in Christendom or a master manipulator, using the island for nefarious purposes. Natalie thought she was clutching at straws, even considering that Liddie was more than a minor functionary. Haddock reasoned that the island was an ideal place to hide something, drugs specifically. The revelation that Alan Greenworthy had been undercover in Cambodia, that Melinda had been Heng's concubine, and that Alice was catering to her benefactor, Clive Morton, who, according to Melinda, was an associate of Heng's, led to the conclusion that Greenworthy had died not as a result of love, but of hate, and that he was a thorn in the side of what was going on, or else his death had been a revenge killing.

Natalie thought it confusing, a dog chasing its tail until ultimately it swallows itself, and then poof, gone, no further investigation, dead ends whichever way they turned.

Haddock didn't have much faith that the crime scene investigators would find more, although he had been right to ask them to keep looking. Not only were the workshops voluminous, but so were the island and the surrounding waters. He considered divers to check under the wharves and in the dry docks, no longer dry but deep and dark enough to hide what others did not want to be found. An exhaustive search of the island would have required more people than could be mustered, and it would need a budget to accommodate the cost. Knowing he would disapprove, there was no point asking Superintendent Payne, and Haddock had to concede he would have been correct.

Clive Morton should not have known his name was being bandied around Homicide, but he did. He phoned Natalie that night and invited her to meet him, a chance to clear the air.

The two met at Catalina's in Rose Bay, one of the best restaurants in Sydney, close to the wharf where a seaplane had taken her and Justice Kline up the Hawkesbury River to the Cottage Point Inn.

Natalie remembered the man she had seen in the foyer, confident that it was Morton:

Morton kissed her on the hand when they met and held her chair as she sat down. Natalie knew this was a dangerous man who oozed charm. She determined not to drink more than one glass of wine and not to let him sway her from the reason for the meeting.

Outside, the harbour, sailing boats, ferries heading up to Manly or coming back, one of the seaplanes taking off, another landing. Idyllic, complemented by the ambience and Morton's attentive manner. He had ordered sea bass for him and barramundi for her. Wine wasn't an option, as he had ordered champagne, Dom Perignon, the most expensive bottle in the restaurant.

'This isn't social,' Natalie said.

'A person close to Alice has been murdered,' Morton said as he clinked glasses with her.

'And your name has come forward. An unusual arrangement with her.'

'Not unusual. A beautiful woman, someone to spend time with. Don't try and read something into it that's not there. And now I believe my reputation is damaged due to scurrilous comments.'

'Whether scurrilous, that's for us to disprove.'

'Which I will. Ask me any questions. How's the fish?'

A throwaway question that had been used to disrupt her chain of thought.

Natalie had met the type before: charming, intelligent, constantly trying to control the conversation, to convince the other person of their innocence. She thought she could counteract the charm offensive, but the champagne was exceptional, and the man was impressive.

'Explain Alice,' Natalie said.

'Why I don't enforce exclusivity?'

'It's unusual.'

'Is it? Have you known many kept women?'

Natalie would have had to admit that she hadn't and that Alice was the first. However, she was well-read on the subject, a rich man's prize, as was a Ferrari, when the speed limit in Sydney was suited to a mid-size runabout, not something with five hundred horsepower.

'I pay for Alice, and I enjoy her company. I met her several years ago, found her delightful, and knew of her and what she was. I asked her to stay in the penthouse. I did not regard her as a rich man's folly but an adjunct to me.'

Natalie thought the explanation was strange. 'I don't understand. She's spending time with Alan Greenworthy, selling herself to other men. How can that be a folly, and what do you mean by as an adjunct to you? Were the men visiting known to you? Did she whore to extract information? To compromise and then blackmail? Married men, pillars of society, men who could not afford to have their reputations tarnished?'

'Information is valuable; knowledge of a person's weakness always assists. So, the answer is that sometimes that does occur, not that Alice has any part in the subterfuge. She spends time with the men, and I know who they are.'

'And sometimes you stake them the money?'

'In business, a gift is sometimes required.'

'Tax deductible?'

'It can be. I'm not a pimp nor a jealous man. Alice gives me joy. You've met her. Do you like her?'

Natalie took a sip of her champagne. 'I do, although I do not approve of her profession.'

'Nor should you. You know of her history, her father, his relationship with Greenworthy senior, and the idiot son.'

'Idiot?'

'Not idiot, but Alice intended to marry him.'

'Something you didn't want.'

'I advised her against taking on the challenge.'

'Her reaction?'

'Adamant, in that she had known the family for a long time, and her father worked with the Greenworthys. To her, it was only natural that she should marry the son.'

'As a child, she might have believed that, but as an adult, she knew the difficulties ahead. Your wealth?' Natalie said, gently pushing the conversation to hear Morton's story.

'Born poor, became rich through hard work and a quick mind. Took advantage of the massive increase in real estate values, leveraged to the hilt, rode out the interest rate hikes, and survived. Not so hard if you're not susceptible to stress, have self-belief, and are unemotional. I use people if I must, but deep love for another is not something I would allow.'

'Incapable?'

'Possibly not, always saw it as a negative emotion. Love flourishes, love wanes, and then the recriminations, the slanging matches, the hatred, and the kids who suffer.'

'Your upbringing?'

'Saw it all. I vowed never to go down the road that my parents had.'

'You're aware of the allegations levelled against you?'

'That I am involved in criminal activity?'

'What do you have to say? Deny or admit?'

'Opportunists, believing I'm an easy target and that I've set up a love shack with Alice to keep a watch on her father, Alan, and his wife. And yes, I know about her.'

'How?'

'Alice told me. You see, I am trustworthy. Alice knew this. Have you considered that those casting stones might be responsible? Easy to blame others, takes focus away from them.'

'Responsible for what?'

'Sergeant, you're being obtuse. Drugs, heroin specifically.'

'Have you been to Cambodia?' Natalie thought going for the jugular might be appropriate, see if she could detect the slightest sign in the man that he was perturbed by the question: a twitch, averting eyes, redness in the face, tapping on the table, gulping down his drink.

'Not Cambodia, but I've been to Thailand. I know of Heng, what Melinda is, and what Alan did overseas. Your next question will be how?'

'It is.'

'What do you know of Melinda Greenworthy?'

'We know what we've been told.'

'The problem, Sergeant, is who do you believe? You don't believe me, not yet. I'm an easy target. And you can't believe Melinda.'

'This is privileged information, Mr Morton,' Natalie said. She pushed her plate to one side, finished her drink and prepared to leave. The conversation had become threatening, and she sensed Morton trying to control it. She knew Haddock was nearby, and she would be safe if she could get to the door.

'It is not,' Morton said. 'Let me explain.'

Nervous, possibly in the presence of evil, Natalie pushed her chair back, not that she thought the man would do anything in a crowded restaurant, but she remembered what Melinda

Greenworthy had said, the treatment she had endured, the treatment Alan had. If the man opposite was involved, was he capable of violence? This was Sydney, one of the safest cities in the world, but crime still existed, injustices occurred, and a basement and chains and beatings, even rape, wouldn't look different from somewhere in Cambodia.

'Make it quick,' Natalie said, aware she would hear another person's slant on the truth.

'Melinda stayed with Alice, you know that.'

'I do. Both women have confirmed it.'

'And Melinda kept to her room or left the penthouse when someone else was there.'

'She said that. We regard Melinda's statements with a healthy degree of scepticism, and this story about meeting Alan, if it's true, and it might be, is a harrowing tale, and you are involved.'

'I am, indirectly.'

'How? A startling admission,' Natalie said. If the man was willing to talk in the restaurant, it showed stupidity or arrogance.

'I know Heng, not through drugs, but through real estate. I would be foolish to deny that I wasn't aware of his reputation. However, in Australia, our dealings were not criminal. He wanted to buy a place in Sydney.'

'Money laundering?'

'I didn't concern myself with that. How much money coming into the country is legal? How much do you reckon that comes out of China and Asia to buy real estate was earned through honest sweat and toil?'

'Some, not a lot.'

'Correct, and the government turns a blind eye to it, as I did. I sold Heng a property. He paid a good price, no issue with the deal, no haggling ad infinitum.'

'The penthouse?'

'Not the penthouse. The place Heng bought is not far away, but it's leased. He's pleased with the deal and offers to buy another. He's paying well; I'm not complaining. I met the man

188

once in Thailand. Only a fool would believe that the man, as successful as he is, wouldn't have taken shortcuts, cheated, and bribed to get where he had. Although, in Australia, a property owner, and if it gets too hot in Cambodia, and he brings enough money, the Australian government will let him in.'

'The penthouse? Alice? Does she know?'

'I know; she doesn't.'

Natalie wasn't sure why the man was telling her this, unless admitting to a minor indiscretion, which might be morally reprehensible but not criminal, hid other indiscretions which could be. Morton had thrust himself into the murder enquiry. She was curious about how he intended to wriggle out.

'You realise that you've opened yourself to further investigation.'

'I do. I haven't committed a crime, but my association with Heng has.'

'Explain this. If Melinda is staying with Alice, is that coincidental? Did you know who she was, of her relationship with Heng, her marriage to Alan Greenworthy? Did you know what Alan is meant to have done in Asia, in the Golden Triangle, in Cambodia?'

'Heng asked me as a favour to approach Alice. I had no reason not to, not for myself, but for him. I assumed he wanted her and had paid for her time once on an earlier visit to Sydney. It was an unusual request; I had no reason not to agree, and he was putting a lot of money my way.'

'She could have come to harm.'

'In Sydney, in the penthouse? I had no reason to believe she would.'

Natalie knew the truth. The man didn't care either for her or what Heng was as long as the money flowed.

'And now, do you know what Heng is?'

'I realise where Alice fits into your investigation. Heng wanted tabs on the woman, aware that Alan might reappear, which he did, and then Melinda was at the penthouse. I'm not introduced, but I've got someone who keeps a watch on the place, the comings and the goings. As part of my agreement with Heng, I update him on who comes and goes.'

'His reaction?'

'Nothing.'

Natalie outlined what had happened in Cambodia to Melinda and Alan, not omitting the details, watching Morton become progressively more distressed.

'True?' Morton asked. He had pushed his plate to one side.

'If you're telling the truth, it corroborates what Melinda told us. And—'

'You don't need to say it. I'm next if Heng finds out.'

'It's not if, but when. You were keeping tabs on Alice; who was keeping tabs on you? Are we being watched? If so, two and two don't make five, but four. I'm a police officer investigating a murder and here at your request. If Heng finds out, what do you reckon will happen?'

'I'll be dead.'

'Death might be a mercy after Heng's men have worked you over. Alan Greenworthy survived because they ultimately believed what he had told them. Melinda survived because Inspector Chong got her out. Who will come for you?'

'No one.'

Clive Morton had come to the restaurant to convince the police that he was innocent of all crimes and that he was only an observer of what was happening, but now, in the restaurant, a different reality dawned: that no one is truly innocent. Each person, including him, is guilty of indiscretion, whether minor or major. And he could see that he would be construed as the latter and that his life was in jeopardy.

'Then level with us. Melinda has told us what you are, and even if she had not been candid, her story is more convincing than yours, and we are inclined to believe that Inspector Chong is substantially trustworthy. You, Clive Morton, have no credibility or support mechanism, and we're the only people who could protect you.'

'Sergeant, I'm not that naïve. I believed Heng to be honest in his dealings with me, but in Cambodia, who knows. We don't always make the best decisions in business, as in life. If it is proven what happened to Melinda and her husband, your police can't protect me, and in prison, death is easy to arrange.'

'The money that was found at Cockatoo Island. What do you know about it?'

'Nothing. I'm not guilty of any crime other than greed. But who will believe me? You don't. Heng? If he is what you've said, and I'm willing to believe it, I am dead.'

'Then tell the truth, throw yourself on our mercy. We're Homicide, interested in solving murder. A plea deal: a few years in prison. Better than the alternatives.'

'I abhor drugs. I'm not involved. You'll have to look to others for answers.'

For some reason, Natalie believed the man. Even though the meal had been ruined by what was discussed and revealed, her conversation with him gave Natalie a clear direction to proceed.

Outside the restaurant, a worried man shook her hand, got into his Mercedes and left. Not far away, Haddock waited. Natalie walked over, got into the passenger seat and told him what had transpired, their conversation, and the way forward.

Chapter 20

Superintendent Payne reacted with alarm that, once again, Sergeant Natalie Campbell had met with a man who might be involved in a case, even though he claimed he wasn't.

'Sergeant, there are procedures to follow. Last time, with Justice Kline, you got into a plane with him and flew off to a fancy restaurant, failing to let anyone know until it was too late.'

'That's not entirely true,' Haddock said.

'Inspector, butt out. She told you too late; lucky she came back alive, considering that Kline's son was a murderer. And then a repeat performance. Granted, some good might have come of it, enough to break the case wide open, but hadn't you considered that Morton could be as guilty as hell, handy with a weapon, syringe in your arm, into his car and away.'

'I was in a restaurant, and Inspector Haddock was outside. I told him to get out to Catalina's and wait in the car park, not to let me get on a seaplane or drive away with Morton unless I spoke to him on the phone.'

'There were also two other unmarked vehicles on the street, depending on which direction he took. The risk was acceptable,' Haddock added.

'Very well,' Payne said. He had not been angry, just miffed. Initiative was good, but stupidity was not.

'Morton's provided the link between Heng and the penthouse,' Natalie said.

'Are you suggesting Liddie knew more?'

'Definitely not a major player, hid some of the money, and probably stashed the drugs.'

'You've not found them?'

'Difficult, too many places to hide them.'

'Needle in a haystack,' Haddock said.

'Find the needle,' Payne said. 'Good work, by the way, Sergeant.'

***

Jeb Barton had confessed to a murder he probably had not committed and was in Long Bay prison licking his wounds, reconsidering if he had been foolish and premature in rushing to the defence of Crystal Andersson. A woman who had accused him of rape, and still he had protected her.

Natalie visited the man and found that he had lost weight and looked unwell.

'I was sacked by the council,' he said.

'Can they do that?' Natalie replied, more to empathise than debate the legality. Ryde Council would have taken legal advice, and Natalie thought a confession freely given was tantamount to guilt, and rape, even if only accused of it, was abhorrent.

'After this, when you tell us the truth and are released?'

'I'm guilty.'

'And Crystal Andersson is a shrinking violet. You were set up, plain and simple, and you maintain this charade. Why? What's to gain? Certainly nothing for you. If she wants the child and a marriage, she will look elsewhere, and what can you offer?'

'In here, accused of rape. You know I didn't commit that crime.'

'I don't, Jeb. She's accused you, and the charge remains until she comes forward with the truth. And then, we've got to find a murderer. If it's not you, then who could it be? It's complicated, getting more so, and if we're right in our supposition, it's nothing to do with Alan and his women.'

'Why? It must be.'

'Unknown facts have come to light. Maybe you can help.'

'I killed him,' Barton thumped the desk. 'Why won't you believe me.'

The man was obsessive in his love for a woman who didn't deserve it. Natalie realised that he was a lost cause.

'Okay, different tack. Alan doesn't work. But could he be involved in something illegal?'

'Drugs, I presume you mean. Not that I ever saw. He didn't even like to be around when we smoked marijuana. I don't think he disapproved of us; just saw it as foolish, which it was. Gus liked it, Minsky occasionally had one, and I would go with the flow. But not Alan.'

'What do you know of his time in Cambodia?'

'Nothing, not really. Besides, it was before the band, no reason to ask, and you know Alan.'

'I didn't,' Natalie said. 'Only what people tell us. Could he have been more than you knew?'

'I never thought about it.'

'Did you go to Cockatoo Island often?'

'With the band, two or three times. Nothing there unless you like decay and convict history.'

'Did Alan?'

'Yet again, I wouldn't know.'

With no more to be gained, Natalie left the prison and returned to Parramatta.

***

In the interview room, another round with Melinda Greenworthy. Frank Addison was at her side.

Some of those being investigated were lying, or maybe all of them, but Natalie and Haddock realised it had to be a judgement call on who lied the most, and Melinda won the top spot.

'This verges on harassment,' Addison said.

'Not harassment,' Haddock replied, 'but a development. Melinda needs to elucidate further what she knows of Clive Morton.'

'Involved with Heng. Nothing specific, the man stays in the background,' Melinda said.

'Did you meet him? The truth.'

'I told you. I kept out of the way. If he had seen me, he might have recognised me.'

'Which means you knew him in Cambodia.'

'I did. Heng lent out his women occasionally. Morton was one he lent me to. He was a man who drank little, made love even less, spoke eloquently, and told me about Australia. This was before I met Alan.'

'What's the proof that he was involved with drugs?' Natalie said. 'I've spoken to him, and he said his relationship with Heng was to facilitate a real estate purchase.'

'I was not present when he met with Heng. It might be true, based on what I saw, but Inspector Chong, who is more knowledgeable on the movement of heroin around the world, would not accept that. The Narcotics Bureau is dedicated to stamping out the trade, and all known associates of Heng would be checked exhaustively. Morton is involved. To what extent in Australia, I don't know.'

Were you here to finalise the divorce or to spy on Morton?'

'Two birds with one stone. Opportune, my travelling to Sydney for the divorce, and Alice in Morton's penthouse.'

'And Heng spying on all parties. Has that been considered?'

'It has. No one that I could see.'

'You're a recent arrival. Before that? Morton knew who was going up to the penthouse. He knew of you, and if you had spent quality time with the man in Cambodia, he would have recognised you or sent the video to someone who might. Melinda, your presence was known, but the reason for being in Australia might not have been.

'What if Morton sends up a flare? The man has kept his head low for a long time, and then someone from the past stumbles into the penthouse. You thought you were smart, hiding out there, ensuring no one saw you, but downstairs, a concierge that knows everybody's business.'

'I pose no threat. My reason for meeting with Alice was legitimate.'

'Then why does Morton set Alice up in the penthouse? According to Morton, it makes sense. You and Alan seriously impacted Heng, causing him to be a pariah. He's monitoring Alan, whose crimes against him are more severe. You've said that Heng was chivalrous with women and that you had been punished and possibly forgiven. But Alan's in Sydney, and Heng knows that subjecting him to torture or death won't be overlooked by the police, and no bribe could be given to make the crime go away. And then you turn up just before Alan's death. Too many coincidences.'

'You might be right,' Melinda conceded.

'The twenty thousand you paid to Claude Liddie. Isn't it about time you told us the truth?'

'Narcotics Bureau, I still work for them. They were aware of Heng's involvement in Australia. There are no details, nothing prosecutable, and Australian criminal justice is slow and bureaucratic. But dealing with Heng and with Morton requires action.'

'Which means you were acting in an official capacity without informing your Australian counterparts.'

'In essence.'

'But why pay Liddie, and why were you at Cockatoo Island?'

'Alan was under suspicion. He might have been working for Heng. Morton might not have known. Alan's not a leader, but he's tactical. Advice is as important as action.'

'But his reclusiveness?' Haddock said.

'Very real.'

Natalie looked over at Addison. 'Cat got your tongue?' she said.

'I'm not sure what else I'm going to hear. Not Alan, surely.'

'Torture changes a person. The victim finding truth in the victimiser.'

'Are you saying Alan was turned? But why? How? And even if it's true, why Alan? The man was odd.'

'Odd, crazy, all the epithets you can think of, but he had one attribute: he blended in. Almost Mr Invisible.'

***

Two actions occurred in the subsequent days. The first was that Alice Minchin reluctantly moved out of the penthouse after the salient facts had been explained to her and was moved into witness protection. Her father, Frank, was informed after the event; her mother was left ignorant of what was happening.

The first action was because feathers were about to be ruffled, to put heat on Morton and, by default, Heng.

The second action was to consider the possibility that Cockatoo Island had been used to bring drugs into Australia. Not so difficult if a ship entered the harbour, tossed a waterproof bag over the side, and a waiting boat picked it up, all under the cover of darkness. And then to hide the drugs on the island and distribute from there. It had seemed far-fetched when Natalie had first suggested it, but the more she detailed her train of thought, the more logical it seemed. This would mean that Claude Liddie was involved in secreting the drugs, which would explain the money. While Natalie wanted to think the best of Liddie's wife, Haddock wasn't sure. The woman's sister had spoken highly of her, apart from her poor choice of a man.

A grid of the island was mapped out, two men to each grid, the size of the largest grid not to exceed eighty square metres, the smallest, if densely occupied by machinery as in the workshops, no more than twenty square metres.

Payne had approved the budget for three days; it was mid-week, so no ferry would stop on the island. A private marina on the other side of the island was effectively separated from the larger area by two dry docks, although it had been decades since they were dry. The police would maintain a presence at the road between the two dry docks, no one in or out. Also, for two days, no access to the marina. It was harsh and bound to lead to criticism of heavy-handed police, but it was unavoidable.

'Complain as much as they like, take it to their local member of parliament, even to the police commissioner, I'll hold firm,' Payne said. 'As for you and your merry band, Haddock, don't let me down.'

The man was watching their backs. All who had been interviewed, suspect or not, waited in Sydney. Natalie hoped some waited with bated breath, worried in case something was found.

Elsewhere, in an undisclosed location, Alice Minchin complained.

Natalie kept in contact with her, unsure if she wasn't involved, if she knew more, or even worse, had been passing on information to Clive Morton.

On the first day of the search, teams moved through the engineering workshops. Natalie and Haddock realised that it wasn't a needle in a haystack but a nail in an engineering workshop, impossible to search in every nook and cranny, every drain and pipe, the machines that remained. Added to that was the height of the workshops, the hidden places up high, where gantry cranes had trundled the length of the workshops. Some cranes were still in place, but most had been removed. A person could climb up to a platform at the height of the cranes to conduct a more thorough search, but this was the police, health and safety to be considered. Checks on the structural integrity of the platform and the stairs leading up would take more time than had been allocated.

'The marina,' Haddock said when Payne asked about the second day's focus.

'Overtime to whoever wants it,' Payne replied. 'In for a penny, in for a pound, better to be hung for a wolf than a sheep. Leave the flak from Accounts to me.'

The next day, just after five in the morning, twenty constables, dressed in protective coveralls and wearing nitrile gloves, gathered at the marina.

Thirty-two boats were out of the water in dry storage, and another twenty-one moored in Sutherland dock. It had once been used as a dry dock but was now open to the harbour. All the boats to be checked were motorised, large enough to pick up a package in the harbour, small enough to avoid suspicion, and insignificant enough not to be bothered by the Water Police or to show on the Port Authority radar.

Searching a boat required instruction, and two officers from the Water Police had given a fifteen-minute demonstration on where to look, the tell-tale signs of the recent lifting of floorboards, whether drugs could be stored in a life jacket or fishing tackle, and if a bulkhead could be removed, and if so, where to look. Also, a sniffer dog would enter each boat first.

It would be a long day, although Haddock intended to stay for the duration. He had a good feeling and felt that the previous day had been a waste: too many people, insufficient focus, and unsure what they were looking for, and the workshops contained a lot of superfluous machinery, whereas boats did not, as space was minimal.

After ten boats, nothing had been found. Focusing on another ten yielded no more. The dogs did their best, but the salty smell of the sea and the odour of fish caught and filleted on the boats made their job difficult.

At two in the afternoon, a small cabin cruiser used for fishing yielded the first result.

Haddock had been nearby, fretting that it would be another wasted day, and there was only one more day, and it had been a hunch to search the island based on what he and his sergeant thought feasible – that the island was being used to bring the drugs into Sydney for storage and from there for distribution, under the watchful eye of a caretaker who might have involved his wife. Natalie gave the woman the benefit of the doubt, considering that her husband would be the person walking around the island, keeping a watch on what was going on, peering into tents, taking delivery of the drugs, storing them, and then, if not distributing them, allowing someone else to come in at night and remove them.

'Bayliner 210, twenty-footer, ideal for fishing or day tripping,' one of the Water Police officers said.

'Low profile,' Haddock replied. 'Confirmed?'

'A compartment inside, hidden under the inboard motor. One of the dogs alerted us. The idiots had left a package there, heroin.'

The marina's owner was summoned and told of the development, expressing disbelief. For now, Haddock was willing to give him the benefit of the doubt. He wouldn't have been on the island if the drug movement occurred late at night.

The owner opened his laptop, checked his records, and sent an email to Natalie at State Crime Command as she sifted through the evidence so far, attempted to calm an anxious Alice, phoned Crystal to see if she was ready to prove that her pregnancy was the result of a weekend away with Alan and maintained the heat on Melinda.

Not believing that someone involved in a heinous crime would give the wharf's owner a correct address, Natalie got in her car after the local police confirmed the house was occupied and there were two expensive cars in the driveway. Following her were two unmarked vehicles, each with three officers, two of whom were armed. They drove thirty-six kilometres west to the foothills of the Blue Mountains.

The address was a house on acreage, set off from the road by fifty metres. Google Streetview had shown several ways in and out of the property and tracks that could be negotiated on a motorbike or a small vehicle.

One vehicle entered the acreage from a minor road at the back; Natalie's car and the other unmarked vehicle stayed on the road at the front. Vehicular access points were blocked. A police helicopter was on standby.

Two officers approached the front of the house; another two positioned themselves at the rear. Natalie was wearing a bulletproof jacket, just in case. It was her arrest, and she intended to be in on the action, expecting another rollocking from Superintendent Payne for placing herself in the line of fire.

Natalie stood behind one of the cars at the property. Both had been wheel-clamped. One officer knocked on the front door and moved to one side, holding a ballistic shield in case those inside had rifles and would use them.

Eventually, after a few minutes, the door opened. A smallish woman stood there. She didn't speak English; she was confused. The house was searched.

One of the tracks leading from the house showed recent usage, muddied footprints, and wheeled tracks. Natalie phoned for the crime scene investigators and a photographer to be on standby.

Natalie stayed with the woman and another officer. He was armed. Additional personnel were coming up from Parramatta, and four officers were coming down from Katoomba, the main population centre in the mountains; the term descriptive, but not entirely accurate, as the highest point was less than twelve hundred metres. However, it could snow in winter, and the roads were occasionally impassable.

Two officers were moving in a circular path, cutting through bush and brambles, while another four were moving down the track. Eventually, at the bottom, still part of the extended property, a large metal shed concealed under a green tarpaulin. Ex-military, one of the officers knew. There was movement in the shed as the metal sides echoed what was inside. Surrounding it, the officers stormed the entrance, catching those inside unawares.

Natalie knew those arrested were not the Mr Big but Thai nationals in the country illegally, with limited English and were addicts. Spaced out often, coherent at other times, not caring that they dealt in misery, addiction, and death.

The crime scene investigators were thorough, checking the house and the shed. The two cars were lifted onto a truck and taken to Forensics. Whoever owned the vehicles and the acreage was important, but that person wasn't at State Crime Command in Parramatta, under the care of a physician, unlike the four from the shed as the heroin wore off.

After a translator had spoken to her in Thai, the woman at the house confirmed her identity, that she had a family in Thailand, and she was at the house under duress. She was moved to Villawood Detention Centre. There, she would receive medical care and housing while her status in the country was confirmed. She would not be deported until the investigation into the house, the acreage, the shed, and those arrested was concluded.

Passports seized confirmed that three of the four men arrested were Thai nationals, and the one remaining was from Cambodia. One of the Thais had residency in the country and spoke acceptable English. The other three did not, although, even if they could, they refused to respond out of fear or because they had no knowledge of the drug operation. Charges would be laid. Resident or illegal in the country, they would serve their sentences in an Australian prison, which Haddock thought would be better than prisons in their homeland. The men were processed, and a translator was brought in to address them. They did not speak, even to the translator, although they ate voraciously the food given to them.

Natalie thought the men were simple people who, out of desperation, were used by persons who treated them with disdain, a pittance given, a pittance to send back to their families overseas, apart from one who was a resident in Australia. He was of interest.

Chapter 21

Niran Bunchuai could not deny his fluency in English. It had been a condition of his citizenship that he conversed in English, could answer general knowledge questions about the political system, and affirmed, with others, at a ceremony in Penrith, close to the acreage, that he would uphold the values of his adopted country.

Legal aid had been organised for him at his request. Soon after his arrest, he stated that he was an employee and did not know who the boss was. Natalie and Haddock were willing to accept the first; the second, they were not.

Further searches had revealed nothing more at Cockatoo Island, although Bunchuai's fingerprints had been found on the boat and the package. Also, one of the other men had been confirmed as being on the boat.

There was one day left for the search on the island. Time was in short supply. Bunchuai, handcuffed and charged, Natalie, Haddock, one CSI, and two uniformed officers relocated to Cockatoo Island. There, alongside the boat, they stood. The marina wharf's owner, who had stayed hidden, stated that he hadn't seen the man and that payments for the wharf had been made online. The boat, which had fishing rods and tackle on board, went out at night and came back in the morning once or twice a month, sometimes every two, and there was no trouble with the boat and the owner, identified as an Australian national, although on checking it was found that the man had died six years prior. Further proof of criminal activity, although no more was needed. The evidence against Bunchuai and others was damning.

'Possible life imprisonment,' Haddock said. 'Unless you cooperate.'

There was no criminal history for Bunchuai, who had once owned a Thai restaurant in Parramatta, which had since closed. The family home was mortgaged, and payments had been made regularly.

Natalie knew the problem: the man had succumbed to heroin, and a restaurant couldn't pay the bills and feed his addiction. He had taken the slippery route to working with those responsible for his addiction.

'Talk, or it's a prison,' Natalie said.

'Talk, and it's death,' Bunchuai replied, confirming the two officers' fears that confession wasn't good for the soul.

'A boat comes into the harbour at night. You've been told where to go. A phone call from someone on the boat, then over the side a heavily wrapped and waterproofed package, a flotation device attached, probably a waterproof beacon. You pick it up, bring it to the island, hand it over to the caretaker, or you secure it a location mutually agreed on, and then you leave, another boat to pick you up, probably a small dinghy to the mainland, or the dinghy is towed behind the boat.'

'You saw the drugs when we were arrested. I can't deny that.'

'Except packages over the side is a risky operation. There are more on the island, a logical place to store it. The caretaker's dead, murdered. Are you next?'

Bunchuai, clearly more astute than he had been given credit for, held out his arms. 'Remove the handcuffs,' he said.

Natalie looked over at Haddock and nodded. 'It's an island,' she said. 'No way off.'

Haddock removed the handcuffs and allowed Bunchuai to walk away, the two officers following. The other officers held back after Natalie gave them a signal not to accompany them.

A man arrested for a serious crime should have stayed handcuffed, but these were exceptional circumstances. Across the road between the two dry docks, Bunchuai walked, hesitant in his movements, unsure if he was doing the right thing. He turned right at the rock face and walked as far as the western end of the dog-leg tunnel, constructed in 1915 to move workers and materials from one side of the island to the other, and then, during World War 11, designated as an air-raid shelter, but never used.

Halfway along the tunnel, at the ninety-metre mark, Bunchuai turned into a small alcove off the main tunnel. Natalie assumed the alcove had a function but wasn't sure what, other than somewhere for a person on foot to get out of the way of a vehicle moving through.

Three metres in, Bunchuai pulled at a rock. It was firmly wedged, but eventually, it came free. Once free, it was evident that the rock was part of a roughly constructed wall and inside, an area of approximately six metres by four metres. On a raised platform, more than two hundred packages, each weighing 1.3 Kilograms, with a street value of eighty-six million dollars. 'Now, keep my family alive,' he said.

'The caretaker?' Natalie asked.

'I never met him; only knew that someone was on the island.'

'And moving the packages from the alcove and out to where you were arrested?'

'At night, placed on the boat and taken across to the mainland. From there, we would bring it to the house.'

Natalie could sympathise with Bunchuai, who committed a crime to feed an addiction. And if what Melinda had said about Heng and the treatment meted out to her and Alan was true, then Bunchuai had reason to worry, even though, in a moment of lucidity, he had done the right thing.

The investigation into Alan Greenworthy's murder and Claude Liddie's was open, all the cards on the table, all persons in place. All that was needed was the link that tied the pieces together.

***

Melinda Greenworthy was thought to be the link, although, on the night of the concert, her husband had died at the place where illicit drugs were stored. Or was that coincidental? Something that Haddock did not believe in. He regarded luck as a word loosely bandied around and coincidental did not figure. Alan's murder was preordained, not by an unseen force, but by a person or persons.

'What if,' Natalie postulated aloud, 'Alan had been turned?'

'It was regarded as a possibility,' Melinda said, seconded by Frank Addison, who did not look pleased to be in the interview room.

'We never considered it before. Opportune, the island, a concert, a woman with the man, make out it's a crime of passion. But it's due to a massive drug importation and trafficking empire orchestrated by Heng, overseen in Sydney by Alan.'

'What about Clive Morton?'

'What about him? Where is the proof? He has admitted to a relationship with Heng, duped into believing that Heng was interested in Alice, not knowing about Alan and Cambodia. He wouldn't have been expected to know, but Heng might, and you definitely did. It's been raised before: what is your role in this? Frank Addison, were you working with Alan?'

'Scurrilous lies,' Addison said. 'Where's the proof?'

'Dead,' Haddock joined in the discussion. He knew what his sergeant was doing, throwing aspersions like confetti at a wedding.

Natalie knew she didn't have much to pin on Melinda or Addison, and Bunchuai's confession would convict him.

'You were rescued in the nick of time, but you said Heng was chivalrous towards women. Would you have suffered as much as Alan, or did you throw in the towel? You told us about pain receptors and how you could dull the pain. True or false?'

'True.'

'Is this a witch hunt?' Addison interjected, only to be ignored.

'And Morton, criminal or dupe? He says he's done nothing wrong but is now frightened. Yet you, Melinda, act as if it's business as usual. How are the renovations going? The title of the house, Alan's money, in your possession?'

'There are delays,' Addison said.

Haddock saw hesitancy in the man's reply. Was it a silent plea for help? Did Alice's father, Frank, know something but was afraid to reveal it? He had been close to Melinda, and he was astute. Had he seen the truth?

Haddock knew he had to talk to Natalie, sound her out, and allow her to add to his thoughts or dismiss them. But for now, the interview would continue.

'Here's what we think,' Natalie said. 'Or let's say it's a supposition, based on facts that we know, ideas that we've added, based on experience in homicide.'

'Okay,' Melinda said. 'Continue with this farce if you must.'

'As I said, Alan's been turned. He's solitary in Australia, talks to very few, and doesn't socialise other than with the band, and sometimes with Alice, sometimes with Crystal. But what if the solitary is in part manufactured. What if he is thinking deeply, planning his next move, either to enhance his position with Heng or to sideline him. He's got contacts in the Golden Triangle, and they trust him more than Heng. It wouldn't be the first time.'

'Alan wasn't interested in money or influence,' Addison said.

'I never said he was. Alan is complex and has a personality that defies logic. He did well at school and university, and then he's in Cambodia, just to be away from the confining atmosphere of his family and Sydney.

'He likes it there, spends time in the girlie bars, a blowjob or two, and then he becomes addicted. You recognise the possibility of the man. You nurture him, get him off the drugs, and give him a challenge. We know that he had no fear. He enters the Golden Triangle, finds his voice, gains confidence, sets up the deal, suffers at the hands of those he needs, and then they trust him. Power and influence are addictive, better than drugs to most people.

'Heng grabs him, further torture and abuse, but what if that is another ruse? Alan's back in Australia, living a miserable life, blowing off steam with the band, spending time with a few women. It would have appealed to his personality, and we know of his bravery.'

'Alan wouldn't involve himself with crime,' Addison said.

'Why? Doesn't he display the personality? Not everyone is a James Bond, drives an Aston Martin, licence to kill. More John Le Carré, if you've read *The Spy Who Came in from the Cold*. Alec Leamas is the archetypal anti-hero, the ultimate spy. But he's committed to good, and so was Alan, but it's a fine knife edge between good and bad.'

'Why Cockatoo Island if your logic is sound?' Melinda said.

'Heng's looking to expand throughout Asia and into Australia and New Zealand. Even if broken at times, the route down to Cambodia is more robust than the other routes out of the Golden Triangle. He has Alan working for him, probably realises that the man's up to mischief, and certainly would know if he had twigged you. The apartment, the car, the cushy life he's paying for. Was that to keep you in view? Did he do that for his other women?'

'Maybe he thought I was special.'

'Melinda, you're not that naïve. If we accept that you have been under the tutelage of Inspector Chong, that means you would have recognised the possibility. Of course, that's assuming you are on the side of good, and we're unconvinced. And here's another angle: Alan's fallen foul of Heng, or the Narcotics Bureau wants to do what they did in Cambodia, although that backfired. Was it intended that you would take over from Alan? Did Alan know or suspect? He's been trained by Chong. He might have known you were in Sydney. Alice could have phoned him, or maybe he had someone watching Alice.'

'Are you saying that Alan duped us all?' Addison said as he sat back in his chair. 'Incredible if he did.'

'Not all,' Melinda said. 'Firstly, I did love Alan. The marriage was not a sham at the time. Secondly, there are these.' She leant over, picked up her handbag, and laid out on the table a diplomatic passport, a warrant from the Australian Federal Police in Canberra to conduct covert operations in Australia, identification showing that she was an officer in the Narcotics Bureau of Hong Kong, and finally, a phone number in Canberra. 'Dial the number,' she said.

Haddock dialled, a man's voice on the other end. 'I was expecting to receive a phone call at some time. This line is encrypted. You are free to speak. I assume you recognise my voice.'

'I do,' Haddock said.

'Very well, an exceptional situation, and from reports I've received, you and your sergeant have done an admirable job. Congratulations to you both. And yes, I do vouch for Melinda Greenworthy on behalf of my government.'

'We need proof,' Haddock said.

'Thirty minutes, you will receive an email, documentation to prove that the woman you are questioning is who she says she is.'

The phone call ended. Haddock looked over at Addison. 'You knew?'

'I do now.'

'Frank's been vetted. He's not involved, nor is Alice.'

'The prime minister? Natalie asked.

'It was.'

'It's a joint operation, three countries, half a dozen police forces. Maximum secrecy, complicated by Alan's death,' Melinda said.

'Was he working with Heng?'

'He was with us before, but in Sydney, he chose Heng, not out of criminality, but because skulking around, being secretive, lent itself to his personality. Sergeant Campbell's analogy, comparing him to Le Carré's master spy, is apt.'

'You killed him?'

'I didn't. His death confused our work, and we didn't want to intervene in the investigation into his death, unsure where it might lead us. Nor did I kill Liddie, but I used sex as a tool. The man wasn't the brightest, and his usefulness to those he worked for was at an end. And then he was seen with me, and I was known to Heng. Liddie, his guilt decided by association.'

'But you gave him twenty thousand dollars.'

'To ensure he held his tongue, a lever on the man. I was there on the night of the murder. I saw more than I should.'

'You saw the murderer?'

'Not the murderer, but Liddie did. But he wasn't going to come forward, not to you. The man had a lucrative sideline on the island. He didn't want it to end. You must have realised there was a degree of complexity in what he was doing.'

'His wife?'

'It can't be proven. It might be best to leave her name out of it, but we believe that she was the organiser on the island.'

'Who saw you with Liddie?'

'Someone as silent as the night, a master of disguise, or, more appropriately, mistress. And then she saw your inspector with him, a quiet night, sound travels.'

'You don't mean…' Natalie realised who Melinda was referring to.

'Alan's murder is unrelated. Your inspector might not believe in coincidences, luck, or serendipity, but that is precisely what it was on the night of his death.'

***

Villawood Detention Centre housed a mix of asylum seekers, people who have overstayed their visas, and Section 501 detainees who have had their visas cancelled following criminal convictions and are awaiting deportation after serving prison sentences.

Initially a migrant hostel, it became a detention centre in 1976. Of those incarcerated there, the majority were Section 501.

Chariya Vaiyasingha, who might be innocent and forced to work illegally in Australia to support a family in Thailand, did not fit any of the regular categories, and the centre provided her with security in case others involved in the illegal importation of heroin did not want her as a witness.

That had been the decision initially based on what the woman had told Achara Masdit, an immigration officer, born of Thai parents in Australia.

'From Northern Thailand, impoverished, entered Australia five years ago on a tourist visa, never left,' Masdit said. 'She's been in several places in Sydney, rarely went out, but otherwise has been treated reasonably well. She's desperate to get back to Thailand, fast track the process if you agree,' Masdit said.

Natalie had visited the woman, who was pleased to be returning home. And no, she didn't know what they were doing but thought it illegal, and yes, she should have been concerned, but who would listen to her, and what about her family in Thailand.

Natalie had been convinced, but now there was Melinda Greenworthy, whose credentials had been confirmed by Inspector Chong of the Narcotics Bureau of Hong Kong, the prime minister of Australia, and the Australian Federal Police.

It was hard to dispute the heavyweights who confirmed that Melinda, regardless of her using sex as a tool, was a servant of good, not of evil, not of Heng, nor of Clive Morton, although his guilt was in question. And now, the focus was on Alan Greenworthy, a silent hero or a hidden villain.

On the second visit to the detention centre, Natalie was not in the same frame of mind. A photo had been sent by Chong, along with a dossier, showing that the diminutive woman who kept house for the four arrested drug addicts was Sansanee Sihalak, born in Bangkok on the 3rd of April, 1977. Her father was a builder; her mother owned a restaurant; she had been educated at a private school, spoke good English, and had entered Australia with a false passport through Darwin in the Northern Territory. Also, she was not the housekeeper, sex slave, or dogsbody.

No longer in an open area in the centre, but a closed room. Natalie cautioned the woman; Masdit translated. She told Sihalak that the ruse was over, and Homicide had proof of her identity and testimony that she had killed Liddie. It was not mentioned that the charge of murder could not be proven, not yet.

The pretence continued, the tears flowed, the pleading with Masdit, the holding of Natalie's arm. Unmoved, Natalie placed a copy of the dossier from Inspector Chong on the table. 'Read this,' she said, not asking Masdit to translate.

Sihalak picked up the dossier and scanned through it, discarding it on the floor and then arguing with Masdit.

'She's adamant that it's not her,' Achara Masdit said.

Natalie realised that the immigration officer did not have the experience to understand when she was being conned.

Outside the detention centre, a police car transported the handcuffed Sihalak to Silverwater Correction Complex, where she would remain until her trial.

Chapter 22

The following day, two events of significance occurred. The first was that Melinda Greenworthy left Australia. Nobody had known she was going, least of all Frank Addison, who, when questioned, said that he believed she was staying, that he would miss her for a while, that he had spoken to Alice, and when the heat died down, they would meet.

Inspector Chong had been contacted and confirmed that Melinda was aware that her part in closing down Heng's drug trafficking into Australia would make her a target. Also, his operative had vanished into the ether and that, in time, she would reappear, not as Melinda, but in another guise.

This meant one thing. If confirmed, the marriage in Cambodia between Alan Greenworthy and Melinda Huang, even if love had existed, was invalid, and her birth certificate and passports were expertly created fakes.

The second event was at two in the morning, eight hours after Natalie had left the detention centre. Sansanee Sihalak had been charged with murder, with further proof of her criminality to be supplied from Chong in Hong Kong and Melinda, wherever she was. The woman, who had not uttered one word in English, was found dead in her cell at Silverwater. The headache pills she had been allowed to keep were examined and found to contain cyanide.

Natalie knew what Melinda Greenworthy would have said. 'Failure is not an excuse, not with Heng. To die by her hand is preferable to what might have happened in Thailand.'

After spending the day at the prison, Natalie returned to State Crime Command, to Homicide, to Haddock's office. She had brought in a pizza to share and was prepared for a long night.

They agreed that they would go through what they had, accepting that Alan was involved in Cambodia and Sydney, although he had switched sides.

'Morton?' Haddock said.

'Someone must have been dealing with setting up the drug importation. It could not have been Sihalak, not totally,' Natalie replied.

'Why not? If her English was good, and she had the backing of Heng.'

'Deals had to be made, occasionally hands shaken. Morton was Australian and would have had credibility; she would not. She played her part well, but sometimes a front is needed.'

Jimmy Rogers phoned and asked Natalie to meet with him. In the excitement of the last few days, she had forgotten that he had been working with the CCTV cameras on the island, sifting through what he could on the relevant days.

'It'll cost you,' he said.

Natalie had been down that road before. A meal, a couple of drinks, and a goodnight kiss on the cheek were the limit of what he would get. She knew he could be trusted to keep to the agreement. 'Fair enough, depends if what you've got is worth it.'

'It is. Two hours, you know my address.'

'No getting frisky,' Natalie said in jest.

She didn't know why the relationship could not progress. Apart from his nerdish manner, he was thoroughly decent, someone a woman should be proud to call her own. But it was the same with Crystal Andersson until she had accused Jeb Barton of rape and had destroyed her credibility – that Barton didn't move her, not the way Alan did.

It was two in the morning. Natalie wanted to sleep, but it was Jimmy Rogers' apartment, untidy, unloved, a man's home. In the kitchen, a half-eaten pizza and a pot of what might have been soup in a past life. Even though she was tired and Rogers was anxious, she took to the kitchen with vigour, transforming it from disgusting to tolerable.

'Bob Prentice updated me,' Rogers said.

Natalie, not as sharp as she should have been due to the hour, had to think. 'One of the constables on the island,' she said.

'He gave me the date and approximate time when Liddie died. Also, an image of the woman. There are not many cameras on the island. A few down below, not up where Greenworthy died. However, the marina has had theft, and boats are stored there. Security concerns them.'

On the computer monitor, Natalie could see the boats illuminated by spotlights mounted high on a nearby building.

'Check the time, just after eight in the evening. It's twilight and a clear night, full moon. Can you see it?'

Natalie could not, but she was not trained to sit in front of a monitor for hours.

'A ripple on the water, just behind a boat, to the left of the screen,' Rogers added.

Natalie could. 'What does it mean?'

'Just wait.'

Natalie did and saw a small boat come into view. In the front, a small hooded figure. At the rear, a man holding the tiller of the outboard motor.

'What does it mean?'

'It's the woman. Five minutes later, when she's sure no one is around, she lowers the hood, looks up at the moon, and over to the other side of the dry docks. Facial recognition software confirms.'

'Coincidental that both Inspector Haddock and Sansanee Sihalak were on the island at the same time?'

'I don't know about Inspector Haddock. Only giving you proof that she was there.'

If she was on the island that night, it meant to Natalie that she had been there before and that Liddie, who did not have a chance to deny it, had met with her.

It wasn't proof that Sihalak had murdered Liddie, as there were no cameras up close to Liddie's cottage, but it lent credence to Melinda's belief that she had been seen with Liddie, probably when she had cemented Liddie's discretion in one of the houses.

'It's not concrete proof,' Natalie said.

'I would agree, but there is more. The road around the island was lit at night. The woman moved over to the stairway leading up to Liddie's cottage. I can track some of her movement, and it's her.'

'But why? Why visit Liddie?'

'From what I was told, the man had taken money from someone else, a bribe to keep quiet about them being on the island, and the woman on the stairs did meet Claude Liddie,' Rogers said. 'Can you confirm otherwise?'

'Not from either two. The woman would not talk, dead now by her own hand, and Liddie's been murdered, not so difficult given the copious amount of alcohol he had downed, along with my inspector. Privileged information, my inspector.'

'My lips are sealed.'

'How did she know about the woman from Hong Kong,' Natalie speculated.

'Maybe the woman told her.'

It was an interesting thought. Jimmy Rogers had hit on a possibility. It was now accepted that Alan had been turned by Heng, but what if Melinda, who had intended to remain in Australia after her husband's death, had been the one turned, and Alan was an unwanted obstruction.

The West was decaying into a quagmire of corruption, but it had existed for centuries in Cambodia and was not regarded with the same disdain as in the West.

Melinda, the widow of a murdered man. No suspicion could be levelled at her, and now, she had left the country and vanished.

Jimmy Rogers would have his night out with Natalie. He had earned it.

***

Superintendent Payne, updated by Haddock after Natalie had told him of Rogers' insight, held court in his office. It was after nine in the evening, and apart from Payne, Natalie, and Haddock, Victoria Adderley was present.

Before entering the office, Victoria had pulled Natalie to one side. 'He's left his wife. We have moved in together,' she said.

Natalie had been expecting it, not that she approved, and thought Victoria, fifteen years younger than the superintendent, was foolish. However, foolishness seemed to be in plentiful supply. Crystal Andersson had phoned that day and told her that she had told her parents and that they had called her all the names under the sun.

Still, she knew they would support her and love the child, and Frank Addison had phoned, told her that he had control of the Greenworthy fortune and that she would be provided for once it was confirmed that the child was Alan's. And that she had agreed to the medical procedure to determine the father.

Also, she had reservations about the claim of rape against Jeb Barton, in that she might have egged him on in a time of emotional fragility; her fault if she had.

Natalie informed her that the charge would remain until she rescinded the claim, formally and in writing, and then apologised to the man protecting her from a murder charge.

Natalie didn't elaborate that the proof against Barton on both counts looked weak. Even though he had not complained about his time in prison, it was clear the last time she had visited him that he was suffering, isolated from the main prison, as he had not been convicted, and for his protection from those who abhorred a rapist, and others who would have regarded him as a plaything, a diversion for the monotony of prison life.

In the office, a jubilant Payne, an embarrassed Victoria, when he looked over at her.

'Inspector, what's your take on all this?' Payne asked as he handed over a can of beer.

'Logical conclusions have been reached, some without irrefutable proof,' Haddock replied.

'And to get proof?'

'Melinda Greenworthy's disappeared, Inspector Chong may be honest, or not, no way to be sure of either. We cannot trust him.'

'Sansanee Sihalak killed Liddie. Hair has been found on the cushion that suffocated him. A lot of hair, initially thought to have been Liddie's or his wife's, and those checked were,' Natalie said. 'Forensics has been busy, checking the cushion, analysing more hair, and finding Sihalak's. She killed the man, the assumption that she knew of Melinda Greenworthy spending time with him, and then further proof when Inspector Haddock was with Liddie on the night of the murder.'

'Why?' Payne asked. 'If Melinda was working with Heng, or it had been Alan, there was no reason to kill Liddie. Given time, our focus would have drifted away, business as usual for those involved.'

'If Melinda was working with Heng, she would have known of Sihalak, and the one hundred and thirty-three thousand dollars confirms that Liddie and his wife were hiding drug packages on the island and paid well for their services. As you say, Superintendent, why not let it continue.'

'Except,' Haddock said, 'Liddie was getting old, showed early signs of forgetfulness, and was about to lose his job. His usefulness was at an end. A new strategy was needed to bring in the drugs.'

'And getting drunk with you,' Payne said. 'The man's worst friend, a drinking buddy, possibly saying more than he should.'

'Already compromised, told us about Melinda and the twenty thousand.'

'Have we been taken for suckers? Led down the garden path, told lies, counter-lies, anything but the truth. What do we know? What can we prove?'

'Only that Liddie was killed by Sihalak.'

'Drugs are not our concern; murder is. Tell me what you want?'

'Surveillance Devices Act,' Natalie said. 'We need to monitor Clive Morton, Frank Addison, and Alice Minchin. Phone calls and messaging.'

'Only them?'

'Theorising, we think Morton might have been involved, although Sihalak slipped under the radar. We didn't see that coming. Melinda might have set up Alan in Cambodia, played the long game, and allowed Sihalak to go as far as she could. She was not in the country legally, but Melinda was.'

'The Golden Triangle, Greenworthy believing he was involved in a noble pursuit.'

'It would have appealed to him.'

'If Melinda had taken over, a massive expansion?'

'Why not? Makes us look like rank amateurs, if true,' Natalie said.

'Victoria,' Payne looked at her again, lingering longer than he should. 'What's involved in listening on mobile phones and reading text messages?'

'I will need a convincing case to get a warrant. I can work with Natalie, take a day to prepare, another to present it to a magistrate or judge.'

'Do it,' Payne said. 'Four days, I want Greenworthy's murderer charged and in custody.'

'Unless it's the missing wife,' Victoria said.

'It's not,' Natalie said. 'She wouldn't have risked it, not if she was to take over from Morton or Alan.'

***

Haddock thought that if Melinda had intended a takeover, where did that place Morton? Was he cognisant of the fact? Had they met in the penthouse?

Inspector Chong wasn't answering his phone or emails, and Morton wasn't to be seen. Alice was at State Crime Command, along with her father. The warrant to monitor their electronic communication had been prepared and granted.

Natalie outlined the scenario to Alice; Haddock outlined it to Frank Addison. The two family members were separated into different rooms.

'We know who killed the caretaker,' Natalie said.

Alice sat calmly, listening to the sergeant. Dressed in a white top and jeans, her hair brushed, not styled, she did not look like the whore she had been.

It was known that since Melinda had vanished, she had spent time with her father, although what was discussed, whether they were cordial, wasn't known. The reason Alice was with Natalie.

'And Melinda?' Alice said.

'Gone. How's your father taken it?'

'Ambivalent. He always said their relationship was casual and that after Alan had died, he had fallen in with Melinda primarily to protect his interests and mine.'

'Yet your relationship, father to daughter, is poor.'

'Not poor, confused. I might not always agree with him, and he disapproved of my whoring, but I hoped he respected my wisdom.'

Natalie could not see much wisdom in screwing men for money, although Alice appeared to think it was honourable. Heng had instructed Morton to buy the penthouse and to ensure that Alice, Alan Greenworthy's childhood friend was installed there, which beggared the question, why? Was Greenworthy guilty of drug trafficking? Had he been turned? There appeared to be no resolve to either question.

Natalie thought openness with Alice might be one way. For fifteen minutes, she outlined the case, including details of Alan's activities in Cambodia, the torture, and his worsened condition on return to Sydney resulting from what he had experienced.

Alice said nothing, just listened, slowly sinking lower in her chair. 'I never knew,' she said.

'No one did, not until Melinda told us, but now, we doubt her. She was in the penthouse. Did she see Morton? Talk to him? Sleep with him? She admitted that she used her body in the pursuit of good, but with her disappearance, was that true?'

'I wasn't there all the time. She might have, but does that make Clive complicit?'

'It does not, although it makes us suspicious. Let me be frank: three persons could have killed Alan. You, although we don't understand why; your father, but the timings wrong; Clive Morton, if Melinda was telling the truth, but we can't believe anything that she told us.'

In another room, Haddock sat with Frank Addison, a police sergeant standing in one corner, just in case.

'Preposterous,' Addison said after Haddock had given a similar version of the story.

'Melinda had the most to gain, but she's gone, no one to inherit the Greenworthys' estate, and apparently, the marriage was invalid. Does it come to you?' Haddock asked.

'Alan's father knew that Alan was incapable, and no, it doesn't come to me, although I have access to it. I can sell off assets, and in time, I could transfer the majority to my account. Is that what you want to hear?'

'A confession might come in handy.'

'I didn't kill Alan, why would I? I made sure he was looked after. And then, I had Melinda, looking over my shoulder, making out I am the great lover.'

'You knew what she was?'

'Devious, possibly criminal, low-level sociopath. I don't think she cared for anyone, not emotionally. When Alan returned and told me about the marriage, I had checks done, knew about the two earlier husbands, and how she met Alan. I never knew that she worked for the Narcotics Bureau. Does it exist? Bona fide?'

'It is, although we can't prove Melinda was playing by the rule book. As you said, she was a smart woman. In Sydney, before Alan died. She was on the island when your daughter and Alan Greenworthy pledged their troth and had sex.

'She might have seen someone else there, apart from Liddie, but she dealt with him in the only way she knew, the same as she did with you. Sex is a powerful weapon, and she used it well. You must have suspected.'

'I was not convinced by the report I received. Specific details were missing, such as her childhood, where she had grown up, her parents. I thought that might be because she had been born on the mainland. It was a disquiet, not a red alarm. Alan told me she was a good person, but they could not be together. Too much had happened. I didn't pursue it; I had known him for too many years to believe he would say more. Life moved on. Alan survived, even though it was a strange existence, and then he discussed a future with Alice. I knew what she had become. I blamed myself, but there was redemption, two troubled souls, and I would ensure both were fine, the way Alan's father had cared for him.

'I never knew about possible links to illegal drugs, would have thought Alan incapable if told. Not a dishonest bone in his body, but do we know a person, truly?'

'Melinda? She appears after Alan's death, although she had been hiding out with Alice – alarm bells ringing?'

'I dealt with the reality, not speculation. All I knew was I had to secure the house and move some money.'

'Are you admitting to fraud?'

'Not fraud. I made decisions on what I could. Melinda could have the house and most of the money, but not all. I trusted Alan's father, I trusted Alan, but I couldn't trust her. The money I took is offshore, not accessible by anyone other than me, and if I feel inclined, Alice.'

'Which means you don't trust her.'

'Not until she comes to her senses, moves into the house, possibly finds another man, and has a child. Until then, she is vulnerable.'

In the other room, Natalie persisted with Alice, who eventually admitted that Clive Morton had met with Melinda and had been sworn to secrecy, and yes, she did know that the man pushed the envelope and he sometimes left the country, and no, she didn't know where, and yes, there had been an Asian man in the penthouse once. She had spoken to him, and Clive had asked her to have sex with him.

Natalie opened her phone, brought up an image and showed it to Alice. 'I think so,' Alice said.

Haddock received the message first. Natalie, soon after.

Outside in the corridor, they met and walked together towards Legal.

'Let them go?' Natalie asked.

'Not yet,' Haddock replied. 'Let's hear from the femme fatale first.'

Natalie thought the reference to Victoria was inappropriate but appreciated the humour at another woman's expense.

Victoria was sitting; another woman stood nearby, one of Homicide's administrative staff.

'Why here?' Natalie asked.

'What I have concerns those you're talking to,' Sharon Wentworth said. 'I know how important it is, and Victoria had obtained the warrant. I didn't want to alarm them by barging in on you.'

Haddock sat, loosened his tie, and undid his shirt's top button. Natalie could not see any love bites, a sign that the relationship with Theresa was waning. 'What is it, Sharon?' he said.

Natalie scanned the transcript of the phone conversation. 'Five o'clock this morning,' she said. 'Has voice recognition software confirmed the voices?'

'It has,' the constable said.

Natalie handed the transcript to Haddock.

The interviews going forward would need to be more formal, as the transcripts had revealed questions that needed to be answered.

Frank Addison sat in the interview room, this time with both officers.

Haddock asked Addison if he wanted legal representation. He declined, but it was moot, and he would have a chance to change his mind later.

Natalie pushed over the transcript of the phone conversation. Addison put on a pair of glasses and read through it twice. He then looked up. 'What can I say?' he said. 'We are all creatures of circumstance.'

'But not murderers,' Haddock added.

'You knew,' Natalie said.

'How couldn't I? I had seen the change in Alan, and so had Alice. You can't know a person for that many years, not if you're close, as Alice was, and I was intimately involved with the family.'

'And dishonest. You had pilfered from the family for decades.'

Natalie read from the transcript:

Frank Addison: *Alan was involved with Heng, but we've always known that.*

Alice Minchin: *And you are involved.*

Frank: *Do you care?*

Alice: *Not particularly. Why should I care about a few junkies? Melinda, when did you know?*

Frank: *I always suspected. She told me the truth one night that Alan had turned, and she knew I was a crook, helping myself to Alan's money, and that she didn't care what happened to me, nor to you. All she wanted was for it to be shut down. But then Alan was murdered.*

Alice: *The house?*

Frank: *I never completed the paperwork, not that she knew, or she might have. She didn't want the house, made out that she did. An admirable woman.*

Alice: *What is there for me?*

Frank: *Stop whoring. You won't ever need the money. Get married, and make out you're purer than driven snow.*

Alice: *That will take some doing, but yes, I will.*

Addison continued. 'No more than Alan's father had done with others. I respected him enormously, but he didn't have Alan's reclusive and secretive nature. You see, and you must understand, Alan was never a criminal. He might have committed crimes, but his motive wasn't money; it was the challenge. I was the criminal who took the money and moved it elsewhere, not a skill he could have mustered or been interested in.'

'What was Melinda's part in this?'

'She was who she said she was. Highly accomplished, and Alan hadn't known. As an organiser, he was par excellence; as a judge of a person's character, he was hopeless. He loved her but realised she would be his undoing in Australia.'

'Where does Alice fit into this?'

'To Alan, the love between them was unbreakable, the love of a sibling. He wouldn't let her come to harm.'

'And Morton?'

'I doubt if he knew. Morton's driven by the ostentatious display of his wealth: a mistress in the penthouse, a Ferrari in the garage, a mansion in Vaucluse. Crime would not have suited him, yet Heng had used him.'

'And now you will go to prison for your crime,' Haddock said.

'Based on a phone conversation? I don't think so.'

Nor did Natalie.

'Unfortunately,' she said, 'since we've been here, our people have been to your house, accessed your laptop, and checked a filing cabinet. Your meticulous attention to documented detail has been your undoing. Also, although it makes no sense, traces of heroin were found by a sniffer dog in the office.'

'I didn't kill Alan,' Addison said.

'We know that. Liddie knew the truth, but he worked for you and Alan, and death didn't concern him. He had seen it before.'

Addison, formally charged with drug importation and trafficking, was led away and down to the cells. He was a broken man.

Alice was accorded the opportunity of legal representation. She asked for her father, which had to be denied.

'He told me he wanted Melinda. I knew she was in the country but didn't know what she was. Alan thought there was hope if he admitted his crimes and blamed his treatment in Cambodia for turning him to the dark side. Hopeful that he and Melinda could eventually sail off into the sunset. Melinda wasn't that person, incapable of the love he wanted, but I was.

'He refused me up on that draughty spot on the island. I killed him.'

'Melinda was there. She saw you, unsure if she saw you murder him, but probably did.'

'She would have.'

Two days later, after the reports had been filed, the prosecution reports prepared, the evidence collated, and the two confessions registered, Natalie and Haddock sat down to talk. This time without Payne and Victoria.

'Why didn't Melinda tell us what she knew?' Haddock asked.

'She made us work for it. She didn't want to be in at the end, nor did she want to bring more focus on her than necessary. Maybe she did care for Alan, although we'll never know. I'm sorry about Alice.'

'Never get emotional. I've told you that before. We did not trust Melinda, but she came good.'

'Did she? Did we ever know who she was? What she might do in the pursuit of justice?'

'Never,' Haddock said.

Three days after the confessions, Crystal Andersson walked into State Crime Command. In her hand, she had a witnessed document stating that she wished to withdraw the rape allegation she had made against Jeb Barton.

Natalie informed her that the man had been released two days before and that he had rescinded his confession, and that the rape charge would be dealt with at another time if Crystal had not come forward.

'Maybe he's not such a bad man,' Crystal said. 'Maybe we can make a go of it.'

Natalie would have advised Barton to run like hell, but she wasn't there as a counsellor. If the man was willing to contemplate forgiving the woman for what she had put him through, he deserved what he might get.

That night, Natalie left the station early. The agreed date with Jimmy Rogers was on. She considered the situation and whether she had rejected him prematurely. He was intelligent, decent, and wouldn't cheat on her. Was it time for her to reconsider? She would see how the night worked out.

The End

ALSO BY THE AUTHOR

DI Tremayne Thriller Series

Death Unholy – A DI Tremayne Thriller – Book 1

All that remained were the man's two legs and a chair full of greasy and fetid ash. Little did DI Keith Tremayne know that it was the beginning of a journey into the murky world of paganism and its ancient rituals. And it was going to get very dangerous.

'Do you believe in spontaneous human combustion?' Detective Inspector Keith Tremayne asked.

'Not me. I've read about it. Who hasn't?' Sergeant Clare Yarwood answered.

'I haven't,' Tremayne replied, which did not surprise his young sergeant. In the months they had been working together, she had come to realise that he was a man who had little interest in the world. When he had a cigarette in his mouth, a beer in his hand, and a murder to solve he was about the happiest she ever saw him, but even then, he was not one of life's most sociable people. And as for reading? The occasional police report, an early-morning newspaper, turned first to the racing results.

Death and the Assassin's Blade – A DI Tremayne Thriller – Book 2

It was meant to be high drama, not murder, but someone's switched the daggers. The man's death took place in plain view of two serving police officers.

He was not meant to die; the daggers were only theatrical props, plastic and harmless. A summer's night, a production of Julius Caesar amongst the ruins of an Anglo-Saxon fort. Detective Inspector Tremayne is there with his sergeant, Clare Yarwood. In the assassination scene, Caesar collapses to the ground. Brutus defends his actions; Mark Antony rebukes him.

They're a disparate group, the amateur actors. One's an estate agent, another an accountant. And then there is the teenage school student, the gay man, the funeral director. And what about the women? They could be involved.

They've each got a secret, but which of those on the stage wanted Gordon Mason, the actor who had portrayed Caesar, dead?

Death and the Lucky Man – A DI Tremayne Thriller – Book 3

Sixty-eight million pounds and dead. Hardly the outcome expected for the luckiest man in England the day his lottery ticket was drawn out of the barrel. But then, Alan Winters' rags-to-riches story had never been conventional, and some had benefited, but others hadn't.

Death at Coombe Farm – A DI Tremayne Thriller – Book 4

A warring family. A disputed inheritance. A recipe for death.

If it hadn't been for the circumstances, Detective Inspector Keith Tremayne would have said the view was outstanding. Up high, overlooking the farmhouse in the valley below, the panoramic vista of Salisbury Plain stretching out beyond. The only problem was a body near where he stood with his sergeant, Clare Yarwood, and it wasn't a pleasant sight.

Death by a Dead Man's Hand – A DI Tremayne Thriller – Book 5

A flawed heist of forty gold bars from a security van late at night. One of the perpetrators is killed by his brother as they argue over what they have stolen.

Eighteen years later, the murderer, released after serving his sentence for his brother's murder, waits in a church for a man purporting to be the brother he killed. And then he is killed.

The threads stretch back a long way, and now more people are dying in the search for the missing gold bars.

Detective Inspector Tremayne, his health causing him concern, and Sergeant Clare Yarwood, still seeking romance, are pushed to the limit solving the murder, attempting to prevent more.

Death in the Village – A DI Tremayne Thriller – Book 6

Nobody liked Gloria Wiggins, a woman who regarded anyone who did not acquiesce to her jaundiced view of the world with disdain. James Baxter, the previous vicar, had been one of those, and her scurrilous outburst in the church one Sunday had hastened his death.

And now, years later, the woman was dead, hanging from a beam in her garage. Detective Inspector Tremayne and Sergeant Clare Yarwood had seen the body, interviewed the woman's acquaintances, and those who had hated her.

Burial Mound – A DI Tremayne Thriller – Book 7

A Bronze-Age burial mound close to Stonehenge. An archaeological excavation. What they were looking for was an ancient body and historical artefacts. They found the ancient body, but then they found another that's only been there for years, not centuries. And then the police became interested.

It's another case for Detective Inspector Tremayne and Sergeant Yarwood. The more recent body was the brother of the mayor of Salisbury.

Everything seems to point to the victim's brother, the mayor, the upright and serious-minded Clive Grantley. Tremayne's sure that it's him, but Clare Yarwood's not so sure.

But is her belief based on evidence or personal hope?

The Body in the Ditch – A DI Tremayne Thriller – Book 8

A group of children play. Not far away, in the ditch on the other side of the farmyard, lies the body of a troubled young woman.

The nearby village hides as many secrets as the community at the farm, a disparate group of people looking for an alternative to their previous torturous lives. Their leader, idealistic and benevolent, espouses love and kindness, and clearly, somebody's not following his dictate.

An old woman's death seems unrelated to the first, but is it? Is it part of the tangled web that connects the farm to the village?

Detective Inspector Tremayne and Sergeant Clare Yarwood soon discover that the village is anything but charming and picturesque. It's an incestuous hotbed of intrigue and wrongdoing. And what of the farm and those who live there. None of them can be ruled out, not yet.

The Horse's Mouth – A DI Tremayne Thriller – Book 9

A day at the races for Detective Inspector Tremayne, idyllic at the outset, soon changes. A horse is dead, the owner's daughter is found murdered, and Tremayne's there when the body is discovered.

The question is, was Tremayne set up, in the wrong place at the right time? He's the cast-iron alibi for one of the suspects, and he knows that one murder can lead to two, and more often than not to three.

The dead woman had a chequered history, though not as much as her father, and then a man commits suicide. Is he the murderer, or was his death the unfortunate consequence of a tragic love affair? And who was in the stable with the woman just before she died? More than one person could have killed her, and all of them have secrets they would rather not be known.

Tremayne's health is troubling him. Is what they are saying correct, that it is time for him to retire, to take it easy and put his feet up? But that's not his style, and he'll not give up on solving the murder.

Montfield's Madness – A DI Tremayne Thriller – Book 10

A day at the races for Detective Inspector Tremayne, idyllic at the Jacob Montfield, regarded by the majority as a homeless eccentric, a nuisance by a few, had pushed a supermarket trolley around the city for years.

However, one person regards him as a liability.

Eccentric was correct, a nuisance, for sure, mad, plenty thought that, but few knew the truth, that Montfield is a brilliant man, once a research scientist. And even less knew that detailed within a notebook hidden deep in the trolley, there is a new approach to the guidance of weapons and satellites—a radical improvement on the previous and it's worth a lot to some, power to others, accolades to another.

And for that, one cold night, he died at the hand of another. Inspector Tremayne and Sergeant Clare Yarwood are on the case, but so are others, and soon they're warned off. Only Tremayne doesn't listen, not when he's got his teeth into the investigation, and his sergeant, equally resolute, won't either. It's not only their careers on the line, but their lives.

DCI Isaac Cook Thriller Series

Murder is a Tricky Business – A DCI Cook Thriller – Book 1

A television actress is missing, and DCI Isaac Cook, the Senior Investigation Officer of the Murder Investigation Team at Challis Street Police Station in London, is searching for her.

Why has he been taken away from more important crimes to search for the woman? It's not the first time she's gone missing, so why does everyone assume she's been murdered?

There's a secret; that much is certain, but who knows it? The missing woman? The executive producer? His eavesdropping assistant? Or the actor who portrayed her fictional brother in the TV soap opera?

Murder House – A DCI Cook Thriller – Book 2

A corpse in the fireplace of an old house. It's been there for thirty years, but who is it?

It's murder, but who is the victim and what connection does the body have to the house's previous owners. What is the motive?

And why is the body in a fireplace? It was bound to be discovered eventually but was that what the murderer wanted? The main suspects are all old and dying or already dead.

Isaac Cook and his team have their work cut out, trying to put the pieces together. Those who know are not talking because of an old-fashioned belief that a family's dirty laundry should not be aired in public and never to a policeman – even if that means the murderer is never brought to justice!

Murder is Only a Number – A DCI Cook Thriller – Book 3

Before she left, she carved a number in blood on his chest. But why the number 2 if this was her first murder?

The woman prowls the streets of London. Her targets are men who have wronged her. Or have they? And why is she keeping count?

DCI Cook and his team finally know who she is, but not before she's murdered four men. The whole team are looking for her, but the woman keeps disappearing in plain sight. The pressure's on to stop her, but she's always one step ahead.

And this time, DCS Goddard can't protect his protégé, Isaac Cook, from the wrath of the new commissioner at the Met.

Murder in Little Venice – A DCI Cook Thriller – Book 4

A dismembered corpse floats in the canal in Little Venice, an upmarket tourist haven in London. Its identity is unknown, but what is its significance?

DCI Isaac Cook is baffled about why it's there. Is it gang-related, or is it something more?

Whatever the reason, it's clearly a warning, and Isaac and his team are sure it's not the last body that they'll have to deal with.

Murder is the Only Option – A DCI Cook Thriller – Book 5

A man thought to be long dead returns to exact revenge against those who had blighted his life. His only concern is to protect his wife and daughter. He will stop at nothing to achieve his aim.

'Big Greg, I never expected to see you around here at this time of night.'

'I've told you enough times.'

'I've no idea what you're talking about,' Robertson replied. He looked up at the man, only to see a metal pole coming down at him. Robertson fell down, cracking his head against a concrete kerb.

Two vagrants, no more than twenty feet away, did not stir and did not even look in the direction of the noise. If they had, they would have seen a dead body, another man walking away.

Murder in Notting Hill – A DCI Cook Thriller – Book 6

One murderer, two bodies, two locations, and the murders have been committed within an hour of each other.

They're separated by a couple of miles, and neither woman has anything in common with the other. One is young and wealthy, the daughter of a famous man; the other is poor, hardworking and unknown.

Isaac Cook and his team at Challis Street Police Station are baffled about why they've been killed. There must be a connection, but what is it?

Murder in Room 346 – A DCI Cook Thriller – Book 7

'Coitus interruptus, that's what it is,' Detective Chief Inspector Isaac Cook said. In a downmarket hotel in Bayswater, on the bed lay the naked bodies of a man and a woman.

'Bullet in the head's not the way to go,' Larry Hill, Isaac Cook's detective inspector, said. He had not expected such a flippant comment from his senior, not when they were standing near to two people who had, apparently in the final throes of passion, succumbed to what appeared to be a professional assassination.

'You know this will be all over the media within the hour,' Isaac said.

'James Holden, moral crusader, a proponent of the sanctity of the marital bed, man and wife. It's bound to be.'

Murder of a Silent Man – A DCI Cook Thriller – Book 8

A murdered recluse. A property empire. A disinherited family. All the ingredients for murder.

No one gave much credence to the man when he was alive. In fact, most people never knew who he was, although those who had lived in the area for many years recognised the tired-looking and shabbily-dressed man as he shuffled along, regular as clockwork on a Thursday afternoon at seven in the evening to the local off-licence.

It was always the same: a bottle of whisky, premium brand, and a packet of cigarettes. He paid his money over the counter, took hold of his plastic bag containing his purchases, and then walked back down the road with the same rhythmic shuffle.

Murder has no Guilt – A DCI Cook Thriller – Book 9

No one knows who the target was or why, but there are eight dead. The men seem the most likely perpetrators, or could have it been one of the two women, the attractive Gillian Dickenson, or even the celebrity-obsessed Sal Maynard?

There's a gang war brewing, and if there are deaths, it doesn't matter to them as long as it's not their death. But to Detective Chief Inspector Isaac Cook, it's his area of London, and it does matter.

It's dirty and unpredictable. Initially, the West Indian gangs held sway, but a more vicious Romanian gangster had usurped them. And now he's being marginalised by the Russians. And the leader of the most vicious Russian mafia organisation is in London, and he's got money and influence, the ear of those in power.

Murder in Hyde Park – A DCI Cook Thriller – Book 10

An early-morning jogger is murdered in Hyde Park. It's in the centre of London, but no one saw him enter the park, no one saw him die.

He carries no identification, only a water-logged phone. As the pieces unravel, it's clear that the dead man had a history of deception.

Is the murderer one of those that loved him? Or was it someone with a vengeance?

It's proving difficult for DCI Isaac Cook and his team at Challis Street Homicide to find the guilty person – not that they'll cease to search for the truth, not even after one suspect confesses.

Six Years Too Late – A DCI Cook Thriller – Book 11

Always the same questions for Detective Chief Inspector Isaac Cook — Why was Marcus Matthews in that room? And why did he share a bottle of wine with his killer?

It wasn't as if Matthews had amounted to much, apart from the fact that he was the son-in-law of a notorious gangster, the father of the man's grandchildren.

Yet the one thing Hamish McIntyre, feared in London for his violence, rated above anything else, was his family, especially Samantha, his daughter. However, he had never cared for Marcus, her husband.

And then Marcus disappeared, only for his body to be found six years later by a couple of young boys who decide that exploring an abandoned house is preferable to school.

Grave Passion – A DCI Cook Thriller – Book 12

Two young lovers out for a night of romance. A shortcut through the cemetery. They witnessed a murder, but there was no struggle, only a knife through the heart.

It has all the hallmarks of an assassination, but who is the woman? And why was she beside a grave at night? Did she know the person who killed her?

Soon after, other deaths, seemingly unconnected, but tied to the family of one of the young lovers.

It's a case for Detective Chief Inspector Cook and his team, and they're baffled on this one.

The Slaying of Joe Foster – A DCI Cook Thriller – Book 13

No one challenged Joe Foster in life, not if they valued theirs. And then, the gangster is slain and his criminal empire up for grabs.

A power vacuum; the Foster family is fighting for control, the other gangs in the area aiming to poach the trade in illegal drugs, to carve up the empire that the father had created.

It has all the makings of a war on the streets, something nobody wants, not even the other gangs.

Terry Foster, the eldest son of Joe, the man who should take control, doesn't have his father's temperament or wisdom. His solution is slash and burn, and it's not going to work. People are going to get hurt, and some of them will die.

The Hero's Fall – A DCI Cook Thriller – Book 14

Angus Simmons had it made. A successful television program, a beautiful girlfriend, admired by many for his mountaineering exploits.

And then he fell while climbing a skyscraper in London. Initially, it was thought he had lost his grip, but that wasn't the man: a meticulous planner, his risks measured, and it wasn't a difficult climb, not for him.

It was only afterwards on examination that they found the mark of a bullet on his body. It then became a murder, and that was when Detective Chief Inspector Isaac Cook and his Homicide team at Challis Street Police Station became interested.

The Vicar's Confession – A DCI Cook Thriller – Book 15

The Reverend Charles Hepworth, good Samaritan, a friend of the downtrodden, almost a saint to those who know him, up until the day he walks into the police station, straight up to Detective

Chief Inspector Isaac Cook's desk in Homicide. 'I killed the man,' he says as he places a blood-soaked knife on the desk.

The dead man, Andreas Maybury, was not a man to mourn, but why would a self-professed pacifist commit such a heinous crime. The reasons aren't clear, and then Hepworth's killed in a prison cell, and everyone's ducking for cover.

Guilty Until Proven Innocent – A DCI Cook Thriller – Book 16

Gary Harders' conviction two years previously should have been the end of the investigation. A clear-cut case of murder, and he had confessed to the crime and accepted his sentence without complaint. But now, the man's conviction was about to be overthrown, but why? And why is Harders not saying that his confession was police coercion? His prints are on the murder weapon, but Forensics has found another set.

Not only is there proof of either the Forensics department's error, incompetency or conspiracy, but Commissioner Alwyn Davies is getting tough on crime, draconian tough.

Detective Chief Inspector Isaac Cook and Chief Superintendent Richard Goddard are under pressure to take sides, aware that a positive return ensures promotion, but at the cost of their respective souls.

Davies has powerful backers, persons willing to make a deal with the devil. To allow violent putdown of those who disrupt the streets and removal of those who cause unsolicited and anti-social crime.

The plan has merits, a return to the safe society of decades past, but where will it stop. Who will say it's time to ease off, and then, what's the Russian mafia got to do with it? Too much from what DCI Cook can see, but he's powerless.

Murder Without Reason – A DCI Cook Thriller – Book 17

DCI Cook faces his greatest challenge. The Islamic State is waging war in England, and they are winning.

Not only does Isaac Cook have to contend with finding the perpetrators, but he is also being forced to commit actions contrary to his mandate as a police officer.

And then there is Anne Argento, the prime minister's deputy. The prime minister has shown himself to be a pacifist and is not up to the task. She needs to take his job if the country is to fight back against the Islamists.

Vane and Martin have provided the solution. Will DCI Cook and Anne Argento be willing to follow it through? Are they able to act for the good of England, knowing that a criminal and murderous action is about to take place? Do they have an option?

Sergeant Natalie Campbell Thriller Series

Dark Streets – Book 1

A homeless man, Old Joe's death was not unexpected. Not until it was found to be murder.

This was Darlinghurst Road, Kings Cross, once a hub of inequity, of strip joints and gentleman's clubs, of licensed premises and restaurants. But now, the area is changing, going upmarket, another enclave for those that can afford it, not a place for the homeless, nor is it a place of murder, but then there is another murder in Point Piper, upmarket and exclusive; a woman, her throat cut.

Detective Gary Haddock's a seasoned hand in Homicide, but he's baffled by the murders that continue. Statistically, Sydney's Eastern Suburbs doesn't have murder, but after four, are they serial or random, and if they are serial, why?

Sergeant Natalie Campbell from Kings Cross Police Station is wet behind the ears when she pairs with Haddock but soon learns she is more astute than he is, although she's a risk taker. He has to protect her, but she will take the investigations forward.

Steve Case Thriller Series

The Haberman Virus – Book 1

A remote and isolated village in the Hindu Kush Mountain range in North Eastern Afghanistan is wiped out by a virus unlike any seen before.

A mysterious visitor clad in a spacesuit checks his handiwork, a female American doctor succumbs to the disease, and the woman sent to trap the person responsible falls in love with him – the man who would cause the deaths of millions.

Hostage of Islam – Book 2

Three are to die at the Mission in Nigeria: the pastor and his wife in a blazing chapel; another gunned down while trying to defend them from the Islamist fighters.

Kate McDonald, an American, grieving over her boyfriend's death and Helen Campbell, whose life had been troubled by drugs and prostitution, are taken by the attackers.

Kate is sold to a slave trader who intends to sell her virginity to an Arab Prince. Helen, to ensure their survival, gives herself to the murderer of her friends.

Prelude to War – Book 3

Russia and America face each other across the northern border of Afghanistan. World War 3 is about to break out and no one is backing off.

And all because a team of academics in New York postulated how to extract the vast untapped mineral wealth of Afghanistan.

Steve Case is in the middle of it, and his position is looking very precarious. Will the Taliban find him before the Americans get him out? Or is he doomed, as is the rest of the world?

Standalone Novels

Malika's Revenge

Malika, a drug-addicted prostitute, waits in a smugglers' village for the next Afghan tribesman or Tajik gangster to pay her price, a few scraps of heroin.

Yusup Baroyev, a drug lord, enjoys a lifestyle many would envy. An Afghan warlord sees the resurgence of the Taliban. A Russian white-collar criminal portrays himself as a good and honest citizen in Moscow.

All of them are linked to an audacious plan to increase the quantity of heroin shipped out of Afghanistan and into Russia and ultimately the West.

Some will succeed, some will die, some will be rescued from their plight and others will rue the day they became involved.

Verrall's Nightmare

Historians may reflect on what happened, psychoanalysts may debate endlessly, and although scientists would attempt to explain, none would conclusively get the measure of all that had occurred.

Others, less knowledgeable, aficionados of social media, would say that Benedict Verrall was mad, or else the events in a small hamlet in the south of England never occurred and that it was a government conspiracy. That Samuel Whittingham was a figment of Verrall's imagination and the storms and their devastation, unprecedented in their scope and deaths, were freaks of nature, not of evil.

The truth, however, was more obscure, and that Verrall was neither mad nor was he malicious. Although he was responsible for instigating what was to happen, that hadn't been his intention.

He did not believe in the paranormal or the metaphysical, but then, he had not considered the brain tumour pressing down on his brain.

Or was it Verrall's madness, either the dream or the nightmare? That will be for the reader to decide.

ABOUT THE AUTHOR

Phillip Strang was born in the late forties, the post-war baby boom in England; his childhood years, a comfortable middle-class upbringing in a small town, a two hours' drive to the west of London.

His childhood and the formative years were a time of innocence. Relatively few rules, and as a teenager, complete mobility due to a bicycle – a three-speed Raleigh – and a more trusting community. It was the days before mobile phones, the internet, terrorism, and wanton violence. An avid reader of Science Fiction in his teenage years: Isaac Asimov, and Frank Herbert, the masters of the genre. Still an avid reader, the author now mainly reads thrillers.

In his early twenties, the author, with a degree in electronics engineering and an unabated wanderlust to see the world left England's cold and damp climes for Sydney, Australia – the first semi-circulation of the globe, complete. Now, forty years later, he still resides in Australia, although many intervening years spent in a myriad of countries, some calm and safe – others, no more than war zones.

In his early twenties, the author, with a degree in electronics engineering and an unabated wanderlust to see the world left England's cold and damp climes for Sydney, Australia – the first semi-circulation of the globe, complete. Now, forty years later, he still resides in Australia, although many intervening years spent in a myriad of countries, some calm and safe – others, no more than war zones.

www.ingramcontent.com/pod-product-compliance
Lightning Source LLC
Chambersburg PA
CBHW022125050726
47590CB00002B/412